"A captivating world of glamour, romance, and intrigue."
— Melissa Foster, *NYT* & *USA Today* Bestselling Author

"Jan Moran rivals Danielle Steel at her romantic best."
— Allegra Jordan, author of *The End of Innocence*

"Jan Moran is the new queen of the epic romance."
— Rebecca Forster, *USA Today* Bestselling Author

Reviews for The *Love, California* Series

"*Flawless* is an astute, intelligent, gripping romance for the modern woman. Jan Moran expertly transports the reader to Beverly Hills and, for a period, Paris, and offers a glimpse of glamour while showing those who work hard behind the scenes to create that glamour. The compelling plot that had me turning the pages faster and faster. The characters reach out of the pages and pull you into their lives, and they stay with you long after you close the book. I love that Jan's writing took me to the edge; that she creates a heroine whom you can't fail to care for and understand. A fabulous first book in this series – I can't wait to read the next one."
— Hannah Fielding, Author of *The Echoes of Love*

"Jan Moran's heroines are strong women who have made their way into the beauty world, have battled against the odds, and have the mental acuity to go head-to-head against the obstacles that fall in their path. They care deeply for their families and for their friends. Their loyalty is without question. They love with great sensuality. Not only are the storylines fast-paced and well written, there are

scenes that leave you in a sweat. Jan is quickly becoming a major contender in the Women's Fiction market for just cause. *Runway* receives a strong five-star rating from this reader, with a strong recommendation to read the first two books in the *Love, California Series: Flawless, and Beauty Mark.*"
— Karen Laird, *Under the Shade Tree Reviews*

From St. Martin's Press

The Winemakers: A Novel of Wine and Secrets
"Absolutely adored *The Winemakers*. Beautifully layered and utterly compelling. Intriguing from start to finish.
A story not to be missed."
— Jane Porter, *New York Times* & *USA Today* Bestselling Author

"Readers will devour this page-turner as the mystery and passions spin out." – *The Library Journal*

"Moran weaves knowledge of wine and winemaking into this intense family drama." – *Booklist*

"Spellbound by the thread of deception."
– *The Mercury News*

Scent of Triumph: A Novel of Perfume and Passion
"A gripping World War II story of poignant love and devastating, heart-wrenching loss. Perfumes are so beautifully described."
— Gill Paul, Author of *The Affair*

"A sweeping saga of WWII. Heartbreaking, evocative!"
— Anita Hughes, Author of *Lake Como*

"A dedicated look into world of fashion; recommended."
— *Midwest Book Review*

Flawless

A Love, California Novel

Book Number 1

by

Jan Moran

SUNNY PALMS
PRESS

Library of Congress Cataloging-in-Publication Data
Moran, Jan.
/ by Jan Moran

ISBN 978-0-9639065-9-5 (softcover)
ISBN 978-0-9639065-8-8 (ebooks)

Printed in the U.S.A.
Cover design by Ginna Moran
Cover images copyright 123RF

For Inquiries Contact:
Sunny Palms Press
9663 Santa Monica Blvd, STE 1158, Beverly Hills, CA, USA
www.sunnypalmspress.com
www.JanMoran.com

Other Books by Jan Moran

Contemporary
The Love, California Series:
Flawless
Beauty Mark
Runway
Essence
Style
Sparkle

20th Century Historical
The Winemakers: A Novel of Wine and Secrets
Scent of Triumph: A Novel of Perfume and Passion
Life is a Cabernet: A Companion Wine Novella to The Winemakers

NonFiction
Vintage Perfumes

Browse her entire collection at www.JanMoran.com
Get a free ebook when you join Jan's VIP list.

1

Verena heard her name called. Despite the uneasy, prickly feeling on the back of her neck, she arranged a smile on her face and made her way to the podium through throngs of well-wishers and clouds of expensive perfume. This was her moment. Amid the thunder of applause rising in the ballroom of the Beverly Hills Hotel, she passed linen-draped, flower-laden tables ringed with women in dazzling designer evening dresses and men in tuxedos.

Tonight was a night that her grandmother, Mia, had dreamed of. Verena wished she could be here, but Mia was at home resting in bed. It was supposed to have been such a happy celebration. A vein pulsed in her temple, twitching her eye.

Lifting the hem of her silvery evening gown, Verena navigated the steps up to the brightly lit stage. She greeted Robert Montreaux with a kiss on each cheek and turned on a radiant smile for the photographers. As head of her family company, Verena performed her job with practiced precision and grace.

She blinked against the camera flashes that left a shower of blue sparkles in front of her eyes, momentarily blinding her.

As her vision cleared, Verena glanced at the crowd that

7

had gathered. She sought out the faces of her friends Dahlia, Fianna, and Scarlett, who had just flown in from New York for the occasion. She drew a deep breath.

At least her good friends were with her tonight. They'd waited patiently through long speeches from other industry professionals who were also being honored for their accomplishments. Verena was seated at a front table for the honorees while her friends had been seated at another table farther back. She needed to speak to them, especially Scarlett, her attorney.

Verena had received a voice mail just moments before she'd left for the awards banquet. Her good friend and banker, Marvin Panetta, had left an urgent message for her to call him, but he hadn't answered when she tried to call him back. *I have bad news*, he'd said. *I need to warn you about Derrick.*

That would be Derrick Logan, her ex-fiancé. The man who couldn't seem to accept no for an answer, in business or in personal relationships. She wondered what he was up to now.

"May I have your attention, please?" Robert Montreaux, the French president of Cosmetic Executives Worldwide, tapped the microphone.

Verena swept her attention back to Robert.

"We're here tonight to honor Verena Valent," he said, in a richly accented voice that commanded attention. "She took over Valent Swiss Skincare ten years ago at the age of eighteen after the death of her parents. Not only did she persevere through that tragedy, but she grew to become the driving force behind the company's recent innovations and expansion. Next month, Valent Swiss Skincare expands into Asia, with debuts planned in Hong Kong, Shanghai, Tokyo, and Singapore. So now, before she jets off to Asia, please join me in honoring Verena Valent, our Executive Visionary of the Year."

Applause exploded in the room. From the corner of her eye Verena saw Greta Hicks, the anorexic-thin, Versace-clad reporter with *Fashion News Daily* who'd also dated Derrick. Greta looked especially haughty tonight, and Verena noticed that she kept glancing in Derrick's direction.

"Thank you, Robert, *merci*, my friend," Verena said, accepting the faceted crystal award he offered to her. "It's such a privilege to be singled out for this award when there are so many deserving people in the industry." She went on to acknowledge the people who worked for her, as well as the department store buyers who had helped make her brand such a success.

She paused, wishing Mia were here. "I'd like to thank everyone who has shared our vision and worked to grow the company that my dear grandmother, Mia Valent, founded in 1948, just a few blocks from here. Today, after several expansions, we continue to manage all international activities from that location on North Beverly Drive. I merely carry the torch for the next generation, as my parents did, and I look forward to many years of continued service and innovation in skincare. In closing, I dedicate this award to The Women in Pink Foundation for cancer research."

As applause rose across the room, Verena saw Greta's hand shoot up and she advanced toward the stage. *What's that about?* Verena wondered. *This isn't the place to field press questions.*

Fortunately, Robert noticed Greta and leaned toward

the microphone. "Verena is too modest to mention the rather large donation to Women in Pink from Valent Swiss Skincare, but I will. Thank you, Verena, and now, I invite everyone to the dance floor."

Stymied, Greta folded her arms and spun around.

Music filled the room while the executive director from the Women in Pink Foundation returned to the stage. As people milled about, Verena posed with Robert and the director for photographs with the award. Yet Verena sensed something was going on.

Avoiding Greta, Verena hurried to her friends. Scarlett, Dahlia, and Fianna were dressed in shades of summer sorbet evening gowns from Fianna's latest spring collection.

"Scarlett, I'm so glad you could make it," Verena said, hugging her friend from New York. Scarlett's pale coral gown set off her olive skin and coppery blond hair. Originally from Spain, Escarlata Sandoval was a top intellectual property attorney. "I thought you had a big court case."

"It settled, so I thought I'd surprise you." Scarlett glanced around. "Where are your sisters and Mia?"

"Mia hasn't been feeling well," Verena replied. "Anika and Bella stayed home with her, but she insists she'll be well enough to take the twins to Europe for their school break soon."

Fianna leaned in. "Look out, Verena, Greta is coming your way." Brushing back her mane of red hair, she glanced over her shoulder.

Verena flicked her gaze to one side. "She's up to something, stay close."

With a cameraman trailing her, Greta marched straight toward Verena. "Would you care to make a comment about

National Western Bank? Will you go ahead with your Asian expansion or put it on hold?"

So there *was* something to Marvin's voice mail. Verena wondered what was going on at his bank. She'd try to call him again.

"Well?" Greta was staring at her and waiting for a response.

"National Western Bank has always been a good partner," Verena said, slipping into her media role. "VSS appreciates its commitment to Asia."

Greta raised an eyebrow and looked smug. "Will you take Herringbone Capital's offer to fund your business in Asia?" She stepped closer, shoving her microphone near Verena's lips. "Are you counting on Derrick Logan?"

Verena ignored Greta's last comment. Although Derrick had often offered his advice on her business, his venture capital group was not an investor in her company. "As I said, National Western Bank is handling our business." Verena felt a chill course through her and shot a look at Scarlett, who angled her head in warning.

"Maybe you haven't heard that the feds are taking over National Western." Greta's lips curled in satisfaction as she delivered her *coup de grâce*. "And Marvin Panetta was just found dead in an apparent suicide."

Verena felt sick to her stomach. "No, he just—" Verena stopped as Scarlett touched her arm. *What had happened?* She couldn't believe Marvin would do such a thing. What did Derrick have to do with this?

"Now would you like to comment?" As Greta waved the microphone, her devious glee was apparent in her voice.

"Leave her alone," Scarlett said, narrowing her eyes.

"Marvin was a friend. You're through here, Greta. Move on."

"And who are you?"

"I'm her attorney. Scarlett Sandoval."

"Lawyering up already?" Greta grinned at Verena. "And you said you didn't know anything about this. Interesting." She turned on her heel and left.

"I would have told her to go to hell," Fianna said.

"Verena is the master of control." Dahlia turned to Verena with alarm in her vivid green eyes. "I can't believe he's dead."

Verena shook her head. "Marvin left a message a few hours ago warning me about Derrick. I tried to call him back..." Could she have stopped him from committing suicide? "Has anyone seen Derrick?" His name tasted bad in her mouth. As much as she hated to speak to him, she had to find out why Marvin had called to warn her.

"By the door," Fianna said. "He's with the L.A. mayor."

Scarlett touched her shoulder. "You don't have to talk to him, Verena."

"Actually, I do." Verena strode toward him, thinking about Marvin. He had a sweet wife and lovely children. She'd never thought he would take his own life.

When Derrick saw her approaching, he stepped aside from the mayor. Arching his neck with authority, he held a hand out to her. "Verena, I hoped we'd talk tonight."

She stopped so close to him she could smell the cologne she'd never liked on him. "I just heard the news about Marvin."

Derrick didn't acknowledge her comment. "The mayor was impressed with your speech. Come, I'll introduce you."

"You knew, didn't you?"

Derrick averted her accusatory glare. "Come on, blue eyes, I didn't want to spoil your special day," he said, smoothing his already impeccable black hair.

"Spoil my day?" Verena was aghast. "I'm not ten years old. Marvin was my friend and mentor."

"We didn't expect this," he said quietly.

"Who is *we*, Derrick? You and Thomas Roper?" Verena had never liked Derrick's senior investment partner in Herringbone Capital.

Before he could answer, Greta appeared behind him. "Aren't you going to tell her?"

Verena stepped back. Greta was tough, but she was a reporter. Her job was to dig up the facts. The cameraman was no longer with her, so Verena said, "One of you better start talking."

Greta put a hand on her slim hips, clearly relishing her role. "None of the Herringbone Capital portfolio companies Derrick introduced to Marvin were paying their loans."

Derrick bristled. "All the indicators suggest we're heading into a recession. I don't know what they actually did."

Verena inclined her head. "I thought those companies were among your most successful."

"Come on, you know our business is complicated," Derrick said, sounding conciliatory.

"I'll say," Greta interjected with a smirk.

"Then why weren't they paying their debts?" Anger gathered in Verena's chest.

"I've been investigating." Greta jutted out her chin.

"Seems they had instructions not to pay their notes. Or threats."

"Butt out, Greta," Derrick said, lowering his voice. "Verena, listen to me. Marvin was already in trouble. Herringbone always advises its companies to conserve their cash."

Verena stepped back, confused as to why he would issue such an order. "I don't understand why you'd do that."

"I didn't order them to do anything." Derrick acted exasperated with her. "National Western Bank was over extended. Whatever actions our companies took were based on their own decisions."

Greta cut in. "But if your portfolio companies had paid their loans, they wouldn't have been in trouble."

"You can't make that stick, Greta," Derrick said. "There were rumors in the financial circles that the bank had serious problems. Now it seems the talk was true." He turned to Verena. "Look, I'm here for you if you need me. For a shoulder to cry on, or advice."

"I don't need either one from you." Verena turned to walk away, but Derrick caught her hand.

"Your business is going to need help," he said, sincerity oozing from him. "Think of your employees."

Verena met his gaze, steeling herself against him. Derrick had one thing going for him; he was convincing. He sold business owners—and women—on their need for him. Once a person stepped into Derrick's arena, he was like a lion sizing up his prey. He'd pace his steps, making them feel like they were special, or painting a picture of a future so compelling that those under his spell willingly went to slaughter. When she'd first met him, he'd suddenly

14

been everywhere she went, and he told her their destiny was fated. *We're meant for each other, Verena.*

"No." She snatched her hand from his grip. She had already made a mistake by getting personally involved with him. Fighting her grief, she blinked away tears and left him with Greta.

As she made her way back to her friends, a tall woman in a sleek ebony dress stepped beside her.

"Congratulations, Verena." She was the new buyer for one of their largest accounts.

"Thank you," Verena said. "I'm glad you could come tonight."

"We've been reviewing our budget for the coming year. Call me so we can discuss."

"I'll be happy to." Although Verena despaired for Marvin and his family, she was also aware of her duty tonight. The woman turned back to her companion and Verena glanced around, noticing the cosmetics merchant buyers in attendance from Nordstrom, Neiman Marcus, and other stores.

As Mia would have wanted, Verena circulated through the room, doing her duty and speaking to the people she needed to acknowledge.

"Congratulations, Verena. A well-deserved honor." A stylish woman with short black hair and burgundy highlights paused to speak to her.

"Thank you," Verena said. Wilhelmina Jones was a beauty industry veteran who'd built an impressive infomercial company specializing in the distribution of fine beauty, health, and fitness products.

"Do give my best to your grandmother," Wilhelmina

said. "I've always admired what your family has done in skincare."

She moved on, and Verena did the same. When Verena finally managed to disentangle herself from business, she returned to her friends.

Dahlia frowned at her. "Are you okay? You look awfully pale, Verena."

"I need some fresh air." Feeling faint, she started for the door. She had barely touched her dinner, and she ached for Marvin and his family.

"We'll go with you," Scarlett said, motioning to Dahlia and Fianna.

Outside the ballroom, Verena started up a circular staircase. The four friends hurried through the lobby to the rear of the hotel overlooking the pool, turning heads in their wake.

Perching on lounge chairs grouped under tall palm trees, they chatted a few minutes, discussing how they could help Marvin's family.

Verena breathed in the mild evening air, feeling thankful for her friends, who shared their thoughtful ideas and formed a plan. "I'm glad you all came tonight."

"We wouldn't have missed it," Dahlia said. Her shiny dark hair and mint green evening gown shimmered in the wavering glow from the pool's soft lights.

"You're all dressed up and you look gorgeous," Verena said. "Why don't you go inside and have something in the Polo Lounge? I'll join you in a few minutes. I just need to clear my mind." Derrick's words echoed in her mind. He was right. Without the financial support of her bank, she would need help.

"Good idea." Fianna pushed her tall, lean frame from

the chaise lounge. "Join us whenever you want."

After her friends had gone, Verena strolled through the deserted pool area, inhaling the sweet scent of jasmine on the summer breeze to calm her nerves. Besides being saddened by Marvin's death, she was also worried over what Greta had said about the bank failure. Marvin had been the banker for her company ever since she had taken the reigns of the company after her parents' deaths a decade ago. Over the years, he had become a trusted mentor and a good friend. She still couldn't believe he would have committed suicide. This act seemed so counter to the strong sense of responsibility she knew he had.

Despair encroached on her thoughts as National Western and the Asian expansion rushed through her mind. Her company's debut in China was mere weeks away. Suppliers and promotional vendors would need to be paid. She'd planned to rely on working capital until sales ramped up, just as many companies did.

Marvin had made the loan commitment a year ago, but now she'd have to look for another bank to make a loan. Could she act fast enough to gain the financing she needed?

She paused, staring at the moon as it crested the Spanish-tiled hotel rooftop. A question nagged at her.

When she had broken up with Derrick a few months ago, he'd told her he wanted to remain friends. He still kept in touch, calling her with the latest news that might affect her business and offering her advice. Derrick had a brilliant financial mind; she had to give him that. She drew her brows together in thought.

Derrick also knew that she banked with National Western. So why hadn't he mentioned his concern over the bank's imminent demise? If he'd warned the other companies in Herringbone's portfolio, as Greta had asserted, why hadn't he told her, too?

After all, he liked nothing more than to boast about his superior knowledge and foresight, and then be proven right after the fact.

Watching the moonlight wavering over the faint ripples on the pool's surface, Verena walked and thought of her grandmother and her parents, and how hard they'd worked to build up the business. *Brick by brick*, her father had often said. Joseph and Angelica Valent were well loved by family and friends. She'd ached for them every day of her life since—

A tall man in a white shirt stepped in front of her. "Excuse me, do you have a light?"

Startled, Verena jerked her head up. "No," she snapped. "And you shouldn't jump out in front of people like that."

"I'm sorry, didn't mean to frighten you." Surprise registered in his voice. His voice was a deep, warm baritone, and he sounded genuinely apologetic. The pool lights behind him illuminated his broad-shouldered physique.

She couldn't make out his face, but she could see a cigarette dangling from his silhouetted fingers. "Besides, you shouldn't smoke." She heard him sigh.

"I know. I quit, but I really need a cigarette right now. It's been one of those weeks."

"Tell me about it," she muttered. He made no reply but remained rooted to the ground before her, blocking her way. She put up her hand to shield her eyes from the light. "I can't see you, and you're in my way."

He stepped aside, angling his face. "Is that better?"

A shaft of light shone on his face. Verena caught her breath. Behind his engaging smile, his white teeth sparkled. His eyes crinkled in a nice way, drawing her in. He looked around her age, maybe a couple of years older—about thirty, she guessed. With sun-streaked, chestnut brown hair, it was obvious he enjoyed the California sunshine. He also had a distinct, inviting aroma about him. She sniffed. Garlic and rosemary. He wore a white jacket with a thermometer in a slender pouch sewn onto the sleeve and casual cotton pants. "Oh, you're a chef."

He laughed and bowed. "At your service."

"You smell wonderful." Verena grew warm. With her fair skin, she blushed easily, and she was glad it was dark outside.

"Hungry?"

"I had dinner, sort of, but I didn't really eat it. Actually, I'm starving."

He raised his eyebrows in alarm. "What was wrong with your food?"

With a start, Verena realized the meal must have come from his kitchen. "Nothing, it was delicious, but I can't eat much before I give a presentation. Audiences make me nervous."

Nodding he said, "Lots of actors have stage fright, too."

Feeling oddly comfortable with this stranger, Verena went on. "I'm always starving by the time an event like this is over. Everyone else has eaten well, and then I have to find a late night diner. Or room service."

"You'll have none of that tonight. Come with me." He took her hand and smiled at her again when she hesitated.

"What's the matter?" He glanced down at her barren left hand. "Boyfriend waiting for you?"

There it was again, that warm feeling that grew along her neck. "No, but my friends are waiting for me in the Polo Lounge."

"They'll be fine, but you should eat something." He frowned with concern. "Look, you're so weak you're shaking. I'll call the maître'd at the Polo Lounge for you. What's your name?"

"What's yours?"

"Ah, my manners. Forgive me, too much time in the kitchen. My name is Lance, Lance Martel."

"Verena Valent."

"Beautiful name for a beautiful woman." A smile curved on his full lips. "You're going to eat well tonight, Verena. Come with me." Still holding her hand, he let his fingers glide to her fingertips in a casual, friendly grasp.

His fingers felt magnetic. She was starving, and he seemed innocuous enough, though he was disarmingly attractive. Not in the powerful, intense way Derrick was, but in a charming, friendly way. She hesitated for a moment and then thought, why not?

20

2

Lance led Verena into the back of the kitchen where the staff was finishing clean-up for the night. "We have a limited menu at night for room service," he said. "Most of the kitchen is clean and we have a skeleton staff at night."

He walked ahead of her, nodding to a few employees that Verena guessed were sous chefs, line cooks, and servers. Drawing up a wooden stool to a stainless steel counter, he waved his hand. "Mademoiselle, your throne."

Before she sat down, Verena ran her finger across one of several large, gleaming knives on the table. "These are amazing."

"And razor sharp. Be careful, we have a lot of dangerous tools in here. I've got the scars to prove it." He pointed to an array of thin scars on his hands.

She tried not to stare. He was missing half of the third finger of his right hand. "That must have hurt."

He grinned at her and flicked up his finger. "Just kidding," he said, chuckling. "Old chef's joke. But you could perform surgery with these knives."

Verena smiled at his silly comment. He clearly liked to entertain people. Lifting her silvery skirt, she slid onto the stool and watched him gather the professional tools of his trade.

He brandished a copper skillet. "Anything you won't eat?"

"Hmm, maybe a Big Mac."

"I don't blame you." He looked up at her and paused, fixing his golden amber eyes on her. "Can I get creative?"

"Sure."

Lance placed the copper sauté pan on a cooktop, poured in a small measure of olive oil, and adjusted the gas flame. He reached for a bunch of fresh green herbs—oregano and basil, she noted—and selected an impressive knife. Wielding it with expert ease, he began to chop with speed and precision. The blade tapped in staccato rhythm against the cutting board. As he chopped, the fragrant leaves spilled forth their aroma. Verena breathed in, savoring the culinary magic.

While she was impressed with his confidence in the kitchen, she was mesmerized by his fluid movements. The kitchen was his domain, just as the skincare salon was hers.

He whipped out a copper saucepan and turned on another flame. Next came whipping cream and sprinkles from stainless steel bins—shallots and garlic—followed by cracked peppercorn. Then, several taps and shakes from a collection of stainless canisters were delivered in rapid, measured paces. Tap, tap-tap, tap. The tendons in his muscular forearms rippled as he worked.

Verena had never seen a professional chef at work, and she was captivated by his natural body rhythm and skill.

He glanced up at her. "You'll eat fowl, won't you?"

Jolted from her thoughtful gaze, she said, "Sorry?"

"Fowl, as in birds. I'll bet you like squab."

A smile danced on her lips. "Of course, I'm game."

"Usually I'm the one cracking the jokes." Grinning at her, he tossed more fresh herbs and ingredients into the mixture. He crossed the kitchen and opened a stainless steel refrigerator door. A moment later, he had his prized squab and set to work trimming and dressing the dish.

"Hey boss," one of the workers called out as he gathered soiled towels. "Need a hand?"

"No, I'll take care of this special order," Lance said with a wink.

Verena cupped her chin and leaned on her elbow, watching with rapt attention. "You really enjoy your work, don't you?"

"What's not to love about it? Feeding people great food makes them happy. And everyone has to eat."

He lifted a corner of his mouth in what Verena was quickly recognizing as a nearly ever-present grin. Many of the men she met were intent on being smooth and sophisticated, or forever youthful in a way that could only work in Los Angeles—and especially in Hollywood. Lots of men in L.A. seemed to be on the verge of an important, too-good-to-be-true deal, or professed to know someone who knew someone who could make their dreams come to fruition.

She'd heard it all at her salon—every story one could imagine. The incessant chatter was enough to make her head hurt at times.

And then there was Derrick—and his senior partner, billionaire Thomas Roper—who exuded the kind of power only derived from marshalling great sums of money. They were the dealmakers. Everyone with a dream of overnight riches seemed to pursue them. However, that wasn't why she'd dated Derrick.

In the beginning of their relationship, he'd been so attentive and focused on her. He told her she was the only one who had ever truly touched him. She also admired his business acumen—he'd had far more experience that she had in structuring business deals and raising money. His thoughtfulness toward her younger sisters had made an impression. With Mia's tenuous health, Verena's younger twin sisters were her responsibility and prime concerns for her.

Yet this man before her, who clearly derived such pleasure from preparing a meal for a woman he'd just met, seemed much more genuine, authentic, and relaxed in his skin. She was intrigued.

"How did you learn to cook like this?" she asked, trailing her fingers along the counter's cool stainless steel surface.

"I've always loved cooking," he said as he arranged ingredients. "While other kids watched cartoons or played video games, I watched cooking shows on television. After my mom went to bed, I'd sneak into the kitchen. Later, I went to culinary school in San Francisco. Even worked in Europe for a while." He paused and gazed straight into her eyes. "Someday I'd like to have my own restaurants and food lines. I have a plan, and I'm saving for it."

"Saving? Or just trying to find investors?" She realized she sounded jaded.

"Saving," he replied firmly. "I make my own way."

Verena felt her cheeks flush. Lance was sharing his most precious goals, she realized, and it touched her. She liked listening to him. His voice was as rich and smooth as the cream he poured into the saucepan.

"Do you pick up hungry women by the pool like this every night?" As soon as the words left her mouth, she regretted them. It was none of her business. What difference did it make to her?

But he didn't take exception to her remark, or if he did, he didn't show it. He shrugged. "Usually I clean up and leave, but it's been a busy week. We're short-handed, and I've had to do more cooking than usual."

When she looked quizzical, he added, "I'm the executive chef, which means I have general management duties."

Verena nodded knowingly. "That explains the smoking."

"Yeah, I'm not proud of it," he said. "Picked up the habit a couple years ago in Europe. Last year I quit for the first few months, and then wham, something set me off again. But I promised myself that this year would be different. I can't afford to kill my taste buds."

She liked what she was hearing. The sauce in the skillet sizzled and popped. "Hmm, smells good."

Lowering the flame, he asked, "Are you staying at the hotel or here for an event?"

"I'm a local," Verena said. "I was at the Women in Pink event."

"That's a great organization. And a beautiful dress," he added. "Which looks quite amazing on you, by the way."

Verena shivered with pleasure. She'd wondered if the silver silk dress that Fianna had designed just for her was too much, but its slim simplicity seemed the perfect backdrop for the iridescent South Pacific pearls that had belonged to her mother.

"I'd seen you near the pool," he said. "You seemed deep in thought."

"I was." Thinking of Marvin and her looming troubles, Verena shook her head.

Lance adjusted the simmering flame. "We have a few minutes until the liquid is reduced." He leaned forward to tuck a wayward wisp of wavy blond hair behind her ear. "Sometimes it helps to talk to a stranger."

The compassion in his eyes drew her in. "I run a skincare salon," she began. "It was my parents' business, and my grandparents before them. I've opened a chain of salons, and I'm in the middle of an aggressive international expansion plan for our product line."

He studied her as he listened. "You're having difficulties?"

"If you own a business, it's always something. Products, employees, financing, government regulations."

"So true. Well, I'm impressed. How long have you been running this business?"

"For the last decade, straight out of high school. My grandparents started it in the late 1940s. I love hearing my grandmother talk about the old days."

Lance started to ask a question, but another young man came around the corner. "Excuse me, boss, but I'm ready to leave." He shifted from one foot to another.

"Glad you reminded me. I'll get your check, John." To Verena he said, "Excuse me for a moment, but hold that thought. I'll be right back." His face lit with an easy smile.

Verena watched Lance leave the room with his employee. *What an interesting man.* Not a bit like Derrick.

Lance's quick smile reminded her of her grandfather Emile, who was so good-natured. As a child, she had loved listening to the stories her grandparents told. After the Second World War in Europe ended, Emile and Mia had moved from Switzerland to America. Emile had made their journey sound so exciting. They'd realized the fulfillment of their youthful dreams where the air was fresh, and sandy beaches sparkled under the warm sun.

After they arrived, Emile was soon earning a steady living as a construction superintendent. Compact stucco cottages with Spanish-tiled roofs were springing up in the surrounding valleys for war veterans and their young families.

Mia began to share her skincare formulas with her new neighbors. American women loved her pampering facial treatments and brought friends from Hollywood, Westwood, and Beverly Hills to see her. Mia converted the dining room, but their small cottage soon proved too small for Mia's burgeoning clientele, so they bought a plot of land on North Beverly Drive in the heart of the village of Beverly Hills.

While Emile and his friends built the new salon, Mia planned the interior, fashioning it after fine salons in Switzerland. She imprinted a grand initial "V" on everything from tea towels to tea cups. Ladies loved the European ambience, and the Valent Salon quickly became a favorite destination.

Verena still loved hearing about the early days of the salon.

"All the biggest stars came to the salon," Mia often told her. She pointed out their guests in movies and on television, and she took her young granddaughter to the salon on weekends. Mia loved to reminisce as she led Verena through powder pink treatment rooms that smelled so fresh and clean.

Mia also pointed out patron photos on the walls. "Here's Grace Kelly. What porcelain skin she had. There's

Marilyn Monroe and Natalie Wood…I always told those girls to stay out of the sun. And here's Doris Day. She was such an animal lover." Contemporary stars and models had their photos displayed, too.

In her private office upstairs, Mia kept a photo of Verena's father, Joseph, when he was a towheaded little boy. But Verena's favorite was a photo of her parents' wedding with her mother in a voluminous white wedding dress.

Verena adored her grandmother Mia, who some people mistook for her mother because of her pale blond hair and smooth, wrinkle-free skin. Mia would smile, tell them about her special formulas, and assure them that they, too, could have beautiful skin. Being helpful and sharing her passion was a natural part of who Mia was.

As a teenager, Verena had observed, listened, and learned, but she'd never dreamed that she would have to shoulder the demands of the business so soon on her own.

Lance rounded the corner. "How's the sauce?"

Pulling herself from her memories, she peered at the simmering pan. "Looks nicely reduced, just as you said. And it smells delicious."

Lance picked up a spoon, stirred the sauce, and checked the squab. Satisfied, he turned back to her. "You were telling me about your grandparents."

She nodded. "Before they left Switzerland, my grandmother created many of the natural products we continue to produce and sell today. Her father was a scientist, so she learned her craft in his laboratory. When I was a little girl, she taught me that any woman can be beautiful. To this day she believes that beauty begins with the way a woman treats herself. And she's right. I can always tell if a woman is tired or has a poor diet."

"How?" Lance asked.

"Everything shows on the face. Alcohol, cigarettes...anything that's toxic will affect the skin. And the sun is extremely damaging."

"Guilty as charged," Lance said, tapping his sunburned nose. His tone was teasing, but he was clearly impressed with her knowledge.

Verena laughed. "A few minutes of sun for your skin to absorb vitamin D is actually beneficial and keeps bones strong." Touching his cheek, she quickly assessed his skin. "Your skin looks healthy. Just don't forget sunscreen."

"Can you help me find one that's not too greasy?" As he spoke, he placed another saucepan on the burner and added a handful of tiny vegetables.

"Of course. I'm working on a new men's line." For a moment, she imagined the pleasure of running her hands over his supple bronzed skin. She cleared her throat and went on. "From the time I was a little girl, my grandmother shared her skincare secrets with me. She still has some personal formulas that must be made fresh with each use, so we can't produce them commercially yet. Some of my fondest childhood memories were of Mia and my mother teaching me about skincare treatments in Mia's private facial room."

Mia always made her feel special by gently cleansing Verena's skin and instructing her on each step and each product, explaining its benefits and how to use it for the best results.

Verena looked up at Lance, who seemed transfixed by her story. The way he stared at her made her chest flutter.

"I didn't realize it at the time, but even then, all those years ago, Mia was training me to take over the business."

"Are your parents in the business, too?"

There it was. The question she always dreaded, the question that always changed the way people treated her. By now, she could forecast the pity in their eyes. She just wanted to be treated normally. But she'd probably never see Lance again, so what did it matter what she said? She swallowed and glanced down at her fingernails, smoothing them out of nervousness. "No, not anymore."

She thought he looked quizzical for a moment, or perhaps she was imagining it.

After pouring cognac into the sauce, he said, "And now for the show." He touched it with a match, sending flames toward the ceiling.

"I'd set off the fire alarm if I tried that," Verena said.

Lance stirred the sauce quickly to thicken it, and then announced, "Ready to plate." He worked quickly to arrange the squab with sauce, petit haricots verts, and pearl onions on a plate.

"*Voilà*," he said with a flourish of his hand. He placed the dish in front of her. Silver utensils and a linen napkin followed. "Wine?"

"Love some."

He pulled a bottle from a shelf. "Chef's choice," he said, uncorking it and pouring two glasses. "To you, Verena," he said, giving her a glass and holding his high in a toast. "May you never go hungry again. Please, begin."

She took a forkful, savoring the delicate flavors.

"And?" He leaned forward, clearly curious as to her reaction.

"Delicious. My compliments to the chef." Maybe it was

the sauce, or the fact that she was famished—or maybe it was the way he looked at her—but Verena thought the dish was one of the best she had ever tasted.

"Leave room for dessert," he said.

While she ate, they continued talking about food and skincare, laughing at little jokes, and sipping wine. Lance leaned on the counter beside her, pointing out the best morsels and explaining how the ingredients melded together for a unique flavor.

They were laughing when the kitchen door burst open.

"My God, Verena," Derrick said, anger etched on his face. "I've been looking all over for you. The security guard said he saw you go in the back door. What are you doing here?"

"Eating." Verena calmly wiped a corner of her mouth. "Lance is the executive chef, and he's prepared a meal for me. What are *you* doing here?"

"You already had dinner." He stood with his hands on his hips, glaring at Lance, who just grinned at him over the top of his wine glass.

"No, I didn't. You know I don't eat much before I get up in front of an audience." She took another bite, chewing slowly. *The nerve of him to track me down.* His possessiveness was one of the reasons she'd broken up with him.

Derrick's face clouded, and his dark hooded eyes flashed. "We need to talk. You've eaten, now let's go."

She gestured to her plate, refusing to be bullied. "I'm not finished, and I'm not going anywhere with you tonight." In her peripheral vision, she saw Lance step toward Derrick.

Derrick huffed. "I'll call you tomorrow for lunch."

"I have an extremely busy day tomorrow," Verena said,

keeping her voice even.

"You have no idea," he said. "Instead of sitting here in a kitchen, you should be worried about how you're going to keep your company afloat without Marvin Panetta and National Western Bank."

"That's enough," Lance said. "The lady's not interested. You need to leave my kitchen now."

With one last stony stare at the pair, Derrick turned and stomped out.

Verena was appalled by Derrick's rudeness. In her position as the head of her company, she didn't accept bullying behavior, and she certainly wouldn't accept it in a relationship—current or past. Not anymore.

She swung back to Lance, who stood taking it all in. "I appreciate that. Now, how about that dessert you promised?"

3

Verena glanced around the posh Polo Lounge at the Beverly Hills Hotel, eager to find her friends. After she'd finished eating, Lance had walked her here to make sure she found them.

"Johnny said they're waiting for you," Lance said, lightly touching her elbow. He'd changed from his chef's jacket into a white open-collared shirt and draped his sports coat over her shoulders when she'd mentioned she was a little chilly.

His jacket was still warm with the heat of his body and it held a citrusy, musky scent in its lightweight woolen fibers. Verena inhaled and drew it closer around her shoulders, drinking in his lingering aroma.

She couldn't remember when she'd felt more relaxed and comfortable with a man. Even after the shock of Marvin's death, Greta's bombshell news, and Derrick's warnings, somehow Lance had made her smile.

"There they are." Verena spotted her friends through the crowded lounge area. Scarlett, Dahlia, and Fianna sat in a plush curved booth, positioned, Verena knew, so that everyone entering would see beautiful women. That's what their friend Johnny Morales, the maître'd, had once told her. Her friends were attractive, but they were also much more than that. They had known each other for years and were smart, independent, and hard-working. Verena made her way through the standing crowd, and Lance followed her.

She saw Scarlett's eyes widen when she saw Lance. "Thanks for waiting for me," Verena said. "I'd like to introduce you to Lance Martel, the executive chef here at the hotel. We ran into each other at the pool, and he made dinner for me. I was absolutely starving. Lance, I'd like you to meet some of my closest friends."

"Very nice meeting you," Lance said. "How do you all know Verena?"

Dahlia spoke first, her green eyes sparkling with questions Verena knew would spill out later. "Verena and I met when we were children. Our grandmothers are friends."

Scarlett added, "I was a salon client—still am, of course. Verena knows a lot of people through her business."

"And I used to help Verena with the twins when they were little," Fianna said.

Lance looked interested in this last comment. "You have twins?" he said to Verena, his face lit with interest.

Verena was used to this response. "My younger sisters. I look after them." *Why elaborate?* Sympathy made her uncomfortable.

Though Lance started to say something, Verena turned back to her friends, eager to change the subject. "Lance whipped up the most amazing dinner. A squab that was absolutely delicious. And an organic tofu dark chocolate mousse that was to die for."

A warm smile grew on Lance's face. "You're a pleasure to cook for. I like women who enjoy eating. A lot of women in the city seem to exist on lettuce."

Fianna pushed her thick, fiery hair back and laughed. "Not us. You can cook for us anytime,"

While Verena slid into the booth, Lance remained standing next to her.

"Derrick was looking for you," Dahlia said, stealing another glimpse of Lance. "Did he find you?"

"Actually, Lance met Derrick," Verena said, while Lance slid a slightly amused, quizzical look at her.

"He stopped by the kitchen," Lance said, never taking his eyes from Verena.

Scarlett frowned. "How did he know where you were? I wouldn't have thought to look in the kitchen. Did he follow you?"

"Evidently one of the security guards saw me," Verena said. Nothing slipped past Scarlett. With reluctance, she removed Lance's jacket from her shoulders and returned it to him. She lifted her hand to shake hands with him. "Thank you for cooking for me, it meant a lot to me."

Instead of taking her hand, he leaned in and kissed her on the cheek, carefully brushing her hair aside as he did. "It was *my* pleasure. Good night."

It was a small gesture, but it made her catch her breath. "Good night, Lance," she murmured.

He turned to her friends. "If you dine with us again, ladies, please let me know you're here so I can take extra good care of you." He grinned at them, and then turned and left.

"Wow, weren't you the lucky one," Fianna said, watching him walk away.

Verena shrugged. "He was nice, that's all."

"I'll say." Nodding, Scarlett sipped her sparkling water with lime.

Scarlett didn't drink; she was always the designated

driver in the group. Verena valued her opinion. Scarlett's training in law had taught her to be observant, to look beneath the surface for clues, and to look for the subtext in conversations.

Scarlett was street smart, too. She and Johnny, the maître d' at the Polo Lounge, had grown up together in the *barrios* of Los Angeles after her family had moved from Spain during a recession. She and Johnny had been as close as siblings, and her brother and Johnny had been best friends before Franco had enlisted. And just look at them now, Verena thought, pleased for her friends. Johnny had also turned out well, and he knew all the important people in town.

Johnny caught her eye and strode to the table, adjusting his fancy red polka-dot bow-tie, his fashion trademark. "Lance called and told me where you were. He didn't want your friends to worry."

Scarlett, Dahlia, and Fianna exchanged looks. Dahlia raised an eyebrow and said, "Only Verena ends the evening with a special dinner from the executive chef."

"And one of the hottest ones around," Fianna added. "I mean, one of the most accomplished. I read an article about him in the *Los Angeles Times*."

Scarlett laughed. "No, you meant hottest."

Johnny smoothed his glossy black hair. "I can assure you, Verena was in very good hands. Lance is a good guy."

Verena started to ask him more about Lance, but another patron motioned to Johnny, so he excused himself. She turned to Scarlett. "How long can you stay in L.A?" After graduation, Scarlett had sat for the California and New York bar exams, two of the toughest in the country, and passed them both on the first try. Law firms had competed to hire her, and a New York City firm had won her with a generous offer. Scarlett was trying to make partner, so she worked long hours.

"Actually, I have an open-ended ticket. One of our major clients here in L.A. has a series of licensing deals I'm working on for them, among other things. Looks like I'll be here most of the summer working out of our local office."

"I'm so glad," Verena said, hugging her. Scarlett was in demand, and she didn't get to see her very often. If one of the top fragrance marketing houses was poised to ink a deal with a new fashion designer, or a retailer wanted to license a designer's name, Scarlett and her team prepared and negotiated the deal, wherever the client might be.

A waiter appeared with a tray of cocktails. "Ladies, compliments of Lance Martel, our executive chef." He placed another sparkling water in front of Scarlett, served Bordeaux wine to Dahlia and Verena, and slid a martini across the table to Fianna.

"Lance seems awfully thoughtful," Dahlia said. "Think you might see him again?"

Verena shrugged. "You all know how hectic my life is." Between her sisters, her grandmother, and the business, Verena hadn't had much time for dating. Derrick had been determined, but in the end, he'd proven too demanding. Lance was different, and if her life were different...but it wasn't.

"Derrick is definitely still interested," Fianna said, wrinkling her nose.

Verena chuckled. "You never liked him."

"With good reason," Fianna shot back.

Fianna was outspoken, and she and Derrick had

clashed from the first time they'd met.

Interrupting, Scarlett raised her glass in a toast. "Here's to Verena, our Executive Visionary of the Year."

"*Santé*," Dahlia said. She swirled her wine in the glass, paused to sniff it with her dainty nose and consider, and finally, sipped the wine. "*Très bon*," she murmured.

Verena smiled as she watched Dahlia. Some people might think such actions pretentious, but she knew it was simply second nature to Dahlia, who came from an esteemed line of French perfumers. Her grandmother, Camille Dubois, had emigrated to the United Sates from France during World War II. Dahlia had grown up working in the House of Dubois and had recently taken charge of the company temporarily during her grandmother's illness.

Camille and Verena's grandmother Mia had met when they were young women just starting their businesses, and they had been close friends ever since. They'd supported each other when their husbands had died, grappled with growing their businesses, and stood up to those who'd tried to take advantage of them. But it hadn't been easy.

Dahlia reminded everyone of her grandmother, not only in the way she looked—petite in stature with glossy black hair—but also in her manner. She was fiercely independent and highly intelligent, with a work ethic that scared most men away. She loved ballet and vintage fashion, and she often lamented that she'd been born a few decades too late.

Scarlett turned to her. "Dahlia, I meant to tell you that we received the red-lined documents back from the other counsel."

Verena knew that Scarlett was referring to a legal agreement that she was negotiating between Parfums

Dubois and a major Hollywood celebrity for a new line of perfumes.

"Wonderful, let's review it tomorrow," Dahlia said, looking relieved. "I just learned we need the final contract before we can renegotiate our bank loans."

"I'm surprised." Verena drew her brows together. Parfums Dubois was a major international company. Something didn't add up.

"You're not the only one," Dahlia said. "Camille has had her banking relationship for years, but it's not only our bank. All the lenders are getting tough."

"Why?" Fianna asked, taking an interest in the conversation.

"Our board said all banks are growing more restrictive in light of the economy." Dahlia sipped her wine before continuing. "Scarlett, Camille will want to read the agreement, too."

"Camille is out of the hospital?" Verena knew that Dahlia's grandmother had been in Cedars Sinai for pneumonia treatments.

"Just this afternoon," Dahlia said. "The doctor won't allow her to return to work, so she's bringing it all home. Her assistants have set up in her living room. She'll have them working harder there than in the office. There's no stopping that woman."

Fianna laughed. "Camille is still fabulous. I want to be just like her when I'm in my sixties."

Dahlia raised a brow again. "Sixties? French women seldom discuss their age, but between us, she's a decade or two past that. Maybe it's because she met Verena's grandmother so many years ago and had a lifetime of superb skincare. Camille and Mia don't look their age."

"Or act it," Fianna added, widening her eyes. "Imagine what they must have been like when they were young."

Scarlett tilted her water goblet toward Fianna in agreement. "Not hard to picture, but I don't think they've changed much. They're both awfully sharp and completely self-trained. If there's even a typo in the agreements we draft, Camille always catches it."

Verena grinned at Fianna, the free-spirited artist of their group. Fianna Fitzgerald had been born in Ireland and graduated from the Fashion Institute of Design and Merchandising in Los Angeles. The youngest in a large family, she'd put herself through school working for Verena. She'd helped her with the twins after their parents died. "How's your licensing program going?"

"Scarlett and I are working on it," Fianna said, as Scarlett nodded in agreement.

Fianna's fledging fashion line was sold exclusively in her boutique on trendy Robertson Boulevard in Los Angeles. Fianna had bootstrapped her company and was struggling to expand her distribution to attract licensing opportunities for handbags, eyewear, and shoes. Verena knew she'd welcome the deals. "Fianna, did you follow up with that public relations person in New York?"

"I did, but I'm waiting on payment on some invoices before I retain her. She's pricey."

"But worth it," Verena said. "I think that's the push you need in the media for more recognition." Fianna's designs had garnered a few small fashion awards, but she still had to build sales. Verena thought Fianna was a natural for media exposure. With her flaming red hair, one blue eye and one brown eye—a condition known as heterochromia—and an exuberant personality, Verena thought Fianna could attract a lot of attention from fashion editors.

Fianna and Scarlett nodded in agreement. After Verena had taken over the skincare company at such a young age, she began a media outreach program, inviting beauty editors and young actresses to the salon for free facials. It was a resounding success and helped to reposition the company.

Fianna sighed and looked up from her martini. "Honestly, I'm a little nervous speaking to the press."

Dahlia and Scarlett both answered at once. "You?"

"I know, but I'm always afraid I'll say something wrong. I'm too blunt."

"You need media training," Scarlett said.

"Well sure, but it's expensive. Takes money to make money," Fianna said, cupping her chin. She turned to Verena. "Do you think the bank problems could hurt your company? Greta sure seemed to think so."

Verena was growing more concerned. "I'll figure something out. We're resilient. But I feel awful about Marvin." Verena cast her eyes down to hide the concern she harbored. Even Dahlia's banker was asking to see contracts, and their company was many times larger than VSS. She sipped her wine, noting the fine vintage Lance had chosen. "Scarlett, let's talk tomorrow morning."

Scarlett agreed. After chatting a little longer, they left the Polo Lounge and walked to the front of the hotel, where they waited under the canopy on a red carpet while the valet attendants collected the car.

"I'll drive," Scarlett said. She slid into the driver's seat of Dahlia's car and the other women got in.

While Scarlett drove the short distance to Verena's home, Verena mulled over the events of the evening, her anxiety rising. *Poor Marvin.* She'd always trusted him. He'd been a true friend and a straightforward businessman. If what Greta said was true, her business—and her family—could be in real trouble.

Verena opened the door to her Spanish bungalow-styled home and slipped off her shoes so her heels wouldn't click across the hardwood floors and wake her family. She stopped at the twins' bedroom and looked in on them. They looked like little blond-haired angels asleep in their beds. She waited until she saw the covers lift and fall in silent rhythm. Quietly, she continued on to her grandmother's bedroom. Her door was open.

"Come in," Mia said, "I've been dying to hear how the event went." She was sitting up in bed reading a book. Her pale blond hair was brushed from her forehead, and she looked small against a stack of pillows. She removed her reading glasses and patted the bed beside her.

"I'm glad you're still awake." Verena gathered her silvery evening dress around her and climbed onto the bed beside her grandmother. Mia looked rested, and Verena was relieved. Due to Mia's bout with cancer, she often worried about her grandmother's health.

Verena took Mia's slender hand. "You were missed, you know. Scarlett is in town, and she asked after you. Many others did, too." She hesitated, hating to have to share the bad news about Marvin's suicide, but Mia had known him, too.

After Verena told her what had happened, Mia shook her head, blinking back tears. "Dear fellow, I never would have suspected that of him. Not at all like him, in fact. Something terrible must have driven him to such an act, something that compromised his values, or made his future seem hopeless. And he left behind such a lovely family."

Verena agreed, something just didn't seem right about his death. "I'll call on them tomorrow to see if there's anything we can do for them."

"That's a good idea." Mia smoothed a wavy tendril from Verena's face. "I wish I could have been there for you, but it takes so much to put myself together these days. I'm saving my strength for the long haul to Europe. I hope you understand."

"Of course I do. Why don't you stop in New York for a couple of days? It's a long haul to Europe from L.A. It might be easier on you."

"In the old days, that was the only route we could take. But I like direct flights. A little wine, a nice dinner, and when we wake up, *voilà*, we're in Europe." Mia touched her hand and said, "I wish you would come with us. We're going to have such a wonderful time. Your sisters will miss you."

"I wish I could, but I'm going to be awfully busy at the salon." Although she'd told Mia about Marvin, she hadn't mentioned that they might have difficulty finding another bank to provide the working capital they'd need for the Asia expansion. *Why worry her?*

Verena removed her small diamond-stud earrings and rotated her neck. She cradled the earrings in her hand, admiring the sparkle of the stones. These were the ones her mother had worn on her wedding day, so she liked to wear them for luck.

What had been lucky about tonight? she wondered. A memory of Lance shot through her mind, and a small sigh escaped her lips. She'd spent a magical hour with a charming man. No more, no less.

That's all it would ever be. She had far more important, pressing matters to deal with as soon as she could.

Mia peered at her. "Something else on your mind, dear?

Verena was tempted to confide in her, but she couldn't bear to burden her. "Just tired."

"Did you see Derrick?"

Her grandmother could always read her. "Only for a short time."

"There will be someone else for you. Be patient."

It wasn't a matter of patience, though. Her life was more complicated that any man could understand. Or perhaps tolerate. No, she suspected her life was already written. She had Mia and the girls to look after, and they came first before anyone else. She'd fought to keep the business and maintain their home just as it had been when her parents had been alive.

Verena rose from the bed, kissed her grandmother good night, and softly closed the door behind her.

But as she walked through her familiar home to her bedroom, Verena had the strange prescience that nothing in their lives was going to be quite like it had been before.

4

After Verena and her friends left, Lance stayed behind waiting for a chance to speak to Johnny, with whom he shared a good friendship. It was after midnight by the time the dining area closed and the kitchen was clean. Lance looked for his friend, anxious to find more about Verena Valent.

Johnny looked up from the reservation book he was making notes on. "Did you have a good night?"

Lance leaned against the host desk. "I'll say. Not often I have a beautiful woman in my kitchen to cook for."

"That's only because you don't let them in. You could have a line out the door if you wanted." Johnny winked and loosened his bow tie.

"Not my style." Lance knew that wasn't the way Johnny operated either. They both worked too many hours and held important positions at the hotel. "More of my brother's," he added. Although Lance enjoyed painting, his free-spirited brother was the true artist, travelling the globe to visit galleries or work on special commissions. Women had always flocked after Adrien.

Stifling a yawn, Johnny asked, "Has Adrien gone back to San Francisco yet?"

"He's visiting our parents in La Jolla." Lance was close to his brothers, Adrien and Rhys, even though they all had different temperaments. He couldn't imagine how his mother had managed three boisterous boys born only a

45

couple of years apart. They'd been a formidable bunch growing up, but they'd all gone their separate ways. He had to admit he missed them now.

Johnny glanced at several business cards that patrons had given him during the evening and made notes on them. "How are the folks?"

"Doing pretty well." His father was a writer and his mother was a costume designer. Creativity ran deep in their family. He'd always admired the way his parents had weathered the vagaries of their careers, yet they'd always made sure their sons had plenty of love and guidance. His parents were his role models, and they generally supported his decisions, although his mother was always straight with him. Lisette Martel didn't hesitate to let her sons know when she thought any of them were in the wrong or could do better. In her mid-fifties, she was still a lovely woman with a slender figure from years of yoga and dance. She'd tried introducing him to women in San Diego, but he hadn't really been interested or had the time. He was waiting for a magical connection, the kind his parents had.

Lance tapped on the reservation book to get Johnny's attention. "So how well do you know Verena Valent?"

Johnny glanced up from his work. "She's a good friend of Scarlett's. I've gotten to know her that way, and through her grandmother. Mia Valent is a regular here."

"And?" Lance rotated his hand in a circular motion. "Come on, help me out here. Is she dating anyone?"

Closing his reservation book, Johnny shook his head. "She was engaged to Derrick Logan, but Scarlett said she broke it off. With good reason, I bet. That guy's a snake."

"What about now?"

"She runs her family skincare salon here, and I gather

she's pretty busy with that and her family." Johnny quirked his mouth in a half-grin. "If you could get through to Verena, she's a keeper for sure."

Taking it all in, Lance nodded. He couldn't put his feelings into words, but Verena had something special. The expression in her eyes, the sound of her laughter, the way she'd shot back at Derrick in the kitchen. She had grace and guts, a formidable combination that he couldn't help but admire.

"Thanks a lot," Lance said, giving Johnny a friendly fist bump.

The next day in the kitchen of the Beverly Hills Hotel, Lance changed into a white chef's jacket and went to work. After meeting with his kitchen crew, he went to the Polo Lounge to survey the busy lunch scene, where celebrities dined with their agents and publicists, fundraisers pitched charity balls, and out-of-town guests relished the glamour.

It was his custom to circulate and visit the tables of the hotel's regular customers and welcome new guests. He would ask how they were, and make sure they were enjoying their meal. By doing this, he learned a lot and the attention made their guests feel special, which was good for business.

As he was chatting with a group of filmmakers, he overheard a conversation behind him. A gruff, older voice asked, "Why won't Verena entertain a sale?"

Glancing over his shoulder, Lance was startled to recognize Derrick, who was dining with one of the most well-known power brokers in Los Angeles, Thomas Roper.

Lance stepped behind a potted palm under the guise of observing the activity in the restaurant. He hated eavesdropping on principle, but he couldn't help himself. Verena had been on his mind all night, and he'd even woken up thinking about her.

"She's emotionally tied to the business," Derrick said. "Told me she doesn't want to sell."

"That was months ago. We need to acquire Valent Skincare," Thomas Roper said, tapping his age-spotted fingers on the linen-covered table.

Lance remembered catering a board meeting at Roper's office when he'd first started. *Everything in Roper's office was designed to intimidate.* The cold sprawling office topped a towering Century City office building. His corner view encompassed the Pacific Ocean on one side, and on the other, the Los Angeles Country Club's groomed golf course, where Lance had heard that Roper was a founding member. Roper wore a black suit, starched white shirt, and red power tie. With steely grey eyes and a perpetual grimace, he looked like he'd sold his soul long ago.

"Did you hear me?" Roper frowned in annoyance. "Like everyone, she has her price. Make her an offer."

Derrick drew a breath. "Yes, sir. But we should look at other companies."

"No. You will do this deal."

Or else, thought Lance. He knew Roper's reputation for taking advantage of people and opportunities. Word travelled fast in the hospitality business. Lance also cooked for private parties, and he had his own celebrity clientele. He'd given interviews and been photographed for plenty of magazines. In the homes of the rich and famous, he'd often heard Roper's name. And a whole lot more.

Roper went on, irritation evident in his voice. "Valent is a well-respected company with a marketable story." He ticked off points on his fingers. "Legendary Swiss formulas, three generations, based in Beverly Hills, celebrity clientele, plus pure organic botanical products. The efficacy of her products is off the charts. She has no idea what that's worth. You *will* get that company in our portfolio, one way or the other." He creased his brow. "You didn't tell her about the clinical tests, did you?"

"No, of course not. I told Verena I wanted to give her products to some VIP clients as gifts. I never told her about the tests or the results."

"Good, don't. We can use that later to boost sales. Look, Derrick, Verena Valent doesn't have the experience to understand the future value of her company after she launches in Asia. The accounts she has are critical building blocks for a cosmetics empire that will be worth billions. I want Valent, and you will get it for me."

"Don't underestimate her, sir."

Lance leaned in. *As if the old man needed the money.*

"And don't let me think I've overestimated your ability." Roper narrowed his eyes and pointed a bony finger at Derrick. "There's a reason I made you a minor partner."

"Let me do it my way."

"Then do it. Valent is on track to make hundreds of millions of dollars, with proper management, of course. We'll send Jimmy Don in. He can handle it."

Derrick cleared his throat. "Verena definitely adds value to the business. She has good relationships with clients."

"They don't care. They'll forget her tomorrow." Roper tapped his glass. "You plan to marry that girl?"

"I told you I will," Derrick said, sounding sure of

himself.

As if he had a chance, thought Lance. He'd only just met her, but she struck him as a lot smarter than that. Not that it was any of his business.

Roper snorted. "You'll *have* to have a prenuptial agreement. She'll want the same. If that's what you're thinking, you won't get the company that way. So, why bother marrying her? Lots of fish in the sea, trust me."

"I understand, sir."

Roper waved a hand for the check. "I've got to take a leak." He left the table, leaving Derrick alone.

Disturbed by what he'd heard, Lance narrowed his eyes. This conversation violated his deep sense of fairness. As Lance started to leave, another man in a dark suit joined Derrick at the table. Lance recognized him from the usual lunch crowd, but he didn't know who he was.

"How's that deal going?"

Derrick glanced around and lowered his voice. "Making progress. VSS is missing piece to the Newco."

Newco. Lance had heard that term used before. It meant they were creating an as yet unnamed new company.

"My people might want in on that. What's the deal?"

"It's going to rival the monolithic beauty companies. Coty, LVMH, L'Oreal, Estée Lauder. Roper's been quietly acquiring smaller domestic companies. VSS is the key to international distribution."

"Nice profit margins there," the other man said. "We like what we see in the beauty industry with the aging demographics."

Derrick nodded. "VSS will give us immediate high level entrée into the coveted Asian market. It's got a celebrity-studded pedigree to boot."

The man chuckled. "Got to hand it to you. You set yourself up pretty well with Roper. Even masters of the universe don't live forever."

Derrick scowled. "I work damn hard for that old codger. He spends every day scheming about how to become even richer before he dies, just so his obit will have a higher score than anyone else's." Derrick glanced around and checked his gold Piaget watch.

"I hear that might not be long. Old guy's not in best of health, is he?"

"Yeah, but he's tough. Roper's heirs will still own the majority share of the firm."

"But you'll run the show. Be patient. You'll be richer than all of us one day soon." The guy shook his head. "How's he do it?"

"It's a formula," Derrick said. "Find the company, whittle its projections, loan them less than actually needed. Lock up the founders with mountains of legal documents. Create complications for them, obtain board control."

They guy laughed. "Man, that's a beautiful set-up for failure."

Derrick shrugged. "We acquire equity, take over the company on technicalities, replace the founders with our management team, grab the preferred stock, and repeat."

"Like shooting fish in a barrel right now."

The two men grinned at each other.

The other man shook his head. "Don't you ever feel a little guilty?"

"I'll make a bunch of charitable donations."

"Think that'll hold your place in heaven?"

Before Derrick could answer, Lance saw Roper coming

back to the table. Spying him, the other man rushed away.

Lance let out a long breath. He couldn't believe people actually acted like that. Sometimes what he saw in real life was worse than any fake reality show ever could be.

As Roper signed the check for the meal, Lance hurried to the kitchen.

He had to call Verena and tell her about overhearing this conversation. If it were him, he'd sure want to know, but she might think he was butting in where he had no business. Maybe she already knew, or maybe this was why Derrick had wanted to talk to her. Should he share this conversation with her?

Lance paused at the door to his office. He didn't care. Verena should know.

5

Verena hummed to herself as she dressed for the day ahead in a cream-colored pencil skirt with a matching silk blouse. Between Marvin's death and the pressing financial issues, she had little reason to feel happy, but replaying last night's scene in the kitchen with Lance at least gave her some respite.

Of all her girlfriends, Verena had dated the least because she had her hands full with her family and the business. Though Derrick was as busy as she was, he'd been persistent about their relationship. She had to give him credit for that. Lance seemed so kind and easy going, but then, Derrick had been different in the beginning, too. He'd presented such positive, powerful confidence and she'd found that appealing, but she began to realize that he wasn't necessarily what he seemed.

A wail arose from the bedroom next door, and seconds later, her sister Anika door burst open, her face flushed with anger. "Bella is wearing my new purple top."

And Derrick would never adapt to this sort of home life. Could Lance?

"Bella, we don't have time for this," Verena called out. The twins were twelve years old and nearly as tall as she was, but at times they acted like they were five. "You'll be late for school. Give it back."

"Can't hear you," Bella yelled. "Let's go!" She jingled Verena's car keys and slammed the front door.

Verena snatched a purple shirt from a drawer and tossed it to Anika. "Here, wear mine."

"Really? I love this!" Anika pulled it over her head.

"Hurry, get your backpack." Verena scooped up her purse and the files she'd brought home from the salon.

Minutes later, they were on their way to school. Anika beamed from the backseat. After Verena dropped them off at school, she drove the short distance to the salon.

She stepped inside the salon and drew a deep breath. Her office always smelled fresh and clean. The unique scent of their products permeated the air, and Verena loved it. The natural aroma always helped her clear and focus her mind.

She picked up the telephone and called Scarlett, who had already confirmed Marvin's death.

Scarlett had started work early this morning. "I spoke with my friend at the coroner's office," Scarlett said. "Although early reports said it appeared Marvin shot himself, an autopsy is being done and the police took forensic samples. There's definitely an investigation underway."

"Why? Isn't it evident?" Verena's hand began to shake and she shifted the receiver.

"I'm not sure. He mentioned something about the angle of the bullet entry. Wait a minute, I took notes."

Verena closed her eyes. "I can't listen to this, Scarlett."

"I understand. We'll talk about it later." Scarlett paused. "On a brighter note, Lance seemed awfully nice. Are you planning on seeing him again?"

"Haven't heard from him. Besides, you know how busy I am. Speaking of which, I've got to go."

After hanging up with Scarlett, Verena dialed the bank.

She spoke at length with one of Marvin's associates at National Western, and then she sat back, dumbfounded. Greta's information had been accurate. The bank could not honor its loan commitment for the VSS expansion into Asia.

She flicked on the television in her office and turned to the business channel. New reports were calling this a credit crisis and bank lending was tightening. Although the company had always had good credit, Verena began to realize she probably wouldn't have much luck with other banks, especially since she wasn't a customer.

Still, her company was profitable. VSS had been in business for decades and had signed agreements with retailers throughout Asia. Purchase orders had been received, product shipped, and invoices sent. She simply needed short-term working capital to cover expenses until they received payment. The product wouldn't sell itself; she needed money for co-op advertising, payroll, training, and travel.

The pressure in her chest grew, and she clicked off the television. Whatever she did, she had to act fast.

She glanced at Mia's portrait, an oil painting by artist Max Band of the Paris School of Artists. It had hung on the wall for decades in the elegant office suite. It was Mia in her prime, before the cancer had robbed her of her indomitable strength. Mia's expression was fearless, proud, and determined. What would Mia do? She'd talk with her once she grandmother was feeling stronger, but today's business climate was much more complex than it had been when Mia was running the business.

How quickly things change. Verena pressed her fingers

against her forehead to ease the growing ache. On the desk sat framed photos of the salon and the street from the early 1950s. She rose and stood by the second story window overlooking North Beverly Drive. At that time, Beverly Hills had been a small village of grocers, boutiques, hardware shops, and silversmiths.

When her grandfather Emile had built the salon for his wife, all the shops were owned by individuals and families. The corporate invasion had not yet started. Today, the small, five-square-mile city was a mecca for luxury shopping with international retailers from Cartier and Gucci to Gap and Victoria's Secret lining the streets.

Verena touched the cool glass, watching the bustling street scene below. She was so proud of the women in her family. Mia had worked tirelessly to grow the business. Many of their current estheticians had begun their careers at the salon and had been trained by Mia.

Angelica, Verena's mother, had also worked in the business. When Mia had been diagnosed with breast cancer while on a trip to Switzerland, Angelica took the helm. Since Mia's husband Emile had died of a heart attack a couple of years before, she stayed in Switzerland with her sister during her cancer treatments.

It was during this time that tragedy struck their family.

Verena blinked back tears at the memory. *Ten years ago, though it still seems like yesterday.* She had just graduated from Beverly Hills High School and had been accepted to Brown University to begin in the fall. She was thrilled to be going with her closest friends, and eager to meet new people.

Angelica was running the salon and looking after Anika and Bella, who were just two years old. "They were a singular surprise, but a double blessing," Angelica used to say. The twins seemed to make her parents young again.

It had been a balmy summer evening, Verena recalled. Angelica and Joseph had gone out to dinner at Trader Vic's restaurant in Beverly Hills. Verena agreed to watch the girls so her parents could celebrate their anniversary. It wasn't far from their home; in fact, it was so close that Verena heard the ambulances and fire trucks, but at the time, she didn't know the emergency vehicles had been called for her parents.

To this day, whenever she heard a siren she always said a prayer for the victims.

Her throat still tightened when she recalled that night. *Died on impact*, she'd been told. *Killed by a drunk driver.* In an instant, her entire world had changed.

Still in the middle of her cancer treatments, Mia was too ill for the long flight home—her doctor sternly forbade it. She did what she could from Switzerland, but most of the work fell on Verena's shoulders. Dahlia and her grandmother Camille, who was Mia's closest friend, helped arrange the funeral. Verena immediately canceled her fall matriculation into Brown University so she could care for her young sisters and run the salon. She hired a nanny, and Angelica's assistant Lacey did everything she could, but it was still a heavy load for an eighteen-year-old.

The summer passed in a grief-stricken blur, and Verena never had the opportunity to go to college. As the business had grown, she'd worked hard to overcome this deficit. As Verena reflected, that was one reason she'd been drawn to Derrick. With his MBA and business experience, he always seemed to know exactly what she should do, and so far, he'd been right. As VSS expanded its product line and began distributing to other retailers, the company had pushed the boundaries of her expertise, although she was definitely up to the task for learning and executing. Derrick had been helpful in crafting her new international strategy to bring the company into the twenty-first century, which she'd undertaken to provide for Mia and the twins. Between the twins' costs and healthcare for Mia's condition, Verena's family budget was often stretched thin.

A knock at the door pulled Verena from her thoughts. "Yes?"

"It's me, Lacey."

"Come in," Verena said.

Lacey shut the door behind her. "I've held client calls for you," she said in a soft drawl, handing her a few phone messages. Originally from Atlanta, Georgia, Lacey had been hired and trained by Mia, and now as Verena's assistant, helped Verena manage the salon business.

"Any luck?" Lacey asked.

Verena shook her head. "Nothing. Although the feds are bailing out some banks, the banks aren't making many loans to small businesses. The banks are sitting on federal funds, strengthening their balance sheets, and protecting their assets."

"*Asses*, you mean," Lacey said with disgust. "But we have accounts receivables from major retailers that pay like clockwork, every thirty days. Nordstrom, Duty Free, LVMH. Don't they count for anything?"

Verena nodded toward the TV screen. "According to the news, that doesn't seem to make a difference, but I'll certainly try."

"Well, I *never*," Lacey said with a huff.

Verena had to smile at Lacey's southern expressions.

Lacey was a smart, loyal assistant, and Verena valued her, quirks and all.

Lacey gestured around the office. "What about this building, the land? I declare, it's worth a fortune. And what about our other salons? We've had our best year ever."

"All the salons were mortgaged for the expansion. Derrick said it was the right thing to do. But I'll figure this out."

Lacey clucked her tongue and placed a stack of papers on Verena's inlaid French desk. "Here are invoices for your approval and checks to sign." She adjusted her stylish red glasses. "This is a good business we have here. It's going nowhere but up. I know you'll find a way. You always have, sweetie pie."

"Thanks for your confidence." After Lacey left, Verena reviewed the documents, made a few notes, and signed the checks. But thoughts of Marvin and the challenges before them made it difficult to concentrate.

She pushed back from her desk, crossed the Persian wool carpet, and made her way down a curved staircase to the salon. At the bottom of the stairs, she stepped into the spa waiting area, which she had recently updated in shades of ivory, taupe, and seafoam green, and added subtle lighting, relaxing music, and elegant recliners.

Out of habit, she surveyed the area, always making sure that everything was perfect and comfortable for their guests, as Verena referred to their clients. In one corner stood an antique hutch with hot herbal tea, china cups, fresh fruit, and chilled water. French doors opened to a private walled Zen garden with a trickling fountain and gardenia bushes. Smooth rocks surrounded the warm water therapy tub and natural stone outdoor showers. She scooped up a magazine that had fallen to the floor and returned it to a table beside a cushioned lounge chair.

Verena wove through the hallway past a labyrinth of rooms outfitted for facial, massage, and hydrotherapy services. She saw Rosa, one her best estheticians who made more than six figures a year, emerging from a treatment room. A tall, willowy young woman with platinum hair followed her.

It was Penelope Plessen, one of the world's most famous, perfect faces.

"Verena, it's been too long," Penelope gushed, "Rosa is sensational, she's a magician, I swear."

"She certainly is," Verena said, giving Penelope a hug. She adored Penelope, who had left her home in Copenhagen at just fourteen years of age to model. Now, a decade later, she was always in demand, and her flawless complexion was one of the reasons. Penelope was a chameleon; her hair was forever changing—color, length, style. With the lift of an eyebrow or a tilt of her chin, she could go from virgin to vixen, from innocent to imperial. She was a designer-favored model for runway and print work alike.

Verena pulled away to inspect the skin on Penelope's face and neck. "Marvelous," she said to Rosa. "Well done. And you're doing your part, too, Penelope. I'm glad you're staying out of the sun now."

Penelope laughed. "I hope to have a long career. At least another ten years. So, have you and Derrick set a date yet? I'm booked far in advance, but I want to be at your wedding."

"Actually, I broke off the engagement," Verena replied,

feeling a small pang of regret, even though she'd known it was the right thing to do.

"I'm sorry, I didn't know," Penelope said.

"That's okay. We're still friends." *His idea.* But then, it was complicated.

"Probably just as well. He always struck me as pretty intense."

Verena nodded. "Anyway, great seeing you, Penelope. Relax, and try our new outdoor showers. There's a special screened roof high above covering the area to keep out paparazzi lenses. I've got to run, but I'd love you to join me and my friends again for one of our all-afternoon Friday lunches. And it's not just girl talk."

"I know, last time I picked up some great stock tips from Scarlett." They traded kisses on the cheeks before parting.

Verena continued to the front of the salon, where the entire line of Valent Swiss Skincare was showcased. All natural, organic botanical ingredients were the hallmark of the line and had been since inception. Worldwide trends had simply caught up with them.

Near the front of the shop Verena saw a famous young British actress, accompanied by her equally famous mother, who was also an actress. Many women passed the VSS skincare regimen through the generations.

Verena paused at the front desk. "How is everything today?" she inquired quietly.

A fresh-faced young woman behind the desk smiled. "Excellent. By the way, a call just came in for you. Lacey said you'd be passing through any minute, so I took the message. Lance Martel asked you to call him. Here's his phone number."

"Thanks," Verena said. "And I'll be out for the rest of the day."

How nice of Lance to call. A spark of happiness surged through her, unbidden. She sighed. Although it had been a nice evening, that was all it was, she told herself firmly. She had too much work to do right now.

After visiting the Panetta family and offering her condolences on Marvin's death, Verena visited several banks, but the answer was the same at each one. They had a moratorium on lending, and they had also cut off many of their best customers. If this kept up, good companies would be forced out of business and many people would lose their jobs.

She was determined that would not happen at VSS.

Verena made several other calls, and then drove up the hills overlooking Beverly Hills to the Mulholland home of David and Marian Cohen, who had been friends of her father. David had run a real estate development company before he retired and was one of the wisest financial minds she knew, aside from Derrick. But even David didn't have a good answer for her dilemma.

"You won't find a bank willing to lend right now," David said. "They're hoarding cash to bolster their balance sheets."

"What are our options?" she asked, perched on a sofa in his home office.

He ran a hand over his bald head in thought. "Private money is all that's left in this market, but be careful who you trust."

Verena shifted with unease. "What do you mean?"

"There are plenty of vultures and sharks out there, just looking for tasty companies like yours to acquire at rock bottom prices."

Verena swallowed. This was worse than she'd thought.

"This is bad timing for an expansion, but your wheels were already in motion. Any way you can slow the expansion? Inventory and retail support is expensive."

Verena nodded. "Product has already been paid for and shipped. I have no choice but to make sure it sells through."

"That's right." David said, shaking his head. "Wasn't like this six months ago. If it's any consolation, no one saw it coming."

"So it's not just me." That didn't help the way she felt.

"No, but you'd better buckle up for a rocky ride," David said. "My wife and I are out of the market and in bonds for our retirement now. If we were younger with a longer horizon to retirement, we'd help you. All I can do now is to advise you to cover your assets as best you can."

Verena left and as she was walking to her car, her phone buzzed. Frowning, she started to send it to voice mail, but then relented and answered it. "What do you want?"

"Look, I owe you an apology." Derrick's contrite voice floated through the phone.

She sighed. "You don't have to apologize anymore. It's not like we're not dating." She opened her car door and slid in.

"No, but as your friend, I do," he said.

She cradled the phone against her ear. "Tell me honestly. Did you direct your portfolio companies not to pay their bank loans at National Western?"

"I swear to you that I did not."

Could she believe him?

Derrick went on earnestly. "I'm sure you've had a rough day. Why don't you let me take you to dinner?"

"Derrick, why are we even bothering?"

"Because I know you're in trouble. Maybe I can help you. Advise you, at least."

Verena hesitated. Some of her girlfriends had remained friends with their ex-boyfriends, even ex-husbands. "I don't know."

"Strictly as friends, I promise. I still care about what happens to you and your sisters and Mia."

She owed it to her family to take care of them. If Derrick could help, maybe she should see him, but only for the sake of her family. "Where shall I meet you?"

"I'll pick you up at eight."

Before she could argue, he'd hung up. She started the car.

6

After Verena left the Cohens' house, she wound down the hill back to her family home just south of little Santa Monica, as the locals called South Santa Monica Boulevard. She pulled her car into the narrow driveway that led to a detached garage in the rear yard. Walking past old vine roses, she drank in their heady aroma. She opened the back door and walked in, her leather pumps clicking across the dark polished hardwood floor.

Their house was modest in comparison to the mansions north of Santa Monica and Sunset Boulevards, but she loved it. It was the home her grandfather had built for Mia, which she'd moved into after her parents had died. It was one of the original cottages on the street, nestled now between larger new homes. She loved it and had always felt at home here.

The twins were at a friend's home, so the house was quiet. She checked on Mia, who was sleeping again, though it was still early. Leaning against the doorjamb, she observed the steady rise and fall of Mia's chest.

Before going to bed, Verena always checked on her grandmother and the twins, making sure they were breathing. It was an odd quirk she had, but after her parents had died, she'd been terrified of losing Mia or the girls. She couldn't sleep until she made sure everyone was safe.

Just as she eased the door shut, Mia called out to her and turned on her lamp, so Verena stepped inside her room. Sitting up, Mia said, "Lacey told me you were out of the office today. Is everything okay?"

Verena summarized her dilemma with the bank. As she spoke, she could see the helplessness in Mia's face, and she felt even worse for worrying her, but she had to ask. "What would you do?"

"Exactly what you're doing. We had good years and bad years, but we always found solutions to our problems. You will, too. I have faith in you, Verena."

"This won't be easy. What if I make a mistake?"

"I made my share of mistakes, but you're creative and strong. You can always find a way to move forward."

Verena bit her lip, fearing the alternatives.

Mia took her hand and stroked it. "You're worried about the impact on me and the twins. Don't. We are all resilient." She smiled and tucked a strand of hair behind Verena's ear as she had when Verena was a child. "I used to ask myself, what's the worst that could happen?"

"How did that help?"

"First, the worst rarely happens, and second, if it does, you can survive it. We did and we will. I believe in you. You may have to make tough choices, but I know you can manage."

"I'll try my best," Verena said, hugging Mia. Knowing she had her grandmother's support meant everything to her. "Get some rest. I'm going out for dinner tonight."

Verena walked into the bathroom and turned on the water in the large, old-fashioned, rose-colored tub. She shed her clothes and slipped into the bath. A generous pour of Valent bath oil filled the air with a relaxing lavender aroma, while the natural oils turned her skin silky smooth. *Just ten minutes.* She savored the quiet.

Her thoughts wandered to Derrick. Perhaps he did have advice that could help her. He dealt with highly sophisticated financial matters and maneuvers that were foreign to her. She didn't have the financial degree that he had, and she'd always felt like she was at a disadvantage when the discussion turned to finance.

Once he'd asked if she'd ever thought of selling the business. She couldn't believe he'd actually asked such a question, and she'd been vehement in her response. *How could I possibly sell this business?*

VSS was the only link to her parents and grandparents, and she loved the work she did. She found it fulfilling to help people discover their own beauty and serenity. If only she could find that tranquility, too. She'd had it once, but then her world had exploded. Now, she tried to summon it whenever she could, but it was becoming increasingly difficult.

Verena breathed in. Speaking to Mia had helped, but issues still had to be addressed.

Mia's cancer was in remission, but someday they would lose her, and then it would be just her and the twins. The girls didn't remember their parents, but she still wanted to preserve the business for them. It was their legacy. Their employees were like an extended family, and she felt a deep sense of responsibility.

Verena eased deeper into the warm bath, stealing a few more minutes. The more time that passed since she'd broken up with Derrick, the more she wondered if she'd ever had true feelings for him. He had been relentless in his pursuit of her, and while it had been flattering, she didn't feel the passion or connection she'd heard friends rave about. Were they exaggerating? Or worse, maybe she simply wasn't a passionate person, or her responsibilities precluded her from yielding fully to love.

In the kitchen with Lance, she'd been reminded of Derrick's jealousy, but she had the right to her own life. She and Derrick were definitely better off as friends, which had been his idea.

Thinking about that evening, her thoughts drifted to Lance. He was so easy to be with—not at all like Derrick. She sloshed water in the tub as she recalled his easy smile. She wondered what Lance had thought of her, and she remembered that she needed to call him back.

Verena yanked the stopper from the drain and stepped out of the tub. She toweled off, and then smoothed a body cream she'd developed from neck to toe. She freshened her makeup and brushed her hair, and dressed in a simple white silk sheath dress.

As an afterthought, she opened the safe and chose a vintage strand of pearls that had been her mother's, taking great care to fasten the intricate antique clasp. Running her fingers along the lustrous pearls, she imagined having Angelica's support. Tonight, she wished she could roll back time to ask for her mother's advice, but she couldn't. That made her even more thankful for Mia.

Checking the time and realizing she had still had fifteen minutes, she picked up her phone and tapped in the number Lance had left. The call went to voice mail. Caught off guard, she hung up. Immediately, she regretted not leaving a message.

A knock sounded on the door. Derrick was early.

"Hello, darling," he said as she opened the door.

"Hi yourself." His old term of endearment bothered

FLAWLESS

her. "You know, I'm really not your darling anymore."

Derrick shook his head. "Sorry, old habit."

"I'll get my purse."

"Thought you might have had another date with the kitchen help tonight."

Verena turned around. Lance Martel had gotten under his skin. She suppressed a smile. "So, this is about the chef. Jealous, are you?"

"Not at all, why should I be? But if we were still dating, which we're not, that cook wouldn't have a chance with you."

"You're impossible." She put her hands on her hips and wondered if dinner was a bad idea.

"I'm just kidding," he said, spreading his hands in an innocent gesture. "Come on, let's go."

They got into Derrick's Mercedes convertible and drove the short distance to Madeo's restaurant. As they drove, he kept the conversation cordial, which put Verena at ease. Perhaps they could be friends.

Derrick pulled alongside the valet parking in front of the restaurant and helped Verena from the car. As soon as they entered the popular Italian restaurant, the maître d' greeted them with warmth and escorted them to a prime booth. Derrick had a taste for the finest, and he frequented restaurants where he was known as a big spender, thus guaranteeing he would receive the best service.

Their usual cocktails—a martini for him and a champagne cocktail for her—quickly appeared at the table unbidden. Derrick nodded to the bartender and raised his glass to Verena.

"To our friendship," he said.

69

"I'd like that," Verena added, though she was still on guard.

After they ordered, Derrick asked about her day, and Verena told him about her meeting with David Cohen and the difficulties she was having.

"David's right," Derrick said. "The credit crisis is virtually shutting down bank lending."

"I was counting on our usual revolving line of credit for our working capital needs, as well as the Asian expansion."

"So what's your plan?"

Verena sipped her cocktail, wondering what her plan was, too. She was getting nervous. "David Cohen suggested I turn to private investors for money."

"Was David willing to invest?"

She shook her head. "He's fully invested in bonds."

"Of course he is. He's not willing to gamble," Derrick said. "Can you make payroll?"

"This isn't a gamble. I'm sure of our business." Verena shifted uncomfortably. "We can pay our employees for a few weeks. Not much longer." This couldn't have happened at a worse time. She had invested heavily in inventory for the Asian expansion.

Naturally, she would pay the employees before herself, though she didn't have much money in savings because she'd been more interested in reinvesting and growing the business than in paying herself a large salary. Her family had always gotten by on her income. She couldn't help but wonder if she should've have taken better care of her financial health and silently chastised herself.

"I might have an idea." Derrick formed a steeple with his fingers. "What's your backup plan?"

"My line of credit was my backup plan. So what's your idea?"

"His dark eyes bore into hers. "Have you thought again of selling the business?"

"That's your advice?" *Why does he keep asking that?* The thought made her uneasy. "I've told you, that's out of the question. This is our family business, and the employees are like family. The company is Valent, and we are Valent. I would never sell it. All we need is a short term working capital loan. Six months, maybe eight or nine at the most."

Derrick's chiseled face was expressionless. "Then I don't have any more answers for you, Verena."

"What about individual investors, someone who can make a private loan? Do you know anyone?"

"These things take time, Verena. The due diligence research, loan documents, negotiation. You don't have much runway. You said yourself that you're almost out of time. You should be thinking about canceling the Asian debut and laying off staff."

"Laying off employees?" How had it come to that so quickly? "No, I can't." Their appointments were always fully booked, and they already had a lean management team. There was no one to spare. She rubbed her pearls between her fingers, thinking.

"Then you'll have to close the business. I'm saying this as your friend. You have to pay employees."

Her chest constricted at his words. He spoke as if the business meant nothing to her. Without employees, they couldn't perform client services. Her mind whirred and she grasped at ideas. "But we have contracts, accounts receivables, and cash business, too."

"Sure, but the financial markets are weakening by the day. Look, I know how you feel. It's just bad luck, Verena."

She gazed across the busy restaurant. Derrick always kept the pulse of the market, and she didn't doubt what he said. *Bad luck?* She'd worked so hard. How could the viability of her livelihood and that of all her employees come down to bad market timing? But there it was. The truth.

She swung her gaze back to Derrick as she drew an uneven breath, hating the decision she knew she must make for the good of her family and all their employees. "Could Herringbone help?"

Derrick tapped a finger on the table. "Verena, you know this puts me in a difficult position."

"Because we're friends, is that it?"

"And because we used to be so much more." He touched her hand. "You were right to leave me. I was at fault.'

"I shouldn't have asked you." Verena slid her hand back. She'd once thought she had feelings for him, but that was in the beginning when she'd believed in the man she wanted him to be, not who he really was. "There are other private sources I can pursue."

"No, I'll see what I can do." Derrick clasped her hand again. "I know all the important players in private capital, Verena. Some of them are a bunch of greedy vultures. I'll make sure that we make you the best deal. I'll talk to Roper and see if I can get him on board."

Although he was frowning, his expression quickly gave way to such a warm smile that Verena was somewhat reassured.

Yet while they had dinner, Verena kept thinking about

her meeting with David Cohen and his advice. *Be careful who you trust*, he had told her.

7

Savoring the early morning quietness in the house, Verena stretched in bed, her limbs aching from stress and lack of exercise. Sunlight streamed through the window.

Saturdays were busy at the salon. She was often there meeting their guests, catching up with their travels and new babies and society galas. Verena liked to listen to their skincare concerns, see how they were responding to treatments, and work with the estheticians on new regimens and products. It was this closeness to their guests that her grandmother believed was the foundation of their success.

Mia always told her, "Listen to our guests. Inspect and analyze their skin. See how they're responding to our products and treatments. Above all, strive to improve on our excellence."

The past week had been grueling. Verena threw off the silk duvet, slipped into a blush pink robe, and padded across the smooth wood floors through the living room. The salon could run without her today. She needed a day to herself to recharge.

Seeing the morning sun glinting on the window made her realize how much she loved this home with its groupings of family photos, overstuffed furniture, and tropical plants, which were placed strategically to remove everyday toxins from the air.

Mia had a special affinity for orchids, too. These flowering plants in blazes of purple and pink and white were interspersed among her collection of cherished Asian antiques.

Stricken by her worries, Verena froze, looking around the serene room. She'd never thought that their business, even their home, could be threatened. Unless she could find financing, they stood to lose all that they had worked for.

Not on my watch, she told herself. She could handle Derrick. For the sake of her family and all those who worked for VSS, she'd have to. After he'd agreed to try to push a bridge loan through the company for her, he'd been a perfect gentleman and taken her straight home. Which was exactly the way she wanted it between them.

Verena tightened the belt around her robe and strode into the kitchen, which was decorated with a cozy mix of antique hexagon tiled counters and stainless steel appliances. Her head pounding, she reached for her coffee.

While it was brewing, she went to her bathroom, washed her face, and applied Mia's new serum to a bruise on her face. She'd tripped a couple days ago while airing the tires on her bike and had struck her head on the handlebars. She inspected the faded purple mark.

Miraculous, it's healing quickly.

Never had she seen such rapid skin regeneration. A frisson of excitement coursed through her. As she camouflaged the faint bruise with thin layers of concealer, foundation, and powder, she made a mental note to discuss the serum with Mia.

She finished by smoothing sunscreen over her limbs, and then changed into slim cotton pants and a sleeveless shirt. Stretching her legs, she decided it was a beautiful day for a beach ride.

She returned to the kitchen and sipped her coffee, trying not to think about business. With a pang of disappointment, she remembered the call from Lance, but she'd forgotten to return his call. *Perhaps it's just as well,* she thought, running her hand over her forehead. As a chef, he probably spent as many hours at work as she did. How could that ever work?

Footsteps clattered through the house. Verena looked up to see Anika sweeping into the room.

"Hey Ver, what do you think?" With her slim, lanky pre-adolescent figure, Anika paused to pose like a fashion model. She wore a leopard print swing coat with a bright coral lining.

"Love it. Looks like you've been shopping with Mia," Verena said, giving her little sister a hug. She adored her sisters and their youthful spirit. *When did I lose that?* she wondered briefly, but she knew the precise date. The twins had been too young to feel the full force of their parent's deaths at the time, though they still suffered from the void left in their lives. "Getting ready for the trip?"

"Bella and I are trying on the outfits Mia ordered for us." At the mention of Bella's name, the other girl bounced into the kitchen, her silky blond hair swirling around her shoulders. She wore a similar jacket in zebra print with a brilliant turquoise lining.

"I'm so excited! Can you believe we're going to Paris? And Switzerland!"

A smile tugged at Verena's lips. Bella had such enthusiasm. She always seemed to speak in exclamation points. Anika was the calmer one of the two, the practical foil to Bella's exuberant nature.

Anika leaned against the counter next to Verena.

"Hmm, smells good, can I try your coffee?"

"I don't know, can you?" Verena nudged her sister. "Use *may I* for permission. And yes, you may."

Anika lifted the cup to her lips with a prim gesture, sipping carefully. At twelve—nearly thirteen, Verena realized—she had a slender, athletic build like Bella, but she handled herself with more maturity. She tried to look sophisticated as she drank, but she crinkled her nose. "It's bitter."

"That's because I don't use sugar, only cream."

"Mia said we're going to visit cafés in Paris, so Anika wants to drink coffee," Bella said, dancing around the kitchen. "I think it's yucky."

Mia walked into the kitchen. Her soft blond hair was brushed back from her face, and a sheer rose tint colored her lips. She wore an elegant, floral-embroidered, pink satin robe and gold-toned, kitten-heeled slippers.

Even in the morning, Verena thought, *Mia looks stylish.*

"Did I hear my name?" Mia asked.

"Good morning," Verena said, kissing her on each cheek. "Did you sleep well?"

"Excellent, yes," she replied, laughing at the twins. "I need plenty of rest if I'm going to keep up with these two in Europe."

Verena turned to Anika and Bella. "Girls, would you like to go biking this morning? Beautiful day for it."

"Mia is helping us organize our traveling wardrobe today," Anika said.

Mia put an arm around each girl and hugged them close to her. "I told them I'd make alterations to their clothes today. They can help me thread the tiny eyes on the needles and show me how much they remember about sewing."

Bella resumed her dance while Anika pursed her lips and made a little moue with her mouth. "Oh, Mia, no one our age sews anymore. It's so old-fashioned."

Mia huffed. "No, it isn't. All the fashion designers know how to sew. You're the exception because you're exceptional young ladies," Mia added, winking at Verena. "You go on, Verena dear, enjoy your ride this morning. We'll be fine today."

"Thanks," Verena said, squeezing her hand in appreciation. "I'll pick up groceries for dinner from the market."

Verena gave them each kisses on the cheek before she left. The three sisters were close because of the grief they'd worked through. Given Mia's medical issues, Verena was half-sister, half-mother to them. Only Verena could keep up with the energetic duo on a daily basis. She hoped their trip to Europe wouldn't be too much for Mia's precarious health, but her grandmother was determined.

Verena went outside to load her bike onto the bike rack on the back of her car. With a clear blue sky overhead, she was soon on her way to Marina del Rey.

She parked and unloaded, hopped onto the bike, and then steered it onto the path that ran along the ocean's edge toward Redondo Beach. The sun beamed onto her shoulders, and she breathed in the fresh marine scents of sea and kelp. A light breeze wafted through her hair, carrying with it the aroma of coconut-scented suntan lotion from sunbathers on the beach. Skaters, bicyclists, and walkers shared the path. An occasional greeting punctuated her solitude.

This is exactly what I needed.

She filled her lungs with salt-tinged sea air, feeling oxygen fill her body with energy.

An hour later she wheeled into Redondo Beach. As she was disembarking, she heard someone call her name. *I know that voice.*

She whirled around. Squinting against the sun, she caught her breath. A half-clothed man swung from his bike. Her heart quickened. *What a gorgeous specimen of a man.*

"I was hoping you'd call," Lance said, grinning. "But this is even better."

8

Verena lifted her sunglasses, shocked by the sight of Lance. He wore faded shorts and his shirt was thrown over the handle bars. With brilliant eyes, muscular arms, and a well-defined chest, he looked more like a bronzed Hollywood star than a working chef. She caught herself relishing the sight of him. "What are you doing here in Redondo Beach?"

"I should ask you that question," Lance said. "I live here."

"Oh, well, I rode down from the marina." Flustered, she swatted damp tendrils of hair from her hot face.

"I must have been just behind you. That's too bad." He knelt to tie a shoe lace. "How about some breakfast? I'm cooking."

"Well, I… I guess so." He was inviting her to his place. Verena hardly knew him. But she'd built up an appetite on the bike. "Where do you live?"

He gestured to a tall, narrow building a short distance away. "I have a condo in that building. There's my balcony."

Before she could resist, she found herself falling in step with him as they walked their bikes beside them.

"How long have you lived here?" she asked.

"Three years," he said. "I bought my place right after I returned from Zurich."

As he swerved his bike past a rock, his arm brushed

against hers, sending a surprising tingle through her. Recovering, she said, "My family is from Switzerland. You lived there?"

A grin creased his face. "For six months. I worked for an international hotel chain, and they moved me around quite a bit. I've also worked in England, South Korea, France, and New York. I was scheduled for Sydney when the Beverly Hills Hotel called me. I wanted to settle down and get a dog." They reached his building and he stopped, staring at her.

"And did you?" she asked.

"Did I what?"

"Settle down and get a dog, silly."

He laughed. "I bought my condo, but the dog, no, not yet. I work long hours."

"I understand. I do, too," she said.

He cocked his head. "Are your eyes really that blue?"

"Why, of course." She blinked. She was often asked that question.

"I thought you might be wearing contact lenses. Your eyes are such a deep shade of sapphire."

Now it was her turn to laugh. "That was my dad's nickname for me—Sapphire, for my eyes."

His eyes roamed across her face, and he frowned. "And that bruise on your cheek?"

"Stupid bike accident," she mumbled. Feeling self-conscious, she put her sunglasses back on. The sun was so bright, it illuminated everything.

He stared at her for a long moment. "Mind if I ask if you and Derrick are still seeing each other?"

"Not anymore, but we're still friends. He gives me

business advice."

"Was it serious?"

"We were engaged, but I broke it off."

After a long moment, Lance nodded and seemed relieved. "Selfishly, I'm really glad to hear that."

A shadow crossed his face, and Verena sensed there was something else he wanted to say, but before she could ask him, he started up a path alongside the building. Verena walked behind him. She couldn't help but admire the firm muscles in his legs.

"Come on in," he said, taking long strides.

"Do you ride often?" she asked.

"I like to ride early in the morning before work. It improves my focus, and since I like to taste everything in the kitchen, cycling keeps me in shape. Occupational hazard, that." Glancing at Verena, he added, "We can leave the bikes in the garage."

She followed him into the elevator and upstairs, where he opened the door.

The view caught Verena by surprise. The condo was a wall of glass on the ocean side, opening onto a wide balcony that overlooked the waves. He slid open the glass doors and stepped out. His skin was tanned to a dark golden shade, and his back glistened in the sunlight.

Drawn to him, Verena followed.

"You should see the sunsets," he said.

"I'd love to." She blinked. *Why did I say that?*

Lance grinned at her again. "I don't have much food in the kitchen because I usually eat at work. How do you feel about French toast?"

"After a ride like that, sure. Besides, I still have to ride back to Marina del Rey."

"Then you need good food for fuel." Returning to the kitchen, he pulled on his t-shirt. He washed his hands, put a white apron over his neck, and then began to pull ingredients from the cupboard and the refrigerator. "The bread's turned green, but I have croissants. You'll eat strawberries and macadamia nuts?"

"Sounds delicious."

He pulled a knife from a wooden block of professional stainless knives. The ebony-stained handles were curved to fit the hand and the blades glinted in the sunlight. Handling the knife with familiarity, he began slicing the croissants with practiced precision.

"You have incredible knives here, too," she said.

"I like to use the right tools." He looked pleased that she'd noticed. "Each one is handcrafted in Japan in the tradition of samurai sword makers."

As he worked, Verena perched on a stool and gazed around. The kitchen was open to the living and dining areas. His furniture was simple but fine. A white canvas couch rested between two polished tree trunks that served as end tables. On one sat a colorful Tiffany-style lamp. On the other, a brilliant, azure blue glass wave caught the sunlight. An antique surfboard stood in one corner, and next to it, a large oil painting of the ocean hung on the wall. She was looking at it when he said, "Like it?"

"I do." She squinted at the signature. *Lance Martel.* "You painted this?"

"Guilty as charged." One corner of his mouth quirked into a grin. "When I first moved here, I didn't have any furniture in this room, so I set up an easel and let the paint fly."

She looked at him thoughtfully, appreciating his skills. "You're awfully creative. You paint, you cook."

"I like to work with my hands. Here, take a look at this."

When Verena saw his creation, her mouth watered. He had piped creamy strawberry filling into the croissants, dipped them into a light batter, and rolled them in finely chopped macadamia nuts. A copper skillet sizzled on the stove.

A few minutes later, they sat on the balcony, enjoying his version of French toast, along with tall glasses of blended passion fruit and pineapple juices. They chatted easily, and Verena marveled at how quickly he had produced such a delicious dish.

"It all starts with the best ingredients," he said. "The best butter, salt, berries—everything. And as fresh as possible."

"Sounds like my formulas for skincare. In fact, my grandmother still whips up masks and scrubs in the kitchen from simple ingredients." She took another bite, thinking about the similarities in what they did. "What are you growing in the planter?"

"That's my herb garden. I have basil, thyme, chives, cilantro, oregano, and rosemary. Only the freshest herbs will do."

Verena could feel his eyes on her as they ate. Without meaning to, she thought of Derrick and the differences between the two men. Lance was so easy going. He seemed to have a perpetual grin on his face, whereas Derrick had always been in a hurry, often interrupting her to take, or make, a phone call. Derrick's job was important, but so was Lance's, and yet, the two men couldn't have been more dissimilar in their temperament.

She shifted in her chair, uncomfortably aware of her attraction to Lance. Having breakfast with a man in his home wasn't something she'd had much experience with.

As they ate, Lance asked more about her business and she found that she enjoyed sharing her ideas with him.

"You said Derrick is helping you with the business," Lance said. "Do you feel like you can trust him?"

"He's brilliant in business."

"That's not what I asked."

Where is this going? "He's always looked out for me, and for the company. Why do you ask?"

Lance shifted in his chair. "Sometimes I overhear conversations in the dining room. Derrick and Thomas Roper were in the other day. I heard them talking about your company."

Verena waved her hand. She didn't want to talk about Derrick any more. "I know all about that."

His eyes widened. "You *do*?"

"Of course. We're discussing a deal." She paused, smiling. "I hope you're not the jealous type."

"Me? No, I just thought you should know, because it sounded—"

"And I do know. I assure you."

"Well, okay then. Maybe it was just guy talk."

"Thomas Roper isn't the most cultured man around." He'd always made her uncomfortable. She knew Derrick had to work hard to keep up with the billionaire. "I can only imagine. But thanks for telling me."

"I'm relieved, I guess."

Verena inclined her head in thought, but before she

could say anything, Lance stood and reached for her plate.

"If you're finished, I'll take that," he said, smiling at her again.

His hand brushed against hers as he collected the dish, and Verena felt something akin to a small jolt of electricity surge through her. *What was that?* She could fall too fast for Lance. Yet right now, he would only distract her from the work she needed to do.

When he returned from the kitchen, she said, "That was a wonderful treat, but I have to go."

He looked crestfallen. "Are you sure? I'm going to the farmer's market. I'd love for you to come with me."

"I'm sure." *The faster I leave, the better*, she thought, because her heart was racing ahead of her. Although she had promised Mia she'd go to the market for dinner.

"Then I'll help you with your bike."

As he wheeled her bike out of the garage for her, he said, "I called you at your office. Did you get my earlier message?"

"Yes, but it was a busy week. I have some pressing work issues."

He stepped closer and swept a stray hair from her lashes. Bending toward her and pausing, he asked, "May I call you again?"

He was so close that all Verena needed to do was lift her lips to his. Tempted, she felt her face grow warm. "I'd like that."

As she spoke, Lance's eyes were on her mouth. "And you can stop by the hotel anytime for a bite. I can always make time to see you."

"I'll remember that," Verena said, sliding her hand over his muscular forearm. Feeling the strength of his pulse, she sensed the power that surged beneath her touch.

Lance smoothed his hand over hers and lifted their clasped hands to his chest. "I'm glad we ran into each other today."

As Lance drew her body to his, Verena leaned in until she could feel his warm breath on her lips. Her own breath quickened, and she ached to feel his mouth on hers. The feel of his arms around her was unlike any embrace she'd ever known. *And yet...* She closed her eyes and lifted her face to his, but at the last moment, she hesitated. Instead of touching his lips, she tilted her head and kissed his cheek.

His chest heaved and he tightened his embrace, burying his face in her hair. "Until the next time," he murmured.

Feeling light-headed, Verena pulled away and got on her bike, cycling away before she had time to change her mind.

Lance stood and watched her until she disappeared into the crowd on the path. His body ached for her. She'd been so close, but he'd sensed her hesitation. He didn't known why, but she was a woman worth waiting for. How could she have ever been engaged to a man like Derrick? At least she'd broken it off, but he'd feel better if she hadn't remained friends with him.

He drew his brows together as he thought of the man. Judging from the conversation he'd overheard, Derrick was still interested in Verena, though not necessarily because he loved her. Lance wasn't naive, he knew people married for all kinds of reasons, but Verena deserved more. Much more.

At least he was relieved to know that Verena was aware of Roper's intentions about her company. As much as Lance disliked Derrick, maybe the guy was playing Roper on behalf of Verena.

Isn't really any of my business, is it?

Still watching her in the distance, Lance was impressed with Verena's earnestness and lack of guile, which was surprising in a city like L.A., where many women were open about exactly what they wanted, and it often involved someone else's money. She struck him as someone who didn't date much, but he couldn't imagine why. Smart, charming, and stunning. What was wrong with the men in L.A.?

Then he remembered a comment about her twin sisters. He liked big noisy families, like the one he'd grown up in. He smiled to himself. There was more to Verena than he knew, and he sure wanted to find out.

But Derrick, *really*? As soon as he'd met him, Lance had suspected that something was amiss. Overhearing Derrick and Thomas Roper at lunch was still confounding, too. On one hand, Derrick seemed to be protecting her, but Lance still didn't trust him, no matter what Verena said. He wondered how much Derrick had really told her about Roper's intent.

It was all pretty confusing, but at least he'd let Verena know about it. He felt better about that.

Finally, Verena disappeared into the crowd on the boardwalk. Lance sighed and turned to go inside, but he still couldn't get Derrick off his mind. He'd bet that guy would take Verena back in a minute if he could.

She doesn't deserve someone like that. And if there was anything he could do to protect her, he would. If she'd ever let him past her reserve.

He couldn't deny the physical attraction he felt for Verena, but he truly liked her, too. It was easy to see the goodness in her. Even if she wasn't interested in him, Lance resolved to watch out for her.

He couldn't stand by and let a woman like her get sucked into going back to a man like Derrick. Her words floated back to him. *I hope you're not the jealous type.*

Lance jutted his chin out. He'd never really thought of himself that way. So, was he jealous about Derrick?

Damn right I am.

9

Juggling groceries, Verena opened the door and made her way to the kitchen. "Hello, Mia. How about stir fry tonight?" She put the groceries on the counter.

"Sounds nice and healthy," Mia said, sipping a cup of tea.

"Where are the girls?"

"With friends, shopping for shoes for the trip. They've grown another size."

Verena pulled out vegetables she'd bought: snow peas, carrots, sprouts, mushrooms, and green onions. She began to wash them.

"I can slice those for you," Mia said. "How was your ride today?"

"Wonderful, it felt good to get some exercise. I love the smell of the ocean."

"It must have been quite a ride. You were gone a long time."

Verena smiled now, remembering her impromptu breakfast with Lance, and the heat that had grown between them. "I ran into a friend. We had breakfast together."

"Anyone I know?"

"Lance Martel." Even the sound of his name on her lips stirred something in her. "He's the executive chef at the Beverly Hills Hotel. I met him at the gala, and he prepared a late night dinner for me after the event."

"Nice to have a man cook for you, isn't it?" Mia's eyes

brightened. "Emile was a great chef. I miss that about him, and so many other things, too."

Verena gave her grandmother a sympathetic hug. Mia had never stopped missing her late husband. *She's been talking about him quite a bit lately*, Verena thought, concern edging into her mind. Mia's indomitable spirit was intact, but Verena was always looking after her grandmother's well-being.

"So, is he nice?" Mia's voice held an intimate note.

"He is." She wished there could be more to their relationship, but her family came first. She wouldn't make the mistake of getting involved with someone right now, especially so soon after Derrick. But oh, she was tempted.

Blinking hard, Verena slid a cutting board and knife in front of Mia and then placed a bunch of freshly washed mushrooms on the board.

Mia picked up the knife and said casually, "So how did you run into Lance again this morning?"

Verena paused, replaying the scene in her mind. "It was the strangest thing. I rode to Redondo, and when I arrived, there he was. He has a condo on the beach, and he was just returning from a morning bike ride, too."

Mia nodded knowingly. "Kismet."

"You know I don't believe in that." She had to be practical. "Anyway, he asked me up for breakfast, and whipped up the best French toast I've ever had. He's an amazing chef. And a fine artist, too. I saw a painting he did of the ocean. It was magnificent." Verena stopped herself on the verge of babbling on.

Mia listened, smiling. "Sounds like a nice young man. He is young, isn't he?"

She shrugged. "Probably a couple of years older than I am."

"Ever married? Children?"

"I don't know…but he wants a dog, and plans to create his own line of food someday."

Mia was methodically slicing the mushrooms, taking it all in. "The twins are older now than last time. And this Lance, he's a good man?"

Verena nodded, thinking about Mia's reference. Verena had been engaged a few years ago, but her fiancé, a character actor named Joe Stuart, had broken off the engagement a week before the wedding and broken her heart. Joe had been overwhelmed with the twins, then active seven-year-olds.

I'm not ready to raise children, he'd told her. *And when Mia dies, that's exactly what will happen.* Joe's words had been like a cold slap in the face to her. When Derrick came along, he'd said all the right things at first.

Verena had dated exactly two men in her entire life. Joe and Derrick. They'd both let her down.

Never again. They'd taught her that love and her family responsibilities didn't mix. But she'd never felt the intense level of physical attraction to them that she did with Lance, and it scared her.

Mia paused and lifted the knife, gesturing with it. "Verena, I love you, and I must be honest with you. I never approved of how Derrick treated you."

"Mia, no one will ever be good enough for me in your eyes. You didn't like Joe, either."

"And look how well that worked out."

Verena winced. Mia was right. *Trust—a woman should trust the man she marries.* Not that *that* was on her mind right now. She blew out a breath. "Let's talk about something other than my disastrous love life."

"As you wish," Mia replied, sliding a glance in her direction.

Verena wondered whether to tell her that she had gone to Derrick about a business loan. It had been years since Mia had turned over the reins to her son, Joseph, and his wife, Angelica. But Mia was well known and friends with many of their best guests. She often advised Verena on new products and helped her test them. And she had always been a good sounding board. "There's something I must tell you. It's about the business."

"Yes?" Mia pushed aside the sliced mushrooms, and sipped her tea.

"As I mentioned before, I can't find anyone to fund our working capital needs for Asia. We're running out of time."

Mia nodded, taking it all in. "I've been following the news about the banking situation. Have you thought of another plan?"

Verena drew a deep breath. "Last night I had dinner with Derrick. He thinks Herringbone Capital will help us with a short term loan."

Mia cast a sharp look in her direction. "Be careful about mixing the business and Derrick." She looked down at her hands. "If it helps, the twins and I don't have to take this trip to Europe right now."

"No, you must go," Verena protested. "You've always wanted to take them to Europe and introduce them to their heritage. Just as you did for me when I was their age. This is important to them, too. *Who knew how long Mia had left?*

Mia smiled, reminiscing. "We had a good time, didn't we? Remember hiking in the Alps? Can't do that now, but it was lovely, wasn't it? Emile and I used to hike every weekend when we were young. The views were magnificent."

"Take the tram, Mia, you can still do that. Anika and Bella must experience the views from the mountains."

"Are you sure? It's an expensive trip. Although I have used the reward points I've saved for the airline tickets."

Mia had always been frugal. Verena had learned how to budget from her. "No, I want you to go. It's a lifetime experience for them, and for you. It's been planned for so long." Verena dried the green onions and transferred the vegetables to Mia's cutting board. "Remember what you've always told me about the importance of making memories?"

"Yes, but if you need my help, you can count on me, Verena."

"I always have, Mia."

Mia sighed. "This is not the first time we've been through perilous times in the business. The economy ebbs and flows, but we have always survived, Verena. Women always want to look beautiful, and feel healthy and attractive. And today, men do, too. Never underestimate the power of determination, my dear. You will find a way."

"I'm sure I will," Verena said, but even as the words left her mouth, she had her doubts.

As if reading her mind, Mia said, "I don't like him, but if Derrick's company is the only option, then you must take care to protect yourself."

After dinner and a walk around the neighborhood with Mia and the girls, Verena went to her room to get ready for bed. As she brushed her hair and changed into a nightgown, she thought about what steps she would need to take if Herringbone Capital did not come through with the deal. Or if they did.

Mia's right, there must be a solution. Three generations of her family had dedicated themselves to the salon. It was up to her to continue the business.

As she mulled over her dilemma, thoughts of Lance kept edging into her mind.

Verena wasn't desperate for a relationship, but she was realistic. She didn't believe in happily-ever-after fairy tales. Her life simply wasn't conducive to such thoughts. How many men would be willing to take on her family? The responsibilities for Mia and the twins would surely spill over into any relationship she had.

As she slid into bed, she reminisced about how she and Derrick had met. She had chaired a fundraiser for orphaned children last year, and he'd attended. At first she thought it curious that he would go to such an event if tragedy had not struck his family, but later he confided that he'd lost a cousin and his wife in an accident in Belize, and that another cousin had adopted their child. He'd even had tears in his eyes.

Maybe we could honeymoon in Belize, he'd once said. But that was in the past.

As she drifted off, she thought again of Lance and wondered if they would ever mean anything more to each other.

10

"Good to see you again." Lance shook hands with the hotel owner's representative as the man's car was pulled under the porte cochère in front of the Beverly Hills Hotel.

"We like what you're doing here, Lance. Keep up the good work." The man closed the door and pulled away.

A fiery red sports car with two attractive older women pulled up. Lance hesitated for a moment, nodding to them in welcome as a valet attendant hurried to the car.

"Welcome, Madame Valent," the valet attendant said, opening the passenger door to the car.

Valent? That was a name Lance didn't hear often.

"Good afternoon, Alfred, always lovely to see you," the woman said, swinging her still-shapely legs out of the low car and accepting the valet attendant's hand. "I don't know how you get out of this car in a dress, Lacey, without putting on a show for all the men," she said, laughing. "But thank you for driving me here today."

The attendant averted his eyes. "Madame Dubois has already arrived. She's in the Polo Lounge."

Lance stepped toward the woman. "Madame Valent? May I introduce myself, I'm Lance Martel, the executive chef here at the hotel."

"How nice to meet you. Mia Valent. I always enjoy dining here."

Lance offered his arm to walk her inside on the red

carpet. "By any chance are you related to Verena Valent?"

"She's my granddaughter." Mia she slid a hand through the crook in his elbow, preening in his company. She looked at him appraisingly and smiled. "Come to think of it, I think she might have mentioned your name."

"I'd be pleased to escort you to the restaurant." He noted her porcelain smooth skin and the sweet smile that lit her face. Verena certainly took after her grandmother.

Mia swept into the hotel, chatting as they walked. "I've always loved this magnificent pink stucco palace. I first visited in the 1950s, when my husband Emile and I celebrated an anniversary—I can't remember exactly which one now—but I'll never forget the weekend we spent ensconced in our room here. God rest his soul, but I do miss him." Her eyes twinkled as she reminisced, and she fanned herself a little.

"We must enjoy every day we're allowed in this life," Lance said.

"Oh yes, we must." A mischievous glint sparkled in Mia's eyes. "I miss the little things about Emile, the touch of his hand, the smell of his hair—always freshly washed with our sandalwood-scented shampoo—even the evening stubble on his chin." She paused, and then added, *sotto voce*, "And my Emile was a wonderful lover."

Lance raised his eyebrows in mild surprise. Mia might be coy, but she was certainly outspoken.

She laughed at his expression. "Don't be embarrassed. Sex is a natural part of life. Young people seem to think anyone over the age of sixty reverts to a state of virginity." She sighed. "I still miss my Emile."

As she walked briskly through the lobby, she

acknowledged the familiar staff with a smile. Mia clutched Lance's arm and went on. "There was a time when I would visit the hotel to tend to celebrities, such as Elizabeth Taylor or Marilyn Monroe, in the pink bungalows. I remember that Marilyn liked bungalows number one and number seven. She used to call me to administer emergency facials the morning after late nights of filming or partying. Such a sweet girl, and such lovely skin."

Lance enjoyed hearing the old Hollywood stories that swirled around the hotel. "Please, tell me more."

Mia smiled up at him. "The studios and stars paid me handsomely. I tucked most of it away in my Swiss bank account for retirement. A woman should have her own nest egg, and my darling Emile encouraged it. He once told me, "If you have the money to leave me, and don't, then I know you really love me." Mia shook her head sadly. "How could he have ever thought I didn't?"

"I'm sure he adored you." Lance kissed her cheek.

She patted his arm and smiled up at him. "You're such a nice young man. I'm glad you met my Verena."

"I'm glad we met, too." In fact, Lance hadn't stopped thinking of Verena. They stepped into the restaurant, and he greeted the maître d', his friend. "Johnny, Madame Valent is dining with us today."

"It's always a pleasure." Johnny inclined his head. "You look beautiful today."

"Hello, Johnny." Mia offered her hand, and Johnny air kissed it. "And what a handsome tie-dyed bow-tie you have on today. That's quite the fashion statement."

"Women seem to like it." Johnny chuckled and smoothed his thick, wavy black hair.

"Of course they do, you're a handsome young man.

But you should be courting Scarlett."

"I couldn't do that, Mrs. Valent. We grew up together. She's like a sister to me." Johnny offered her his arm and Lance stepped aside.

Mia adjusted her colorful silk scarf and pearls before turning back to Lance. "Come with us to the table, dear, I'd like to introduce you to my friend."

Lance trailed behind as Johnny escorted her through the restaurant, returning nods to those they passed.

Mia continued. "It doesn't matter, Johnny. My Emile and I were neighbors. She's a fine girl, that Scarlett, a smart one, too."

"Yes, ma'am, she certainly is. Too smart for the likes of me, I'm afraid. But I'm proud of her."

Lance suppressed a grin. Clearly Mia loved making an entrance into the Polo Lounge and enjoyed dispensing advice.

Amid chatter that rose across the restaurant, Johnny guided her through pink stucco arches to the patio, where bracelets of pink bougainvillea flowers brightened the festive, open air dining area bathed in California sunshine.

"*Bonjour*, Mia." A chic older woman welcomed his companion with a kiss to each cheek. Johnny and Lance helped Mia with her chair.

"*Bonjour*, darling. Hmm, I believe, you're wearing my favorite Dubois perfume." Mia smiled with pleasure. "Camille, I've never seen anyone emerge from a hospital looking so beautiful. Is that a new Chanel?" she asked, admiring her friend's woven emerald green jacket and jacquard silk scarf. "It sets off your eyes so well. And I love it with those black slacks."

"Chanel, *oui*, but not new. Timeless, though, no?" Camille touched her friend's shoulder. "And I've always loved this shade of mauve on you. Blondes wear it so well." Camille turned to Johnny. "I remember when Marlene Dietrich had the *No Slacks for Women* dress code dispelled here at the Polo Lounge. Back in the 1940s, it was. Did you hear of it?"

"Madame Dubois," Johnny said, his dark eyes flashing. "If I may say so, I believe it was you who inspired Ms. Dietrich."

Mia said, "Camille, I'd like to present a new friend, Lance Martel, the executive chef. My dearest friend, Camille Dubois, the founder of Parfums Dubois."

"Madame Dubois, it's an honor to meet such an icon of beauty, and a beautiful woman, too." Camille held a hand to Lance, but instead of shaking it, he took her hand and executed a perfect air kiss over it, just as Johnny had. Legendary women should be shown respect.

"So nice to meet you, and what impeccable manners you have. American men seldom do that." Camille turned to Johnny. "No need for menus, I'll have my usual Maine lobster salad. Mia, your Wagu beef salad today?"

"Why not? And let's share a slice of the chocolate pistachio roulade cake. Damn the cholesterol. I survived cancer. I might as well live a little."

Johnny winked at Lance and smiled at the pair of old friends. "And your usual champagne?"

"But of course," Camille replied, glancing around the restaurant. "These young people, sometimes I wonder—were we ever really that young?"

"I still feel the same on the inside, Camille. It's these old bones that betray me."

"Nonsense," Mia said. "Your old bones are still gorgeous. Look, there's Pierre Chevalier looking your way."

Camille slid a glance at a nearby table, where two elegant, silver-haired gentlemen sat drinking cocktails. "No, he's looking at you. He always had eyes for you, Mia."

"Poor Ondine. They were such a love match. She went so quickly." As she spoke, Pierre lifted his hand in a small wave, and Mia smiled in acknowledgement.

A waiter appeared with a bottle of Veuve Clicquot. With an expert hand, Lance poured the pale bubbly champagne into two crystal glasses for them.

Camille looked at Lance. "You've spent time in Europe, no? France, perhaps?"

"I worked for the Hôtel Ritz in Paris one summer."

"How well I remember the Ritz," Camille said, a wistful look crossing her face. "Did you like Paris?"

Lance nodded. "Loved it. In fact, I'm returning soon for a special engagement."

"Engagement?" Mia asked. "To a lady in your life?"

"No, I'm not that fortunate. It's a competition among the leading chefs in the world. I'm honored to be invited."

Mia inclined her head. "A handsome man like you, there's no one special in your life?"

Lance hesitated for moment. "Let's just say, no one who returns the sentiment."

Mia leaned forward with interest. "My granddaughters—the young twins—are going with me to Paris soon. Verena might even join us. Perhaps we'll be there at the same time."

Lance was interested, especially if Verena was going, too. "I'm leaving in a few days."

"Really? Why, so are we. And where are you staying?"

"At the Villa and Hôtel Majestic in the sixteenth *arrondissement*." A friend of his managed the hotel. "And you?"

Mia waved her hand. "I don't recall. My travel agent takes care of those details. But it's a small world, perhaps we'll run into one another." She took a sip of champagne.

Camille slid her eyes from Lance to Mia, and pursed her lips.

"It's lovely to meet you, Lance," Mia said, brightening. "I hope we'll meet again soon."

Lance excused himself. He stopped at another table to say hello, but he could still see and hear Mia and Camille talking.

Camille could barely contain herself. "What was *that* about?"

"I have no idea what you're talking about," Mia replied nonchalantly.

"Mia Valent, you cannot lie to me. I know you too well." Camille sipped her champagne, studying her friend. "Are you playing matchmaker?"

"What if I am?" Mia tilted her chin and sniffed. "He seems like a nice young man."

Camille shook her head. "You're unbelievable. Isn't she engaged?"

"Verena had the good sense to break it off. Besides, did you see ever a ring on her finger? I didn't, and I never liked that Derrick. If only her father were still alive, poor Joseph, and Angelica—" Mia's voice broke. "I miss my son and his beautiful wife every day. I only want the best for their children, my grandchildren." She pressed a hand against her chest. "Dear me, I have to watch my blood pressure. I shouldn't interfere with Verena's love life, but I feel so strongly that she should find a fine young man someday."

Lance saw Mia glance discreetly in his direction.

Camille covered Mia's trembling hand with her own, and said, "There now, like you, I believe in kismet. It will happen when the time is right."

Mia nodded, brushing tears from her eyes.

A moment later, Lance saw another one of their elegant older guests, Pierre Chevalier, saunter toward Mia. He whisked a monogrammed linen handkerchief from his jacket and presented it to her. "I hate to see a beautiful woman in distress."

Mia blinked and looked up into his kind face. "Why, thank you, Pierre." She accepted his offering and dabbed her eyes. "But I'm not crying. It's my allergies."

Lance grinned at her charming mannerisms. He couldn't help but adore Mia, and he now understood where Verena got her allure. Would Verena be like that someday?

Pierre smiled down at Mia. "Terrible this season, aren't they?" He touched his head in greeting to Camille. "Ladies, enjoy your brunch," he said, and then returned to his table.

"They don't make men like that anymore," Camille said, watching him go.

Lance grinned. He could still hear every word they said. He continued watching the two women, pleased for them that they still attracted the attention they deserved.

Mia folded his handkerchief and studied it for a moment. After that, their food arrived, and the waiters presented their plates with discreet, courteous service. Mia recovered her composure and slipped Pierre's handkerchief into her purse.

Camille raised her glass in a toast. "*Santé*, my dear, to your voyage."

"And to yours, and your health," Mia said, raising her glass, too. "And may those who carry our torches into tomorrow find nothing but happiness and success."

A soft clink of crystal sounded, and Lance watched the two doyennes of beauty sip their champagne. He passed another table and stopped to say hello, still keeping an ear open to the conversation between Mia and Camille, an art he'd perfected after years in the restaurant business.

Mia said, "Verena tells me you're working from home."

"I was for a short time," Camille replied. "I love my home, but I can't bear not going to the office. Honestly, there's nothing better than a day of good work to soothe my soul. I still have so many ideas, so much to create." She tapped the table, her brilliant green eyes brimming with excitement. "Did I tell you about the new celebrity line we're making? I'm blending it, but Dahlia is overseeing the deal, and she's doing a marvelous job."

"She reminds me of you when you were young. Amazing that our grandchildren are taking over the businesses we began so many years ago." Mia shook her head in amazement. "We barely had two coins to rub together when we arrived in America."

"We ate a lot of bread and soup in those days, too," Camille said, nodding in agreement. "My granddaughter Dahlia is so talented. I just hope she doesn't make the same mistakes in love that I did."

"I was so lucky with Emile, but I fear for Verena."

"Is she going with you to Europe?"

"I wish she were, but Verena is staying here to prepare

for the launch in Asia. So, it's just me, Anika, and Bella." She leaned over and patted Camille's hand. "At our age, we have to make every day count. You should come, too."

When Lance heard that, his hopes sank. He'd hoped he might run into Verena in Paris.

"Actually, I intend to go with Dahlia later this year, but she doesn't know it yet. She's quite busy right now. We've had to renegotiate our bank loans." Camille gazed over Mia's shoulder at Lance and arched a finely drawn brow.

Lance nodded to her, feeling slightly embarrassed, and turned back to the kitchen. Had Camille realized he'd been listening to their conversation? He chuckled to himself. A man could learn a lot in a restaurant.

Back in the hotel's gleaming stainless steel kitchen, Lance skirted the precision dance of the sous chefs and line cooks who moved in unison to produce gastronomic delights for the daily cadre of discriminating guests.

Even so, he couldn't help thinking about Verena and why she had hesitated in his arms at the beach. Would he get another chance with her? He stopped and tapped his forehead.

Of course, he thought. *Mia Valent is the key.*

11

The brilliant stone caught the sunlight through the window, reflecting an arc of rainbow colors against Verena's white blouse.

Perched on the edge of her office desk, Verena stared at the solitaire ring nestled in the robin's egg blue jewelry box. She was utterly dumbfounded.

"What is this?" she asked uncomfortably.

"A perfect diamond. About three carats," Derrick said, sliding next to her in his custom gray suit. "It's D grade for colorless, and FL IF. That means it's flawless. Just like you."

Irritated at his presumption, Verena flung up her palm. "That's not what I meant."

He went on, unfazed by her anger. "I saw it in Tokyo at Tiffany's. I want you to know my feelings for you haven't changed."

"Did you feel guilty about being too busy to shop for rings when we were *actually* engaged?" Verena snapped the lid shut. "I can't accept it."

"I wish you would." Before she could resist, he pulled her into his arms and ran his hands over the back of her slim black skirt. "I've really missed you," he murmured.

Reflexively, Verena pushed him away and held out the small box. How dare he take her friendship toward him as an invitation to reopen their relationship? "The answer is still no."

Derrick lifted a corner of his mouth in a confident

smile, and then shoved his hands into his pockets. "Keep it. You might change your mind."

Exasperated, Verena placed the box on the edge of the desk, and then walked to the other side, sat down, and steepled her hands. "Let's get back to business. Have you spoken to Roper?"

He took his phone out and nonchalantly tapped it. "Sure did."

"Well?"

After sending a text, he looked up. "Roper has agreed to lend the money you need after the due diligence proves satisfactory. We'll have to review your contracts and finances."

"That shouldn't take long."

"We'll work as quickly as we can." Spreading his hands on her desk, he leaned in, his dark brows drawing together. "Is there anything we should know about?"

She shook her head. "I have no secrets, Derrick. But we do need to meet payroll soon, as well as the obligations for the marketing in Asia."

"Don't worry, Verena. You're doing the right thing." His phone buzzed and he checked it. "Just got a message from Roper, have to go." He paused, and then added, "I'll have Jimmy Don send you the details that we need to begin the due diligence."

"Who's Jimmy Don?"

"Jimmy Don Herald is a twenty-four-year-old whiz kid we hired. Has degrees in business and chemical engineering. Real bright. He can help you crunch numbers." He tapped his watch. "Got to run, Verena." He leaned in to plant a kiss on her cheek, but Verena shifted, averting him.

Is this what she was going to have to contend with?

A bemused expression lit Derrick's face. "Whatever you want, Verena. You know I can wait."

"You'll be waiting a long time. Take the ring," she said, shoving it firmly in his hand.

A moment later, Derrick was out the door. As he rounded the corner, she heard him say good-bye to Lacey.

Perturbed at his cocky attitude, Verena turned her attention to her computer screen. Derrick might be awfully sure of himself, but she wouldn't give in. *Not this time.* Better to keep him as a friend and professional associate. That she could handle.

Lacey walked into Verena's office with a startled expression. In her outstretched hand, she carried the small blue box. "Derrick just left this on my desk. What does this mean?"

Verena rolled her eyes. *The temerity of that man.* "Absolutely nothing."

Later that afternoon, Lacey showed a pasty-faced young man in an ill-fitting suit into Verena's office. With her eyebrows arching toward her hairline, Lacey shot Verena a warning look as she spoke. "Jimmy Don Herald to see you."

Verena wondered what was wrong. "Good afternoon." Verena stood to meet Derrick's associate, and they shook hands. "I'm glad you could start so quickly."

"I'm here to collect financial statements and documents for Herringbone's due diligence." He looked around her office and sat down. "I'll wait."

"I beg your pardon?" Verena gave him a tight smile, but the expression did not reach her eyes. No *hello*, no *nice to meet you.* She stared evenly at him. "I can have everything you need tomorrow."

"No, I need it all now."

Her trouble detection meter immediately soared. "My controller is off today and will be back tomorrow."

Jimmy Don smirked. "I've heard that before. I wouldn't advise you to change any numbers."

"Excuse me? Are you accusing me of altering my financials?" She was incredulous. *Why, the nerve of this kid.*

He shrugged. "Like I said, I'll wait."

She slid a folder of financial documents across the desk to him. "You can take these now and come back tomorrow. I assure you that you will find everything in order. We have a very competent controller."

"Let us be the judge of that."

"Good day, Jimmy Don. I'll be in touch with Derrick." She turned her attention back to her computer screen, fuming inside. In less than a minute, he'd managed to completely alienate her. *Was he being rude on purpose or was he just socially inept?*

She glanced back at him. He hadn't budged. "What else can I help you with?"

He whipped a piece of paper from his briefcase and tossed it across the desk.

Verena stared at him. *Correction. He's a complete jerk.* She scanned the long list. Jimmy Don had a sneer on his face that she wished she could slap off. She said evenly, "This will take quite a bit of time. Derrick said you're going to assist me with the financials. Why don't you start with the projections?" She slid the paper back across the desk. Lacey can show you to our meeting room. You may work there."

He seemed to consider this. Finally, he stood. "I'll start by interviewing each employee."

She glared at him. "They're busy with clients and cannot be interrupted."

"It's necessary."

"I can assure you that we're all professionals here."

He grunted. "Rubbing creams on old ladies' faces? I don't think so."

"*What?*"

"I said, rubbing creams—"

"I heard you the first time." Verena narrowed her eyes. "I'm calling Derrick."

Another smirk. "Go ahead, call your boyfriend."

A burst of anger exploded in her chest and threatened her composure. "I will not be disrespected. Out of my office. Now. And Derrick is *not* my boyfriend." She swiveled around in her chair, putting her back to him.

Jimmy Don did not move.

She swiveled around to face him again. "What's the matter with you?" she snapped.

"I have my orders. You want the money?"

Furious, Verena marched past him into Lacey's office. "Deal with this idiot, please. He wants to interview each employee. I'm imposing a five minute limit during their break, and do not let him interfere with guest appointments."

She saw Lacey's eyes widen and travel up, and her lips parted. "Well, I never," Lacey muttered.

Verena whirled around. Jimmy Don was towering behind her, uncomfortably close. She shoved past him and returned to her office, slamming the door behind her. She grabbed her phone and angrily punched in Derrick's number.

When he answered, she blurted out, "Who is that obnoxious cretin you sent here?"

A long pause. "That would be Jimmy Don. Didn't he introduce himself?"

"Get him out of here."

"I can't do that, Verena. He's in charge of due diligence for Herringbone." Derrick's cool voice floated over the line. "He might be a little unpleasant, but if you want to deal with Herringbone, you'll have to deal with Jimmy Don."

Verena couldn't believe what he was saying. "His behavior is completely unacceptable. I will not tolerate such belligerent, condescending, demeaning treatment in my own company."

Another long pause.

"Did you hear me?"

Derrick sighed. "Listen, we don't have to do this deal, Verena. Honestly, we're only doing it as a favor to you because I know you can't get the working capital you need elsewhere. I don't want to see your business go under. I care about you and your family."

Verena grew quiet. If Herringbone pulled out, she would have no other options. Panic seeped into her mind like a fog, obscuring her reasoning.

"What'll it be, Verena?"

She gritted her teeth, weighing her options and wishing she could tell him and Jimmy Don to go to hell. "Carry on," she managed to say before she hung up, feeling frustrated and angry.

Three days later, Verena leaned on the edge of

Scarlett's office desk and watched as she reviewed the Herringbone documents that her corporate attorney, Jack Epstein, had received. Jack had been counsel for Valent Swiss Skincare for many years and technically, he represented the company.

This division was important because the company was a corporation, which existed as a separate legal entity. Verena and her family were shareholders of the company, and as chief executive officer, Verena was also an employee of the company. It was complicated, but it was simply the way corporations were run.

Scarlett acted as Verena's personal attorney, and negotiated Verena's employment contract with the small board. It had always been a friendly, beneficial relationship. But now, after her initial review of the documents, Verena feared that her family's business was going to become substantially more complex. With a major international launch underway, the timing couldn't have been worse.

Scarlett put her pencil down and rocked back in her chair. "If you want the money, you have to agree to their terms."

Concern creased Verena's forehead. "Can't we negotiate more?" She slumped into a chair.

Scarlett punched a line on her phone. "Please hold my calls." She turned back to Verena. They were in the Century City office of her law firm's west coast partners, where she worked when she was in Los Angeles.

"Do you have any other options, Verena? Other banks or investors?"

"No other options. I've checked everywhere I can." She pinched the bridge of her nose in thought. "A lot of our competitors are laying people off in advance of a domestic crisis." Still, there *had* to be another answer. She didn't want to lay off good people when the company was so close to its Asia launch. Preorders had been strong and all signs were pointing to a smashing debut.

What *could* she do?

Lacey always said that Verena never took *no* for an answer.

It was true. Verena had always found a way to work around problems, mostly through sheer determination and creative thinking. But this time the financial markets were different and solutions eluded her.

"I can advise you, but you have to make the decisions." Scarlett pursed her lips. "It's going to get worse, Verena. The word out of the financial circles in New York say this could be the worst recession since the Great Depression. Can you make some cuts?"

"I terminated our newest hires, but our core employees are necessary. And they're loyal. They've been with us for years. I know their families, their children. Besides, we're booked solid."

Scarlett leaned across the desk. "Can you halt the Asian launch?"

"It's already in motion." Verena pressed her fingertips to her temples. "The money has already been spent on product. Inventories have already shipped, so we must support it in store. That's the only way we can recoup the investment."

"Then you have no choice. It's this or bankruptcy. The Asian launch was a big gamble."

"And it's the right one. But we expected to have a line of credit at the bank to handle it." Verena blew out a breath of exasperation. "Why is Roper doing this?"

"He makes the terms," Scarlett replied. "He knows the financial markets and knows it's tough out there. Some investors—the unscrupulous ones—go in for the kill when you're at their mercy. Believe me, it could be a lot worse."

"Don't know how."

"Listen, you must be careful, Verena. You can't deviate one iota from these restrictive financial covenants. You can be extremely profitable, but if you don't hit their mark for whatever reason, Herringbone can call the shots. You can bet that Roper will conduct regular reviews, beginning immediately."

A chime sounded on Scarlett's computer. "Here's another email." She squinted at the screen.

"What does it say?"

"They want Jimmy Don to run product development. They think the costs are too high in that area." She swiveled the computer screen. "And here's his very healthy salary requirement."

"That's impossible, he has no idea how to do that. Besides that's *my* job." Verena sprang from her chair and began to pace the office. "He's a disaster in the office. He's creepy. None of the women like him, or the way he looks at them. He's disrespectful, he's uncouth, he's—"

"Hired, if you want their money." Scarlett shook her head. "This is terrible, I know. Start a file on his behavior immediately."

Verena felt as if she'd been punched in the gut. She could hardly breathe. Crossing her arms, she said, "I can't agree to this."

"Okay, here goes." Scarlett tapped out an email reply. Thirty seconds later, the response came back. Scarlett lifted her gaze and shook her head.

Verena said nothing. She picked up her purse and stormed from the office.

"I didn't even say good-bye to Scarlett," Verena said. She had just arrived home and found Mia clipping roses in the backyard garden. "This rotten deal isn't her fault."

Mia rested the basket of cut roses on the patio table under the awning and sat down. "Scarlett understands, Verena. You've been under so much pressure since your parents died. I wasn't well enough to help you with the business then, and I've always regretted that." Mia shook her head. "You were so competent that I found you didn't need me much. Still, maybe I should've been there more for you."

"You have been." Verena couldn't have made it without Mia's emotional support. After her parents died and before the doctor would release Mia to fly, they had spoken every day on the phone, sometimes for hours. She had often gone to sleep listening to Mia's soothing voice over the phone.

Mia placed a hand on her shoulder and looked directly into her eyes. "I have some money set aside in Switzerland, my dear. It was for Anika and Bella's college fund. It's not much, but we can put it into the business."

Verena raised her brows. "Absolutely not. Besides, it's probably not enough to make a difference, but thank you for offering."

"Don't give in to Roper yet," Mia said, methodically stripping the excess lower leaves from the roses she had clipped. She arranged the flowers in a vase. "When do you have to provide an answer to Herringbone?"

"Ten days."

"I spoke to my old friend in Paris, Henri Becaud."

Henri was the managing director of Rose Beauté. She remembered him well. "He was interested in buying VSS two years ago. That's the last time we spoke."

"Well, he's willing to speak to you again."

"About a sale? I don't know..." Rose Beauté was one of the largest beauty conglomerates in the world.

"There are other options. Perhaps he'd buy a stake in the company and you could continue to run it."

Verena mulled this over for a moment. Mia had a point. "I can call him first thing in the morning, Paris time." That would be about midnight in L.A. Her pulse quickened at the thought of speaking to Henri Becaud, a legend in the industry. Hope surged within her. Perhaps there was an option to Derrick's company, after all.

Mia frowned. "Oh, no, you can't deal with a matter such as this on the phone. Face to face, Verena, that's the only way." She fluffed the flowers in the vase.

"Then I'll have Lacey book an overnight fight if she can. I'll start packing." She didn't have a moment to waste. "I only wish you could be in that meeting, too."

"What a thought..." Resting her hand on Verena' arm, Mia's face brightened. "Why don't we travel together?" A smile danced on her lips. "In fact, I'll have my travel agent arrange the flights and accommodations. We can all go tomorrow."

12

"This fit is magnificent," Verena said, turning in front of the three-way mirror in Fianna's Robertson Boulevard boutique.

Lacey had booked the first flight she could for the next evening for her. Verena needed an appropriately chic outfit for Paris, so she'd called Fianna last night, and her friend had come to her rescue.

Verena tamped down her anxiety. Their livelihood and the continuation of the business hinged on the Rose Beauté meeting with Henri Becaud. She'd hardly slept worrying about it.

Verena smiled at Fianna in the mirror. When Fianna had realized her state, she had brought Verena a cup of mint tea and turned up the music. Verena was so thankful for friends like Fianna and Scarlett.

"I knew that dress would be perfect on you, and the style is just right for your meeting in Paris." Fianna finished zipping the black lace and silk sheath dress and fastened the hook. "Or a date with a hot chef. Have you heard from Lance?"

"I ran into him, but we're both so busy." Verena told her about their chance meeting at the beach and the brunch he'd made for her. As she thought of him, heat prickled her neck and a pang of regret shot through her. Lance was the first man who'd made her tingle when she was near him, yet she came with far too much baggage and no time for a man.

"I can't even think about him right now." That wasn't exactly true. Thoughts of Lance encroached on her mind every day. It was all she could do to keep them at bay to focus on urgent matters.

Fianna gazed at her with understanding. "You'll have more time when the twins are a little older. Still, he seems nice, and the way he looked at you..."

Verena squared her shoulders. "What should I wear over this?"

Fianna clucked her tongue and reached for a black cape with a scarlet lining. "Try this." She unfurled the cape and draped it around Verena's shoulders.

Sizing her up, Fianna added a vivid print scarf at Verena's neck. "The ivory background in this scarf captures the highlights in your hair and softens the look. In fact, wear your hair in a French twist. You'll have to wear your black Louboutin shoes, too, of course. The red soles will be a classy accent." Fianna stepped back to admire her work. "It's very Grace Kelly."

Verena wound her blond hair into a makeshift twist. "How's this?"

"Perfect. Elegant and modern. For stylish women at the top." Fianna put a hand on her hip and grinned. "Like you. You're my muse, Verena, you and Scarlett and Dahlia—and all our other girlfriends in the beauty business. You have to look glamorous on the job."

"What I need is a glamorous suit of armor," Verena said, her voice edged with weary sarcasm. She'd had too much of Jimmy Don, spreadsheets, and legal documents in the past few days. "The beauty business is plenty hostile, believe me."

"So is fashion." Fianna met Verena's eyes in the

mirror. "But I wouldn't do anything else."

That's what Verena liked about Fianna. Her determination, as well as her creativity. That's what it took in their work. "This new line is your best work yet," Verena said, glancing at several garments that hung from a rack. "But you must let me pay you for these outfits."

Fianna shook her head, her brilliant red mane swaying around her shoulders. "These are samples, Verena. All I ask is that you wear this dress when you meet with your buyers at the department stores. I'm finally ready."

"We sell into Nordstrom, Neiman Marcus, and Saks Fifth Avenue," Verena said, ticking off her best retail chain partners. "I'll make some introductions for you after I return." She glanced around Fianna's boutique, which was brimming with a sumptuous array of unique styles in the finest fabrics. "They're good accounts, but be ready for them to ask you for an exclusive."

Fianna frowned. "Is that good or bad?"

"Depends. Sometimes you have to commit to selling your line to a chain on an exclusive basis, and nowhere else. If the merchant is willing to support you with enough sales and promotion, it can work. But if not, you'll get locked into a relationship that can't support you."

"Can I limit it, say for a few years?"

"That's a good negotiation point. Or require a minimum annual buy. There are lots of ways to create a deal. Talk to Scarlett. She's the best dealmaker I know." Verena picked up another scarf and held it up against her neck. "She's amazing at brainstorming how deals can be structured."

"I'll do that before she returns to New York. What

time did you say your flight is?"

Verena checked her watch. "Ten o'clock tonight on Air France. "I'll arrive in the morning. My meeting is the next day, and then I depart the following day."

"Sounds busy." Fianna scooped up the clothes. "While you change, I'll wrap these clothes in tissue paper so they'll travel well. Might not prevent all the wrinkles, but proper packing can eliminate a lot of them."

"Thanks, it *is* an important trip." Verena made her way back to the dressing room. As she changed, she thought about how critical this meeting was. If Jimmy Don's demoralizing meetings with her employees was any indication of the tone of future dealings with Herringbone, then it was imperative to explore alternatives.

Verena emerged from the fitting room, smoothing her crisp white shirt and slim eggplant-colored slacks. "Here's the black dress, Fianna." She ran her fingers over the exquisite fabric. "I love the way it feels, especially how it conforms to the body."

"Nothing like a silk lining—done right, that is. Here, I'll wrap that up, too."

Verena opened her purse to look for her sunglasses. As she rummaged through it, a robin's egg blue box tumbled out.

Fianna spied it. "Oh, Tiffany. What's inside?"

Flustered, Verena said, "Nothing. Just something I have to return to Derrick."

Fianna's eyebrows shot up. "I'd love to see what *nothing* from Tiffany looks like."

"It means nothing to me." Verena flipped open the blue box. "I'm giving it back to him."

"What a shame," Fianna said, slipping the diamond

onto her finger. "I don't remember you ever wearing this."

"That's because he never got around to giving me a ring when we were engaged. He only recently left this in my office."

"Why?"

"He's deluded, I suppose. I gave up trying to figure Derrick out."

"Smart move." Fianna gave her the ring back. She slipped a couple of fragrant sachets into the package of clothes. "Here's something sweeter for you. These sachets are from Dahlia's company. And some for Anika and Bella and Mia, too," Fianna added, tucking a few more in. "We've watched the girls grow up, haven't we? They'll be old enough to wear my designs before long. Maybe I could start a younger line, something fun."

"Anika and Bella would love that," Verena said. "I knew you were destined for greatness, Fianna. You always had incredible talent. Surely success is right around the corner for you."

"I hope so. This boutique and the new lines cost a fortune. Every penny I make seems to go right back into the business. If I can expand distribution, which takes more investment in inventory, then Scarlett can work on the licensing deals she has in mind."

"Sounds like you have a plan."

"You bet I do," Fianna said, her mouth set in a determined line. "Here's your traveling wardrobe." She handed the package to Verena. "Have a great trip."

"Ah, the glamour of travel," Mia said facetiously as she, Verena, and the twins prepared to go through the airport security line on their way to France. Verena was glad that Mia had managed to obtain a ticket for her on the same flight they were taking.

Verena removed her shoes, belt, and jacket, emptied her pockets, took out her laptop, tablet computer, and phone, and placed everything in the bins on the conveyer belt for scanning. Between the four of them, Verena had twelve bins to organize.

"And the twins think this is fun," Mia said, watching Anika and Bella relish the new experience.

Anika looked at Mia and Verena. "May I go through the line first?" she asked, while Bella was hopping from one foot to another in anticipation.

"Sure," said Verena. "You have to wait for the security personnel to give you clearance before you go through. Remember to watch your belongings and collect your bins."

As Verena prepared to go through the line, she caught a glimpse of the back of a man who had just gone through one of the other security lines in front of her. She blinked. *No, it couldn't be.* She squinted and tried to get a better look. *Is that Lance?* She could have sworn it was, but she hadn't seen his face. She shook her head. No, it couldn't be. *This is ridiculous.* Why couldn't she get him out of her mind?

"Verena, are you going?" Mia was waiting for her.

"What? Oh, no, you go ahead, Mia." Verena watched her grandmother walk through the scanner. Though she was still in great shape for her age, despite her bouts with cancer, Verena noticed her slowing step. Although this was far from a carefree trip, she was glad that Mia had suggested coming along with the twins. She never knew how much time her grandmother had left.

Once they'd made it through security and boarded their Air France plane, the four of them settled in for the long trans-Atlantic flight. After the in-flight meal, they took turns going to the tiny bathroom to perform their nightly skin cleansing ritual. Verena replaced the girls' shoes with fuzzy socks, tucked them into their reclined seats with thin flight blankets, and watched as they fell asleep.

Several hours later, Verena woke to the smell of coffee. She was still groggy in her half dream state and disturbed by her nocturnal fantasy. *What was I dreaming?* She realized with a start that she'd been dreaming of Lance. *What's the matter with me? A man cooks two meals for me and I can't get him out of my mind?* She stretched and rotated her cramped neck.

Mia was next to her, watching her with interest. "Good morning. Sweet dreams?"

Verena shrugged, trying to forget how sweet they were. *Just once in my life*, she thought, thinking about how nice it would be to have a real-life man like that in her life. Her body still ached with dream-laden desire. Just once she longed to have the kind of wild romantic experience others talked about, but she had never known.

"Seemed like it. You were talking in your sleep." Mia had an amused look on her face.

"Don't tell me. I'll get coffee." Verena threw off her blanket. The plane was dark, and most of the passengers were still sleeping. She padded down the aisle to the galley, where a flight attendant prepared two cups of coffee for her. As she waited, she peered into the cabin in front of her. She looked for the man that had been ahead of them in the security line, but she couldn't see much.

"*Crème?*" the flight attendant asked.

"Oui, merci."

"Sucre?"

"Non, merci."

She carried the cups back to her seat, pausing as she watched Mia, who was arranging her hair, and Anika and Bella, who were still sleeping. Mia had an array of small travel-sized VSS skincare products on her tray: toning lotion, moisturizer, eye cream. And her special serum. Verena loved the subtle, fresh smell that hadn't changed in years. To her, it had always been the scent of morning.

Verena sat down and placed the cups on her tray. "Here you are."

"Thank you, my dear," Mia whispered.

Verena touched a spot on her face. "Your serum worked wonders on a bruise I had. Did you change the formula?"

A smile played on Mia's lips. "I might have. Glad you like it."

"It's a shame there's nothing we can do with it right now."

Watching the girls sleep and her grandmother conduct her beauty ritual, even on an airplane, made Verena realize how much she loved her family, and how much they depended on her. *This is an important trip.* The business, their livelihood, their way of life—everything was at stake.

A little while later, after a breakfast of croissants, yogurt, and fruit, the flight began its descent into Charles de Gaulle airport outside of Paris. Anika and Bella took turns gazing from the window.

"Look at the patches of farm land," Bella cried, "I thought Paris was a city."

"Of course it is," Anika answered. "But they don't land

airplanes there."

Verena remembered her first trip to Europe with Mia. She had finished the school year with good grades—just as Anika and Bella had—so her parents had rewarded her with the trip for her thirteenth birthday. Mia had been an energetic woman; her battle with cancer was still five years away. Mia insisted on showing Verena her favorite museums—the Musée d'Orsay, the Louvre, and the Rodin—as well as her favorite skincare salons and fashion boutiques, often followed by tea at the Hôtel Ritz.

Mia glanced at the twins and smiled. She turned to Verena. "Remember the first time you and I came here?"

"I was just thinking about it. Shall we show them the same sites?"

"Absolutely." Mia made a small moue with her mouth. "I'd love to visit the d'Orsay and the Rodin, but let's start with the Louvre. We can save the others for another trip." She stretched and rotated her ankles as she spoke. "Verena, I've been thinking about Henri. You should go to the meeting at Rose Beauté by yourself. I've been away from the business for so long, I can't really add to the meeting."

"Nonsense, Mia, you're the founder. You'll always be the face of VSS."

Mia patted her arm. "I had my turn, but today you're the face of VSS." She looked at the twins, who were thrilled that the airplane was about to touch down. "They'll have their turn, too, someday. If I were there, Henri and I would waste time going down memory lane. You'll need all the time they've allotted for you. Be thorough. Henri will listen, but he will also be honest with you."

As Mia turned her attention to the twins, Verena

leaned her head back, mentally preparing her presentation to Henri. Could she make an agreement with Henri without Mia?

Yet in the last ten years, lining up funds to finance the company's growth had been one of Verena's most important activities. Valent Swiss Skincare was a first class product line, always on the innovative edge, and their customer service was second to none. To stay at the forefront of skincare innovations required more than dedication—it required financial investment. Henri would understand and appreciate that.

Fortunately, they had an impeccable credit record with their banks and vendors. Mia had always prided herself on that, and Verena assiduously protected their reputation in business circles.

By tomorrow, she had to have a concise, persuasive presentation. She massaged an ache in her neck. During the flight her muscles had tightened and spasms stung her shoulder blades. She didn't have much time. As the plane touched down on the runway and hurtled to a halt, she set her watch to the local time.

Gazing out the window, Verena prayed she could steer their company to a safe landing in Asia as well. Everything her family had worked for depended on her efforts.

13

"Welcome to the Villa and Hôtel Majestic," the doorman said as he opened the door to the limousine.

Verena smiled at the girls, whose eyes were round with curiosity and delight. Anika and Bella had been so excited to ride in the sleek black car. In Beverly Hills, they often saw limousines, especially the lumbering black SUVs and sedans of the much longer stretch variety. But cruising through the café-lined streets of Paris and around the Arc de Triomphe on their way to the hotel was a new experience for them. Verena was glad they weren't jaded by life in L.A.

"Here we are," Mia said.

"*Bonjour madame, mesdemoiselles.*" Accepting the distinguished doorman's proffered hand, Mia slid out of the car first.

Verena gazed up, admiring Mia's hotel selection. Balconies laced with flowering vines rimmed the top of the exclusive boutique inn. A pair of navy blue uniformed young men whisked away their luggage.

"Can we go out now?" Bella asked. "I'm hungry."

"We have to go to a café and sit outside," Anika added with a sophisticated arch of her brow. "It's the thing to do in Paris. Meadow Dylan said that's what she did last summer."

Verena smiled. Miss Dylan was Anika's French teacher at school, and Anika adored her.

Mia glanced at Verena. "We could use a glass of

champagne and hors d'oeurves, *n'est-ce pas?*" When Verena hesitated, Mia put her hand on her shoulder and said, "After we check in, let's have a relaxing meal."

Verena saw Bella stifle a yawn. "It's the jet lag."

They were shown to their suite, which had a small kitchenette, high ceilings, a large bathtub and separate shower. It was tastefully decorated in the French style with sumptuous taupe and burgundy fabrics and draperies, silver gilded furniture, a shaded chandelier overhead, and a polished parquet wood floor.

"Isn't this lovely," Mia remarked.

"You have a great travel agent," Verena said, admiring the comfortable rooms.

Mia looked nonplussed for a moment, before she replied, "Of course, the travel agent. Mariana is excellent."

"Isn't she the one who suggested this hotel?" Verena asked.

Mia waved her hand. "I'd forgotten. At my age, I sometimes forget my name."

Anika and Bella dissolved into giggles.

After unpacking, they set off toward Place Victor Hugo, a sprawling roundabout where ten avenues fed into it. Fountains of water soared in the center and stylish shops and cafés rimmed the perimeter.

"Here's the one I like," Mia said, catching Anika's hand. "Miss Dylan would approve, I'm sure."

At the Café Le Victor Hugo, they sat under apple red canopies and ordered croissants, salads, and *foie gras*, and the twins had ice cream for dessert.

"Here's to a successful trip for you, my dear," Mia said, raising a glass of champagne to Verena. "Trust that you are ready." She gave her a confident nod. "Life is shorter than we think, so we must always make the most of it."

Verena clinked glasses with Mia. She sat back to watch the girls and observe the simple joy on her grandmother's face. Mia had faced illness and death so often. *I'll do anything to make her life comfortable*, Verena thought with sudden conviction. *And anything to preserve the company Mia built.*

Observing cars circling the roundabout, Anika said thoughtfully, "We should have more roundabouts at home. Look how easily traffic flows around them. Whoever thought of that was very wise."

"There's certainly something to be said for them," Mia said, lifting a brow at Verena.

"They'd be chaos at home," Bella said.

The girls were growing up, crossing the chasm between childhood and the women they would become. Soon they would be joining Valent Swiss Skincare and working by Verena's side, continuing the family tradition.

As long as Verena could produce the funding needed. *If I can,* she wondered, concerned about her meeting.

After they ate, they strolled along Avenue Victor Hugo. The twins loved going into the boutiques. With their slender figures, it was easy to find clothes, and they were excited to find a pair of new outfits that Mia had promised them. The day passed quickly, and soon they were enjoying a light supper at another brasserie on the corner of Avenue Kléber.

Verena saw Bella's eyelids flutter from exhaustion. "We should go to bed early for a good night's sleep. The first day is always difficult with the time change."

When they returned to the hotel, Mia and the girls prepared for bed, but thoughts of tomorrow's meeting still spiraled through Verena's mind.

"I'm going downstairs to the pool for a swim," she told Mia. "I need to clear my head."

"Good idea. I'm sure we'll all be asleep when you return."

Verena slipped into her sleek, cream-colored maillot swimsuit, which she preferred for serious swimming and always carried with her when she traveled. She threw on a white cotton hotel robe and took the elevator down to the lower level where the spa, fitness room, and pool were located. She noticed that it was only seven in the evening, and after a quick calculation, realized it was mid-morning in California, but she hadn't slept much on the airplane.

She stepped out of the elevator, walked past the massage and fitness rooms, and opened the door to the pool area. *Good, it's deserted. Plenty of time to think in silence.* She removed her slippers and stepped into the foot bath to cleanse her feet before entering the pool room.

To her left, glass-walled topiaries were illuminated with subtle colored lights that rotated between soft shades of cornflower blue, shamrock green, lemon yellow, and cherry red. A few cushioned chairs and lounge chairs surrounded the pool, while at the far end of the room water trickled over a pebbled wall, which sounded like a natural waterfall. The soothing spa music lifted another degree of tension from her shoulders.

After draping her robe across a chaise lounge, Verena stepped into the pool. The salt water felt silky against her skin, and she appreciated its therapeutic value. The water temperature was perfect—warm enough not to jar her, but cool enough for a vigorous swim. Stretching and lengthening her body through the water, she began to swim.

The water muted the world around her, and as she coursed through the water, she thought about her meeting with Henri, what she would say, what he might say. In her mind she rehearsed her replies, as she did before every important meeting. She revisited their revenue numbers, the Asian expansion timeline, and the marketing plan. She felt lighter, sleekly skimming through the water from one side of the pool before turning and continuing to the other side.

The financial numbers were fresh in her mind after the exhaustive due diligence that Herringbone had ordered. Unbidden thoughts of Jimmy Don intruded, and his pasty white face floated into her mind. He had spent hours gleefully grilling her about procedures and costs and operations. She submerged, swimming deeper under water as if to escape his omnipresent smirks.

Powerful strokes propelled her through the water. The muscles in her arms began to burn.

A foreboding sense deep in her gut warned her against the Herringbone alliance. If Henri Becaud could help, they'd have no need for Herringbone. But if not... She'd have to do the best she could.

Thomas Roper. She'd only met the head of Herringbone Capital once. He had a smooth complexion for a man his age, but it wasn't from years of proper skincare. There were no creases around his eyes from laughing, no furrows between his brows from worry. Nothing, even, to suggest a life well-lived. *That's it*, Verena realized, catching her breath as she broke the surface slightly. He had the waxy, expressionless complexion of a sociopath.

Tension gnarled between her shoulders. The

Herringbone deal disturbed her. It made sense on paper, but every time she thought about it, agitation rose within her. She fought against the feeling now, flipping in the water when she touched the edge of the pool, speeding to the other end, and repeating.

She cut through the water—faster and stronger with each length—her chest feeling as if it would explode, frustration welling in her chest.

Her breathing was labored, but she kept on, slicing the water with powerful strokes, pulling herself through the currents her body created. *Stroke, and stroke.*

Pushing herself farther and harder, she thrust herself forward as she had in school swimming competitions, only now it was the ultimate competition that drove her, the fight for survival. *We can do it, we will win, we will win....*

She tried to expunge images of Derrick and Jimmy Don and Roper from her mind. Exertion and anger overtook her judgment. *Faster, faster.*

She approached the end of the pool, nearly ready to flip again, but blinded with rage and determination she miscalculated, her unbridled power driving her headfirst into the wall.

A splitting pain shot through her head, while the rock-hard thud stole her breath.

She gulped reflexively, and salt water poured into her lungs. Her chest threatened to explode, and her limbs thrashed ineffectively. *No,* she screamed in her mind.

Her head throbbed. She tried to pull herself to the surface, but she was disoriented and drove to the bottom instead. Her breath spent, she choked and sputtered, the taste of salt water pungent in her mouth. Water surrounded her in swift blackness, and she felt herself separating from consciousness.

Slipping away, she saw herself floating in suspension in her watery grave. Relishing the peaceful feeling devoid of worry, she wondered if she could stay in this muted existence, though she felt persistent pulls from both sides of her pleasant cocoon.

Suddenly, a wave crashed her against the wall of the pool with a deadened thud, shattering her solitude. At once, white hot pain seared her lungs.

A split second later, a muscular arm rushed her to the surface, and frigid air blasted her face. Thrust from the pool, she landed on her stomach. A man flipped her slippery body over and pressed her chest in rhythm, which purged salt water from her lungs. Gasping for breath, she began heaving and coughing. *What had happened?* She was an expert swimmer.

"That's better," she heard a male voice say, his fingers on her pulse. "Just breathe, try to relax."

Struggling to a seated position, she opened her eyes.

"Verena?"

The room swirled hazily around her. She could barely make out the form of a man crouched beside her, water dripping from his hair. *How does he know my name?*

"Verena, look at me." He cupped her face in his hands.

Her eyesight came into focus, and she could make out familiar features. *Why, he looks like...but no, it can't be.*

Still in a stupor, she wondered how it was possible that she was looking into the eyes of the man she'd dreamed about on the plane. Or was she dead after all?

Blinking, she tried to recall where she was.

Paris.

"Verena, stay with me."

But he has an American accent.

She pushed her hair from her face. "Lance?"

He grinned as she blurted out, "What are *you* doing here?"

"I could ask the same of you."

Verena managed a small laugh, and then she glanced down and saw he wasn't wearing a stitch.

Lance became aware of her gaze, and he shifted his thigh with modesty. "My robe's over there," he said, nodding to the edge of the pool, where he'd clearly flung it off before diving in. It was half in, half out of the water. "I was waiting for a massage, relaxing on the chaise lounge, when I heard you go down." He grinned again. "You're a mighty powerful swimmer. Impressive."

She wiped spittle from her mouth. "Yeah, that was pretty impressive."

"I've never seen anyone head butt the pool."

Verena felt her face grow warm—the curse of having such fair skin. She couldn't keep her eyes off this handsome, well-built man. And he was a sight to behold. She motioned to the other side of the pool. "I have a robe over there."

"I'll get it for you."

"No, for you," she said. "You must be cold."

"Never say that to a naked man," he said, laughing.

"I didn't mean it that way." *Not at all.*

"I'm glad you're okay. I'll get a robe for you."

She angled her face while he stood, but once his back was turned, she couldn't help peeking. *I nearly died, didn't I? So, a girl can look.* Watching the sensual movement of his powerful hips and thighs as he crossed the room, she felt her body respond. He wrapped a towel around his hips and picked up her robe. She clamped her eyes shut when he turned around.

"You can open them now," he said, walking back to her. He paused to pick up several towels.

A woman opened the door. "Monsieur Martel, are you ready for your massage?"

His gaze rested on Verena. "Something else has come up. I'll reschedule tomorrow." The woman nodded and closed the door, leaving them alone.

Shivering from a combination of cold and shock, Verena sat clasping her legs.

"You're shaking pretty bad." Lance knelt beside her. He quickly draped her robe around her shoulders and a towel over her wet head. "You need to warm up. Can you walk?"

She nodded and he helped her to her feet, sliding his arm around her waist to steady her. His grasp was strong and sure, but more than that, it felt natural.

"I know just what you need," he said, supporting her weight. "Hot sauna. Come with me."

Wrapped in terrycloth, her teeth chattering, she leaned on him to walk from the pool but after a couple of steps, her knees buckled.

"I've got you," he said, scooping her in his arms.

Water droplets glistened on his skin, and she wrapped her arms around his neck. "I'm so glad you were here," she said.

"So am I." His golden eyes mesmerized her. When they reached the sauna, he gently set her down. "Can you stand yet?"

She nodded. She could stand, but he had taken her breath away.

As he opened the door to the private steam sauna, eucalyptus-scented steam billowed out. "They have one of the greatest *hammams* around," he said.

Warmth cloaked her icy skin. "This is heavenly," she murmured, sinking onto a broad bench covered in azure-colored tiles. Clouds of mist enveloped them as heat seeped into her skin. The herbal aroma soothed her roughened throat and sinuses with every breath.

"This is one of my favorite saunas," Lance said, laying out towels on the tile.

Verena closed her weary eyes. Moments later, Lance brought in a cup of cool, lime-infused water and pressed it to her lips. After drinking, he leaned her head against the tiled wall, grateful that he'd been there to save her.

"I might have drowned." She shuddered.

"It was close." He held the cup to her lips again, and she slid her hand over his to steady the water.

For the next few minutes, they sat in silence, both breathing deeply in the steamy sanctuary.

Finally, Verena asked, "So what are you doing here?"

"I'm here for an international chef event representing the Beverly Hills Hotel. Lots of publicity, that sort of thing. It's a lot of fun. I even get to save beautiful women. How about you?"

Verena cleared her scratchy throat. "My grandmother and sisters are here on holiday, and I came for an important business meeting. Unfortunately, I won't be here long." She saw perspiration gleaming on his chest. She had to admit, he had a nice physique. "Funny how we keep running into each other. Seems like an awfully big coincidence."

"I call it a really nice coincidence," he said, spreading his arms across the tiled riser in back of him. "Want to tell me what happened in there? You were swimming like a woman possessed."

She shook her head, recalling the thoughts that had consumed her. "I've got a lot on my mind. It's just business."

"I'm a good listener."

This wasn't fair. He was the complete package. "I'd rather talk about something else. Besides, you're the one leading the glamorous life."

"Me?" Lance said, pointing to his chest. "You really don't know what a chef does, do you?"

"Besides cook for strange, wayward women?" She laughed. "I'm sure it's a lot of work with long hours. In fact, people usually say I'm the one with the glamorous life."

"I'd agree with that. Look at you, jetting to Paris for a meeting. What, can't get a phone call through?"

"It's an important meeting, and better conducted face to face." Verena stopped, noticing how easy it was to talk to him. *Too easy.* She rubbed her arms. "I'm warm now, I should probably go." *Before we take up where we left off at the beach.* She started to get up.

Lance touched her hand. "It's still early. How about a glass of wine? We can relax by the pool, but no more swimming for you tonight."

She should turn in and put distance between them, but she was so drawn to him that her words tumbled out despite her better judgement. "I'd like that," she said. Masking her attraction to him, she turned slightly to stretching the tension from her back. "Good for jet lag, I mean."

"Just get in?"

She nodded. "When did you arrive?"

"Today."

"On Air France?" When he nodded, she paused, thinking back. "I thought I saw you at the airport, but I figured I was imagining things."

A teasing smile danced on his lips. "Seeing me in your dreams, too?"

"You flirt." Thank goodness for a wave of steam rising between them to obscure her guilt. "Come on, let's go."

"I'll order wine while you shower." He stood and ran a hand through his hair. Opening the door for her, he asked, "Have you had dinner?"

"We had a light supper." She padded toward the dressing area. "See you soon," she added, smiling at his spiky sauna hair.

She stepped into the shower and let cool, refreshing water sluice over her warm skin. She could hardly believe Lance was here. In all her travels, she'd never been to Paris with a man. *A friend*, she corrected herself. *Who just happens to be a man, a very real man.*

She turned off the water and stepped out of the shower, toweling dry. Catching a glimpse of her lean body in the mirror, she stood tall, realizing that she was as prepared as she'd ever be for her meeting tomorrow. She knew her business well. It would do her good to relax.

Looking around the well-appointed dressing area, she saw it had everything she needed. She rinsed out her swimsuit, dried her hair, and then put on a fresh white cotton robe she'd found in a locker. After strolling back to the pool area, she made herself comfortable on a chaise lounge, thoughts of Lance uppermost in her mind.

Her thoughts wandered, and with a start, she found herself comparing Lance and Derrick, weighing their attributes. But there was more to this accounting than that.

If she was truthful with herself, she'd often felt there was something missing in her relationship with Derrick, even in the beginning, but she'd been attracted partly out of curiosity. His power and intellect had been compelling. She'd never met anyone like him.

Still, the few times she'd seen Lance, he had stirred feelings deep within her that she'd never known before. As much as she fought it, she had a visceral reaction to his presence.

There, I've admitted it, she thought. *Now what?*

Lance sat in the intimate lounge area waiting for his order to be prepared. While working in Paris at the Ritz, he had met the manager of the Majestic, and as they became friends, Lance had spent a lot of time here.

He stroked his chin, remembering the day he'd spoken to Mia Valent and Camille Dubois at the Polo Lounge. They had talked about Paris, and Mia had asked him where he was staying. He'd lay money that Mia had arranged this coincidence. He thought about it a moment and then laughed to himself. *That sweet woman is playing matchmaker.*

"Then I won't let her down," he murmured to himself. Nor would he let Verena in on the plot. Mia could prove to be a powerful ally.

Verena Valent. *What an incredible woman.* He'd known a lot of pretty women, sophisticated women, wealthy women, but he'd never known anyone like her. She seemed completely unaffected by the life in the fast lane in L.A. She had an innate sense of grace. The first night he'd ever seen her, he had stopped by the ballroom at the Beverly Hills Hotel to observe his banquet team in action. She was speaking at the podium and accepting an award. But he hadn't caught her name. Who was she?

It was as if he'd been struck—not by lightning, but by enlightenment. He had stood in the back of the room, transfixed by her melodious voice and the passion in her words. Instantly he understood the passion she had for her profession; he felt the same about his cooking. It was as if she were the woman he'd been waiting for. He had to find out who she was. He'd even made a note to ask the banquet manager.

He remembered the dress she'd worn that night, a silver-colored evening gown that set off her pale golden hair. The meeting at the pool later that evening really had been a coincidence, yet he was quick to seize the opportunity to cook for her and learn more about her.

A young man carrying a tray of food emerged from the kitchen. "Shall I take this to the pool room for you?"

"No, I've got it, thanks," Lance said. He took the tray, and then punched the elevator call button. The doors slid open, and he stepped in.

When he opened the door to the pool area and saw Verena, he could hardly speak. He ached to have someone like this in his life—*no*, he corrected himself. He wanted *her* in his life. Seeing her lounging in her robe, her hair freshly washed and her face devoid of makeup, made him imagine what it would be like to wake with her in the morning. *Have patience.* His gut tightened.

"Your order, mademoiselle," he said, placing the tray

on a small table between their chaise lounge chairs. He poured a small amount of golden-colored wine into a crystal glass and handed it to her. "Try this."

Lifting the glass by the stem, she sipped the wine. "Marvelous," she said. Her hand quivered slightly.

"Chateau d'Yquem. Some call it liquid gold. It's one of my favorite wines with dessert or *foie gras*. Its magic is derived from botrytis cinerea, or noble rot."

Watching her, he finished pouring the wine. Removing a cover from a plate, he revealed a selection of colorful macaroon treats arranged in a checkerboard pattern. Rolled white chocolate straws separated the treats, and blueberries and raspberries garnished the plate.

"Thought you might like to have something festive to celebrate your survival." He selected a raspberry macaroon for her.

"Looks delicious. My stomach hasn't adjusted to the time change yet. I don't know if it's time for breakfast or dessert." Biting into the sweet macaroon, she added, "Yum, definitely dessert."

Lance watched her lick the delicate, creamy filling from her fingers, and felt himself fall for her even more. *She has no idea the effect she has on me.* He poured more wine into her glass, and then filled his own. It was going to be a beautiful evening after all.

Against the rippling sound of the pebbled waterfall and the low illumination that cast colorful, flickering shadows across the shimmering pool, they sipped wine and nibbled, sharing stories of Paris. Soon they were talking and laughing with the ease of good friends.

At one point, Verena stifled a yawn. "I have no idea

what time it is," she said.

Lance gazed into the deep sapphire blue of her bright eyes. "Does it matter?"

A brief smile lit her face, and then slid away. "My meeting is tomorrow morning."

He sighed. "You need sleep," he said with reluctance. He stood and took her hand to help her from the chaise lounge. As she rose, their bodies naturally came together and Lance bent toward her.

This time, Verena lifted her face to his without wavering. He paused for only a moment before his lips brushed hers, softly at first, as if in question, and then, as she responded, with increasing fervor.

Lance was transported to a new dimension, and he wrapped his arms around Verena, deepening their connection. And then all thought left him as pure sensation coursed through him, full and loving and urgent. He ran his hands through her loose, fragrant hair, stroked the warm length of her neck, and then, as her robe parted, the smooth skin on her shoulders. Longing filled his soul as their lips met over and over, moist and yearning.

Verena was the first to pull away, demurely shifting her robe to cover her shoulders. "Lance, I never imagined…."

"I did," he said, kissing her again as her face colored. *She had, too, he suspected.*

After a few more moments, Verena raised her eyes to him. He melted into the twin orbs of endless blue that shimmered with emotion. Savoring every detail, he fixed each movement in his mind to recall and relish. The clean smell of her skin, the taste of her tongue, the fullness of her rosy lips. *She's incredible*, he thought, wondering how he could make her his own.

Wordlessly, she slid her hand into his and led him to the elevator.

She pressed the call button, and as they waited, Lance turned her face up to his, drinking in the lovely angles of her face and her slightly quivering lips.

"I'll see you to your room," he said.

She shook her head. As the door slid open, she touched his face and kissed him with the softness of butterfly wings.

When he opened his eyes, she was gone.

As the elevator rose through the floors, Verena sank against the wall with her eyes closed, wishing the moment had never ended. She touched her lips, still tasting him on her mouth.

Had Derrick ever brought forth such emotion in her? She couldn't remember and suddenly didn't care. The only thing that mattered was the passion Lance had ignited within her. *A feeling I never want to lose.*

A soft murmur escaped her lips, as she realized the intensity of her feelings for Lance. *What have I done?* She was aware of the complications in her life that their actions would pose, and yet, she had been a willing partner.

A vision of Lance floated through her mind. His lean, nude body bending over her beside the pool, his strong arms around her, how he looked above her, so close to her… She recalled the musky smell of his wet hair and perspiration in the *hammam*.

Despite the strange turn of events, tonight had turned into the perfect evening in Paris.

Warmth flooded her body, along with an almost

overwhelming urge to return to him. The elevator slowed to a halt at her floor and the doors opened. An elegant, chandelier-lit hallway loomed before her, its loneliness sparking questions about the pathway of her own life.

14

"*Enchanté,*" Henri Becaud said, greeting her. "It's nice to meet in person. You have your grandmother's lovely eyes, I see."

"*Merci, monsieur,*" Verena replied, as they exchanged kisses on the cheeks. Verena detected a discreet *parfum* emanating from his neck and recognized it as one of Rose Beauté's classic masculine fragrances. She was glad Mia had bought a feminine perfume from Rose Beauté for her to wear today.

"Let's sit here," he said, motioning to an antique inlaid table surrounded by four chairs.

Verena sat down, draping her cape over the polished arm of the chair and smoothing her black lace shift dress. Fianna had supplied her with just the right ensemble for this important meeting.

The private office was spacious and orderly, yet comfortably appointed. Verena couldn't help but admire the original artwork on the walls. *Degas, Picasso, Manet.* Evidence of the billions of dollars of market share the company controlled around the globe.

A slim middle-aged woman clad in black entered on silent feet and placed a coffee serving before them. She poured coffee, asked Verena how she liked it, and then completed her task and left the room.

Henri and Verena exchanged pleasantries and sipped coffee. The tall, silver-haired man was as elegant as his office, Verena noted. She'd observed his hand-stitched custom suit, understated black shoes with a small Louis Vuitton emblem, and slim wristwatch that shone discreetly from beneath a fine, starched cuff. His courtly manners reminded her of her grandfather, Emile, Mia's husband. As she spoke, his keen, inquisitive eyes never left her face.

"Mia mentioned your expansion into Asia," he said. "Tell me about your plans."

This is it. Henri's comfortable manner put her at ease, yet she knew that he was weighing every word she said. *He's brilliant*, Mia had told her. And he had a pristine professional reputation.

"We've been working on this deal for more than two years," she began. "The initial inventory has shipped, and we've committed to marketing, advertising, and public relations for the debut, as well as continuing market support." She went on to explain their plans for the future, quoting figures with confidence when he asked for specifics.

Henri nodded. "You are quite prepared. Mia mentioned that you have financing needs."

"Due to economic uncertainties in the U.S. market, our bank withdrew its commitment for working capital to fund the launch and for ongoing support."

A shadow crossed his face. "Do you wish to be acquired now?"

That question again. "We take pride in our family business. We're looking for working capital, but we're open... to other possibilities." Even though it pained her to say that, she knew that for her family's sake, she must.

"At some point, it's a good idea for families to diversify their holdings." Henri sat back and crossed his legs. "We would have liked to acquire your company, full or in part, a few years ago," he said. "But times have changed."

Verena found the warning note in his voice unsettling. "Do you expect the credit crisis in America to affect your business in Europe?"

"When America catches a cold, the rest of the world is at risk for pneumonia. In recessionary times, we must be especially proactive to protect our assets. The luxury and Asian markets are trending up, but losses in America could offset gains."

Henri continued sharing his perspective of the road ahead, and as she listened, Verena wished once again that she'd had the benefit of more education. Henri was way ahead of her. He wasn't trying to impress her, in fact, he was speaking to her as an equal, but she still had difficulty following everything he said.

Henri paused and added, "How else might I help you?"

Verena swallowed hard and met his direct gaze. "We are looking for a lender, *monsieur*. A bank, perhaps a private individual."

"The smart money everywhere is pulling back, preparing to weather a storm. Unfortunately, our portfolio has companies in similar situations to yours. At this time, we must focus on our commitment to them. If I hear of any suitable financiers, I will be pleased to make the introduction. However, if I were you, I would proceed with caution and make reductions."

Despair fogged her mind. At least he was honest with her.

"You have a fine company," he added, his voice kind. "I wish we could help you, but we are already fully committed to those in our portfolio. Once this storm blows past, we might speak again, I hope."

"I hope so, too." She inclined her head in appreciation. "Thank you for meeting with me."

"We have entered a difficult era. You must do what you can to save your company." He walked her to the door, where they exchanged kisses on the cheek again. "Please give my regards to your grandmother," he added with a cordial smile.

"I will, *merci*." Blinking back her disappointment, Verena left the office building and walked out onto the bustling boulevards of Paris.

Eschewing the taxi line, she walked for a long time, past fragrant perfumeries, decadent chocolate shops, fashionable boutiques, and throngs of tourists. Her chest clenched with frustration and her mind racing, she strode on, navigating the cobblestone sidewalks that threatened her high heels.

Her options—or rather, her lack of options—became clear.

I have to make the deal with Herringbone, she realized, turning over her dilemma. *Which means I have to call Derrick.*

She had a grave sense of portent. Mia believed in that sort of thing—kismet, karma, intuition—but Verena had always laughed and told her that she'd been living in California too long.

She stepped from the curb, but the blare of a car horn startled her. She felt a firm hand on her arm, tugging her back from the street.

"Good Lord," she exclaimed as a car whizzed by barely missing her, and so close that she felt the rush of air against her hair. She caught her breath and turned to thank the stranger. But when she did, there was no one around her.

No one at all.

Shocked, Verena stood rooted to the ground. This was the second time in less than twenty-four hours that she might have died.

When Verena entered the Majestic, she heard someone call her name.

Lance was striding toward her. "*Bonjour*," he called out. When he reached her, he kissed her on the cheek, lingering at her neck. "You look stunning. Join me?" He motioned to a small table in the lounge.

Taking her hand, he led her through the foyer past a dazzling white floral bouquet. The scent of lilies and tuberose filled the air, soothing the raw edges of her distress. "How lovely," she said as she passed the arrangement. "My favorite flowers."

"Wait," Lance said, gazing at her. "I have to have a picture of you right there with the flowers. He drew his phone out. "That's perfect."

He clicked a photo, grinned, and then leaned in for a selfie of the two of them.

Verena peered at the shots. "Send those to me?"

"Sure."

She tapped her phone number in.

Lance took her hand again, guiding her into the lounge. "How did your meeting go?"

Verena shook her head. So many emotions warred within her, but hearing his voice and gazing into his eyes provided a welcome reprieve. "Mia had high hopes, but unfortunately, Rose Beauté can't help us either. I'll have to tell Mia right away."

Lance looked concerned for her. "Sit with me and chill. Besides, Mia and the girls aren't back yet."

"How do you know?"

"I arranged a car for them."

"You didn't need to do that," Verena said, sharper than she'd meant.

"Relax, the manager is a friend of mine. It's a hotel car. He also arranged special passes to the Louvre." They sat down and he motioned to a waiter. "Rough day, huh?"

"The man I met with was kind enough, but...." Her voice trailed off and she shrugged. She was resigned to do what she must, as Henri had advised. She'd have to call Derrick. But for now, the only man she wanted to talk to was sitting with her, filling her mind with even more uncertainties, however enticing.

"Here, try this, it's an apéritif." He handed her a small stemmed glass.

She sniffed the fine bouquet, and let it flow over her tongue. "Tastes like walnuts."

"You have a good palate," he said. He motioned across the small salon to a table, where several plates rested. "We've been experimenting in the kitchen. Here, try this." He handed her a toast point spread with something that smelled delicious.

The savory treat melted in her mouth, and she realized she was starving. She rarely ate much before important meetings, and today had been no exception. "This is marvelous, what is it?"

He laughed. "A little of this, a little of that. Mushrooms, herbs, cheeses, infused oils. The real work begins tomorrow. You should come to the chef's event.

The food will be incredible."

"I wish I could," she said. "But I fly home tomorrow." As she said it, she realized how disappointed she was to leave him.

Or is it simply Paris and its magical spell?

He studied her over the rim of his glass. "At least join me for dinner."

"I'd like that, but I'd promised Mia and the girls that we'd have dinner tonight."

A mischievous smile tugged at his lips. "Will everyone eat crab?"

"Yes, but—"

"Then I know just the place for us. Excuse me."

Verena watched him cross the room to speak to someone at the front desk. Lance wore black jeans and a black cotton turtleneck shirt with the sleeves pushed up to reveal his firm forearms. A light grey scarf was casually draped around his neck. If she didn't know better, she would have thought he was French. He was a chameleon, blending in with his surroundings, yet standing out among men. Glancing around, she noticed she wasn't the only woman watching him.

"It's all set," he said as he sat down beside her, rubbing his hands together in excitement. "You'll love this place. It's a legend and very hard to get into."

The joy on his face was apparent. "You love food, don't you?"

"*Good* food," he said, his eyes shining with excitement and his fingers pressed together in a gesture of emphasis. "Food is a primal urge, but good food is an art form. It might be the most flavorful garlic mashed potatoes you've ever had, or a duck confit so sublime it melts in your mouth. It doesn't matter if food is simple or elegant, as long as the ingredients are fresh and natural, and the dish is well prepared. That's artistry."

Verena appreciated his passion for his craft. "It's wonderful to see someone who loves their work."

"It's not just work, it's my life. I love to take care of people." He took her hand as he spoke. "When customers leave my restaurant, I want them to feel thoroughly pampered, to sense the passion that went into each dish, and to appreciate the creativity. Most of all, I want them to say 'wow, that was a damned fine meal.'"

"That's how I feel about my work, too," Verena said, getting swept away by his enthusiasm. "I want every one of our guests to feel cherished when they visit our salon, or when they use any of our products. It's a ritual of self-love that people should do every day."

"We share the same philosophy, the same dedication to excellence." He twined his fingers with hers.

His touch sent a surge of energy coursing through her. *What just happened?* The feel of his hand against hers set off sparks in her soul. *Is this why people call Paris the city of love?*

"I'm glad we ran into one another again here," he said softly.

"So am I," she said, finally feeling like smiling again.

"When we return home, why don't we actually plan to meet, instead of leaving it to chance?"

"Chance has worked well for us."

"But it's… chancy." He grinned, and his amber eyes held her gaze.

"Oh, that was too obvious," she said, laughing, and then caught herself. *What am I doing?*

Lance seemed to take this in. "If you ever need me, I want you to know that you can call on me. For anything." His voice was husky and he caressed her hand as he spoke, trailing his fingers along hers. "I care about you, Verena. Last night was just the beginning."

His words held an intensity that scared her. She lifted her glass. "To the beginning of a beautiful friendship in Paris, how's that?" Even as soon as she spoke, regret flooded her. The words seemed to hang in mid-air, dividing them.

"We'll see," he said with confidence, rising to her challenge.

Behind them there was a commotion in the lobby as Mia and the twins walked in. Anika and Bella were wearing the new clothes they had bought yesterday, and they both had their hair styled differently.

With a start, Verena noticed they were attracting the attention of several young men in the lobby. The girls were maturing; they were on the cusp of womanhood. *They're like lovely young swans, and I must protect them.* The weight of her responsibilities bore down upon her again.

"Hey, what's the matter?" Lance asked.

"I just realized they're almost grown. Sometimes I don't notice. I get so overwhelmed with business."

"You have a wonderful family." He looked directly into her eyes. "You're doing a fine job with them, and I know you'll continue to do so, but you deserve a life, too. A good life."

She stroked his hand. *He understood.* "Then let's enjoy the evening."

Mia spotted them in the lounge. "Why, there you are,"

she said, starting toward them.

Verena quickly slid her hand away from Lance's, but not before Mia had seen them.

"We had such a wonderful day," Mia said, beaming. "Lance, thank you for arranging the car for us. What a difference it made. I couldn't have managed these two energetic girls without it."

"I'm glad I could help," Lance said. "The day isn't over yet. I've booked a special restaurant for dinner. Nothing fancy," he added, nodding toward the twins. "But good, fresh food in a great atmosphere."

"Sounds wonderful," Mia said. "Girls, let's go. We'll freshen up, and meet you downstairs." When Bella started to protest, Mia shot her a firm look.

"Eight o'clock—early for Paris, but probably better for the twins," he said.

"We'll see you then," Mia said, excusing herself to take the girls upstairs to their room.

"I should change, too." Verena glanced down at her black lace dress.

"You look exquisite, but you'll be more comfortable in casual clothes tonight."

She rose, and as she did, Lance stood and gave her kisses on her cheeks. Unable to resist, she nipped her lips and he responded with a lingering kiss on her mouth. "I mean it, you deserve a wonderful life," he whispered into her ear. "And someone who'll be good to you."

Energy surged between them, and Verena's nerves tingled. "I'll see you soon," she murmured.

As she turned away from him, her face grew warm, but this time, her coloring wasn't from embarrassment, but from a feeling that was infinitely finer. And as she walked away from him, she was glad he couldn't see the delight on her face.

So much for her idea of friendship. Lance was irresistible.

After all, this was Paris.

15

"*Bon appétit*," the waiter said as he delivered an enormous platter of steamed crab to the table. The scent of fresh seafood and homemade bread filled the air, and laughter bubbled around them.

Verena laughed as she watched Anika and Bella, their eyes widening with delight. She loved having her family together in Europe, just as Mia had always dreamed.

Sitting beside Mia, she saw her grandmother slip her hand into her pocket, pull out a handkerchief, and run her fingers over the monogram. She'd seen her do this a couple of times on their trip, but she couldn't remember Mia ever carrying one of her husband's handkerchiefs before. Or did it belong to someone else? Verena tried to see the initials, but Mia slipped it back into her pocket.

"I'll tie your bibs," Lance said, chuckling as he helped the girls put on bright blue fabric bibs with the words *Le Crabe Marteau* emblazoned across the front. "And now for you, *mademoiselle*," he said to Verena.

"Oh, no," she said, holding up her hands.

"What? Are you too proper for a bib?"

"*I'm* not," Mia said, turning a coy smile on Lance. "You can help me. It's so nice having a man around to help. Especially you."

"It's an honor." Lance tied Mia's bib around her neck with a flourish.

Other diners in the restaurant wore the cloth bibs, too.

Fishing nets and lures hung from the walls, along with a chalkboard that featured the specials of the day. Butcher paper covered old wooden tables, and the waiter had left a heavy wooden mallet to crack the freshly steamed crabs.

Verena was glad that Lance had chosen such a delightful restaurant. Everyone was having fun. The meeting today had been disappointing; if Henri couldn't help them, then the economy was definitely in trouble. But that was for tomorrow to think about. Determined to enjoy the brief time she had in Paris, she gazed around the table, happy that Mia and the girls were having a good time.

"Now you're the only one left." Lance stood by Verena with a bib in hand.

"Oh, all right, get on with it. But you'll never see me with a bib in Beverly Hills." She shot him a warning look.

"Come on, don't be a snob," he said.

The twins looked at one another and burst out laughing.

Verena lifted her wavy blond hair to let him tie her bib. As he did, he brushed his fingers discreetly across the back of her neck, and she thrilled to his touch. Her skin grew warm, and she noticed Mia watching them.

"You look happy, Verena," Mia said. "Look at us all, what fun we're having." She took Verena's hand and gave it a quick, meaningful squeeze. "I'm so glad you came with us to Paris."

"Now that you're all tied up, let me explain this meal to you," Lance said, sitting next to Verena. He picked up a wooden mallet. "We'll use this to beat the crab into submission."

Bella's eyes widened. "It's not alive is it?" She poked

one of the orange-red crabs on the thick cutting board in front of her.

"Watch out," Lance cried. "They'll pinch you."

Anika and Bella screamed and then fell against one another, giggling with glee.

Regaining her composure, Anika said, "I'm trying to become a vegetarian."

"I respect that," Lance replied, looking concerned. "I can speak to the kitchen, have them make something for you."

Anika eyed the crab and licked her lips.

"It's really no trouble," Lance said. "A smart chef always accommodates dietary preferences."

"I'll resume my diet tomorrow," Anika said, a shy smile lighting her face.

Verena observed Lance with the twins. He was good with them, and they liked him. *Better than they liked Derrick.* Mia was watching their interaction, too.

"Let me show you how it's done." Lance took the mallet to the steamed crabs and began to crack them with gusto.

Verena picked up a bowl of red potatoes with herbs to serve Mia, the girls, and Lance.

"We have a good Chardonnay, too," Lance added. "Mia, would you care for wine?"

"Of course, my dear." Mia's face lit with pleasure. After he poured a small amount into her glass, she swirled it to aerate the bouquet and then lifted the wine to her nose and inhaled. "Quite nice." She sipped, savoring the taste on her tongue before swallowing. "A fine choice, Lance." She nodded her approval.

"Just a simple wine to go with this hearty fare." He

poured more into Mia's glass and then matched the pour into Verena's glass.

Verena glanced at the label. "Not that simple." Her eyes met his.

"You know your wines." Lance looked at her with admiration.

"My grandmother taught me." Verena could feel the electricity sparking between them. Turning to Mia, she added, "In fact, I believe you began your instruction when you brought me to Paris the first time."

"But you were our age then, Verena," Anika said, darting a look at Bella.

"So, can we have wine, too?" Bella asked.

"Now, you two know you're not crazy about wine," Verena said.

Mia smiled at the younger girls. "Your sister is right. We'll develop your palate later."

Lance passed cracked crab around, and soon everyone was eating and exclaiming over the food.

Verena looked around the table, a rush of joy filling her heart. Everyone seemed to be enjoying themselves. *This is a perfect evening.*

As they ate, Lance turned to Mia and asked, "What are your plans in Switzerland?"

"We'll stay with my sister Lara in Vevey," Mia said. "That's a quaint little village on the banks of Lake Geneva where we were born. We'll tour with Lara and her daughter, drive around Fribourg, sample cheese in Gruyères, and wine in the Valais. We'll take a tram into the Alps, too. So much lovely country to explore. There's never enough, though."

Anika and Bella looked at Mia with excitement. Everything was a new experience for the girls, and Verena was glad they were enjoying the trip.

After they finished the meal, Mia said, "It's still early by Paris time. Verena, why don't you and Lance leave us at the hotel and go out for a nightcap?"

"She's right," Lance said, taking Verena's hand. "Paris is magical at night."

Despite her worries, Verena felt a wave of anticipation. "I suppose. How often do we find ourselves in Paris, right?"

Surely there was no harm in spending the rest of evening with Lance.

After Verena and Lance left Mia and the twins at the hotel, they strolled along Rue la Pérouse in the cool evening air. The magnificent Arc de Triomphe loomed ahead in the center of an impressive roundabout, which yawned toward the grand Avenue des Champs-Élysées.

"I know a place you might like," Lance said. "Are you up for walking?"

"I'd love it. It's such a beautiful city. And it's my last night." *Before returning to reality.*

"On this trip," Lance said, touching her shoulder. "I'm sure you'll be back."

They passed an outdoor café where a group of people were engaged in a heated political discussion over a table littered with wine, coffee, and cigarettes.

Verena brushed his hand. "You haven't been smoking here. Did you quit again?"

"I haven't touched a cigarette since you chastised me about it. Although I have to admit I'm tempted here in

Paris."

"Don't do it," she cried. "Remember your skin—and the rest of your body."

Taking her hand, he said, "For you, anything."

She squeezed his hand, feeling a thrill at his touch. They walked toward a nightclub where the music was throbbing and fashionable people were milling around outside on the sidewalk. Everyone was having a good time.

Lance stopped. "Do you ever go to nightclubs in Paris?"

She laughed. "That's not usually on my agenda."

"It should be, it's fun." He looked at her and brushed away a strand of hair that had blown into her eyes. "Come on, I know a jazz club that I think you'll like. You can dance, can't you?"

"Of course I can." She shook her head in amazement. He was a man of many surprises. Though the night was cool, his hand felt warm and sure. A connection flowed between them, linking them in a manner she had never known. *Not with Joe. Not with Derrick.* Was this one of those signs Mia often spoke about?

They continued wending their way through the streets until Lance found the street he was looking for. "*Voici la rue Jean Giraudoux, mademoiselle.*"

Hearing Lance's rich, gravelly voice in French was almost too much for her to bear. Turning onto the lane, Verena shivered with excitement.

"And here it is, Le Speakeasy." At the entry, Lance spoke in French to a slim man, who quickly swept them into the dimly lit club, which was styled in chic 1920s fashion.

They wound through a young, stylish crowd, past a long bar with ruby-red covered stools and into a room filled with black sofas, tables, and chairs.

They slid onto an ebony leather banquette near a piano, where a Josephine Baker look-alike was draped across the polished wood, cooing a sensual jazz tune in French that made Verena feel like she'd been transported back in time.

Lance put his arm around her shoulders and leaned in to her. "This isn't a traditional French club, but it's fun. It's a mix of French and American jazz."

As he spoke, his breath was warm on her neck and each puff sent a tingle through her.

"I love it," she said. There was that word again: *fun.* When was the last time she'd had any fun? "I didn't know you spoke French."

"*Un peu,*" he said, grinning. "When I worked in Europe, I picked up a smattering of languages. It sure helped in the kitchen. I can say 'that's burning' in half a dozen languages."

Verena laughed. "I have to admit, cooking is not my strongest point. But I can bake."

"Really? Then we're a good match. That's quite a science; I usually leave it to the pastry chefs."

"Mia and my mother taught me when I was young. The three of us used to gather in the kitchen, with Mia showing my mother how to make old family recipes. Tartes, brioche, and pastries." Verena gazed off, remembering the good times they'd had and how much she's taken for granted.

"Does your mother work in the family business, too?"

Verena hesitated, carefully choosing her words before she spoke. "She did. In fact, she was wonderful at everything she took on. But my mother and father died in a car accident when I was eighteen."

Lance's face was etched with shock. "I'm sorry, I didn't know."

"How could you?" Verena lifted a shoulder and let it drop. "It's been ten years, but I still miss them. I think about them so much, often wondering what they would do in this or that situation. How would my mother handle a marketing issue, or how would my father deal with the bank? They ran the business together after Mia stepped down, but when they died, it all fell on me."

Lance didn't speak, but covered her hand with his, and she could feel emotional strength flowing from him.

Idly tracing the thin scars on his fingers, she continued. "When it happened, Mia was in Switzerland undergoing intense cancer treatment. She was quite ill. Instead of going to college that fall, as I'd planned, I accepted the responsibility for the business and the twins." She blinked, remembering. "That helped occupy my mind."

"You were so young," Lance said softly. "Did you have help?"

"The staff at the salon rallied around me. They taught me everything I needed to know. They were—and are—so loyal to our family." She shook her head. "In my last year of high school, I became licensed and worked part-time giving facials, but I was unprepared for the financial, marketing, and human resource sides of the business. I was so inexperienced."

Lance was taking it all in. "How did you manage with the girls?"

"I hired a nanny when Anika and Bella where little, and a few years later I hired Fianna—you met her at the Beverly

Hills Hotel—to care for the girls after school. Fianna was working her way through the Fashion Institute of Design and Merchandising at the time. The girls loved her, and it gave me time to throw myself into a hands-on crash course on business. That's when I began expanding the company."

He stroked her hand, listening. "You've certainly succeeded, Verena."

"If I succeeded, it was only with the help of my assistant Lacey, and that of my accountant, attorney, and banker. They took time to teach me, but I had to learn fast, because important projects were in progress. My first job was to expand the product line and sell it into luxury department stores. My father had started the process, but I had to implement the plan. Next, we expanded the salons across the country."

"Sounds like it was rough, but you came through it."

She nodded, recalling the difficulties. "After that, nothing seemed insurmountable. When you've faced the worst that life can serve up, and pushed on, moment by moment, day by day, until you've finally overcome your challenges, there isn't much that can ever faze you again." Or was there?

"You were strengthened by fire." Lance searched her eyes. "But there's something troubling you, isn't there?"

She found it so easy to confide in him. "Am I that transparent?"

"Only to me." He angled his head with interest. "You're worried. Your meeting today didn't go as you had hoped. Is that what's bothering you?"

"It is." She closed her eyes, thinking.

"Do you have another plan?"

An image of Derrick flashed through her mind. She

raised her eyes to Lance. "We have an investor." Tomorrow, when she landed in Los Angeles, she'd have to call Derrick. She sighed. *And this—whatever this is—will have to end.*

As Lance gazed at her, a new song began, and a few couples near them began to sway with the slow, soulful piano tune. "Dance with me?" he asked.

The music had a cool, sexy vibe, and it struck a chord of need deep within her.

Verena hesitated for only a moment before following him to the dance area. She moved into his arms, surprised that the movement felt so natural.

He held her close, their bodies melding together as they moved in rhythm to the music. His sure touch sent a wave of relaxation through her, and the disappointments of the day were swept away, at least for the moment.

Pressing against him, she felt the beat of his heart in his firm chest. She sucked in a breath. Never had she felt such a strong physical attraction to a man, including Derrick, who had pursued her with such persistence that she'd finally agreed to go out with him.

And look how that had turned out.

She hardly knew Lance either. Yet she could not deny their natural affinity, their easy connection. Tuning out her better judgement, she let herself go and looked up into Lance's sparkling eyes.

A smile curved his mouth and she reached up to touch his inviting lips. He kissed her fingers, teasing her the tips with his tongue. Trailing her fingers across his chin and slight stubble, she explored his face, his neck, his chest. She liked what she was seeing.

He slipped an arm around her waist, moving gracefully with her in unison to the smoky vocals and jazz piano.

Leaning in, he said, "Verena, you're an amazing woman." His voice was thick with emotion. "You must know how deeply you've affected me."

His words were a panacea to her soul, a caress to her heart. "As you've touched me," she whispered.

He ran his thumb along her neck and bent to kiss her. Verena responded, awash in pure pleasure. Their surroundings seemed to fall away, and they danced as one, their desire mounting.

"Never stop," she whispered, and he kissed her again.

Another song began and they continued dancing, blissfully gliding from one tune into another, until finally, Verena pulled away, breaking the spell. "It's getting late," she murmured.

Lance found her mouth again and left a kiss lingering on her lips. "As you wish," he said, and then guided her back to the table.

After paying the tab, they stepped out into the night. Lance put his arm around her and drew her close to his side.

Verena rested against him, content for the moment despite her inner turmoil. As they strolled through the streets of one of the world's most romantic cities, she smiled to herself. *It's true what they say about Paris.*

As they walked, Lance hugged her close to his side. "Verena, I understand your situation. I know things are difficult for you, but you can't deny what we have."

His words were like a soothing balm, but she had to ask, "What do you think we have, Lance?"

"A deep connection. Surely you feel it, too."

She smiled up at him. "This has been a magnificent evening. I can't think of anyone I'd rather be with in Paris."

"Or anywhere else?" he asked, grinning at her.

Unable to answer, she looked into his eyes, her mind riddled with worry over what awaited her at home. Their timing was awful. She didn't dare commit, not now. Not after two failed relationships and the responsibility of a family that depended on her to do the right things.

They strolled on in silence, savoring the moments they had and slowing as the neared the hotel. When they arrived, Lance walked with her upstairs to her suite. They stopped just outside of the room.

"Here we are," he said, kissing her on the nose.

"I had a wonderful evening. Thank you for making this trip special." She inclined her head toward the door. "For all of us."

"And for you?"

"Especially for me. Paris is magical."

"It's in us now." A slow smile played on his lips. "Wherever we are, I promise to keep the magic alive for the rest of our lives."

Lance kissed her, and this time their connection was deeper than ever before. She threaded her fingers through the back of his hair that curled along his collar. She pulled him to her and found his lips, yielding to her desire.

At last, their lips parted with reluctance.

"Good night, my darling Verena," Lance said, his voice thick with passion. "I wish you were staying longer."

"Me, too." She cradled her head in the crook of his neck, regretting leaving him, and regretting even more what she knew she must do.

He trailed a finger along her jawline. "Paris won't be the same without you."

"Nor my life without you." Verena hesitated. "I'm sorry, I can't continue seeing you after we return."

Shock registered on Lance's face and he fumbled for words.

But before he could speak, Verena swiftly closed the door behind her and leaned into it, her heart bursting, hardly daring to believe what had happened on this trip, or that she had just told Lance good-bye.

16

"Thank you for the ride, George," Verena said.

The driver turned into her driveway and stopped. "It's my job, Miss Verena." The well-built older man got out of the car and made his way to the trunk.

"I'll help you with the bags," she said, sliding out. Years ago, her father had hired George to ferry guests to and from the salon—the elderly, the city dwellers who didn't drive, the sweet sixteen party-goers. He made product deliveries and airport runs, but more than that, he'd always been like an uncle to her, listening to her travel woes on her extensive travels to visit retail store buyers and conduct training across the country for them.

"Nonsense, it's part of my exercise," he said, hoisting the bags. "Makes lifting weights easier."

"How's your writing, George?"

"New detective book coming out next month," he said with pride.

"Someday you're going to sell the film rights and become a big Hollywood writer, and leave us all behind," she said, joking with him.

"Hasn't happened yet, but I still enjoy it. I think it's important to have a creative outlet and take the time to do something you love."

George often shared his thoughtful views on life with her. Verena thought about how much she loved helping people feel attractive and pampered. For many of those who lived hectic, time-starved lives, their visit to VSS was the only time they had to themselves. She'd seen the ravages that stress could cause in a person's life, and she loved seeing their customers emerge from treatments feeling relaxed and happy.

Verena truly cared about the people she saw at the salon and those who bought their products. She felt she was doing her life's work, and she felt fully alive and engaged when she knew she was helping people.

But the financing deal and her doubts about Derrick were taking a toll on her. Now she was the one who needed a therapeutic massage. She couldn't wait to slip into a whirlpool tub and close her eyes.

Verena opened the front door, and there in the small foyer was an enormous vase bursting with fragrant white lilies and tuberose. The scent was intoxicating.

"My goodness, someone missed you an awful lot." George placed her bags inside, said good-bye, and closed the door behind him.

Verena saw a note on the table from their neighbor, who had taken delivery and brought the bouquet over while they were gone. The family had lived next door to Mia for forty years, and they trusted each other with keys to keep an eye on their homes when they traveled.

She leaned in to smell the flowers. Derrick used to send flowers a lot. He had even joked that he had a standing order at the florist.

A pang of guilt shot through her. She hadn't called him when she touched down. Mentally, she was still in Paris, still with Lance, although was trying to forget hm. *Time to re-enter real life.* A life that had no room for Lance right now. She pressed her palm to her forehead.

She thought of all the people who depended on her— not just her family, but her employees and their families. She had to be responsible. There was no time to waste.

Sighing, she called Derrick's number to make arrangements to go forward with the Herringbone financing.

As the phone rang, she plucked a tiny envelope from the bouquet.

Derrick's voice boomed from the phone. "Hi, are you back in L.A.?"

"Yes, I am." She could hear loud noise in the background and a woman's familiar laugh. She heard him excusing himself and the woman said something she couldn't make out.

"Listen, I can't talk."

"Was that Greta?"

"No, I'm at dinner with a client."

"Oh. Well, I just called to tell you that I'd like to go forward with the deal."

"I knew you would. We'll celebrate."

She glanced at the bouquet. He was as presumptuous as always. "And thank you for the flowers. They're beautiful."

Derrick paused. "I didn't send you flowers."

"No?" She opened the envelope and slid out a small card. *A remembrance of Paris.* She caught her breath as she remembered where she'd seen a similar bouquet. In the foyer at the Majestic. With Lance. Her heart twisted with regret. She had mentioned how much she loved the floral arrangement. "Ah, they must be from Mia."

"But you just left her."

"She's thoughtful," Verena said. "I'm here alone until they return."

"Mia spends a lot of money, Verena. This trip with the twins, for example. Was it really necessary?"

Where did that come from? Verena didn't know what to say. Mia had never been extravagant. She had saved money for her retirement, and she certainly wasn't a spendthrift.

"Listen, I'll call you tomorrow," he said. "We have things to discuss."

Click. Verena stared at the phone, and then her eyes fell on the note card. It was simply signed: *Lance.* Sighing, she ran her fingers across it and slipped it into her purse.

17

The next day, Verena continued trying to resist thoughts of Lance by spending hours reviewing financial documents in preparation for her meeting with Derrick. He'd called that morning and invited himself over, saying that he wanted to talk to her in private tonight. He even had a special request: *Can you make my favorite Beef Wellington?*

If she hadn't been desperate to get this deal done, she'd have told him exactly what he could do with his Beef Wellington.

Verena glanced at the clock on the stove. Derrick was late, which wasn't like him. She opened the oven to check the pastry covered roast, which was baked to a rich golden brown. This was a special dish she'd enjoyed making for her family for Thanksgiving. When they'd been dating, Derrick had spent a couple of hours with them that day before flying out to Shanghai. Tonight, she was so worried that she'd derived little enjoyment from cooking. Especially for Derrick.

The doorbell chimed.

"Verena, wonderful to see you again, babe," Derrick said as Verena opened the door. He took her in his arms.

"Babe?" She laughed and pulled away. "You've never called me that. And I'm not your girlfriend."

Something seemed different about him and it made her uncomfortable, but she couldn't articulate the change.

Maybe it was because she now compared him to Lance.

And Derrick fell far short in comparison.

As if on cue, her phone rang in the kitchen.

Derrick caught her hand. "Can't you turn that off? We have a lot to discuss tonight."

"Of course not, it could be Mia or the twins." She raced to answer it but she was a second too late. Lance's missed call appeared on the screen. She drew her fingers over the message, wishing she could talk to him and explain herself. Yet she'd made her decision. Her life was about to get even more complicated.

Derrick had followed her to the kitchen. "Was that Mia?"

"No." Verena snapped off her phone and whirled around. "Dinner is almost ready. Would you care for a glass of wine?"

"Sure. Smells delicious." He made himself comfortable at the kitchen table while Verena turned to her salad preparations.

"This is a wine I discovered in Paris," she said, handing him a bottle. "Open it for me?"

"Sure. How was Paris?" he asked, watching her.

"It's an incredible city." *Made even more so by Lance.* Biting her lip, she rinsed off a handful of vegetables from Mia's garden.

"Get your business done?"

"I made an important connection, and kept the trip short," she added, remembering what he'd said about the cost of the trip. She'd never had to justify personal expenses to anyone before, but now that Herringbone had been researching the company—the due diligence—she felt she had to explain the expense to Derrick.

He nodded. "Speaking of expenses, we've been going

over the numbers on your company."

Her controller had sent the last financial statements to her by email, and she had gone over them on the plane, and again that morning, analyzing their position.

Now that Rose Beauté had passed, she had few others to turn to, even though she'd still made a few calls to other financiers. At this point, Herringbone was the only one willing to lend to VSS, and if it didn't make the loan soon, she'd have to start terminating employees.

Wielding a large knife, she sliced through a carrot with vengeance. She didn't even want to think about that. "How do the financials look?" she said, trying to keep concern from her voice.

Derrick pulled the cork from the bottle. "Good news. There's a deal on the table, Verena."

She paused, her knife suspended in one hand. "What does that mean?"

"Herringbone is willing to do the deal. But the terms have changed a little." He took a wine glass from the cupboard, poured wine for himself, and took a swig.

"The amount of the loan hasn't declined, has it?" Verena felt a chill creep up her neck. The company couldn't get by on much less.

"It's not that. You'll actually have a lot more money to work with," he said, sounding confident.

Verena stared at him. An alarm went off in her head. "Why would I want to borrow more than we need?"

Derrick shifted in his chair, picked up his wine glass, and swirled it in the halo of the overhead light. "Good color. You discovered this wine in Paris?"

"That's what I said. And I wouldn't mind a glass."

Verena cast a cool glance at Derrick. *He's stalling, he knows I won't like the terms.* After emptying sliced carrots, romaine lettuce, and sweet peppers into the salad bowl, Verena took the roast from the oven to rest. Satisfied with her work, she wiped her hands on a towel, got her own wine glass, and sat across the kitchen table from Derrick. "Tell me about the deal."

As he made a show of pouring wine into her glass, he began. "Herringbone will make the loan, and you'll have access to whatever else you might need in terms of management talent, lines of credit—you name it. It's a good deal."

Swirling her wine, Verena narrowed her eyes at him over the glass. "We have a good management team already."

Derrick shifted in his chair. "As you expand, you'll need a more experienced team. Of course, you'll remain at the helm as CEO, but you'll need a broader knowledge base on board."

"We've been in the skincare business for decades."

"Right, but there's a new opportunity you're going to need help with."

Verena arched a brow. She didn't like what she was hearing.

Derrick licked his lips and went on. "Herringbone has another beauty company that we want to fold into VSS. We believe VSS can be a beauty powerhouse, and this will be the first step."

"We're running at full capacity as it is. Why would we want to dilute our efforts when we have such a tremendous opportunity already in progress in Asia?"

"You have to think big, Verena. This nail care

company has a great product line, but the management was lousy. With our help, you can turn it around."

Verena pushed back from the table. "*Nail* company? That's not what we do. We focus on skincare."

"Close enough. Look, it did well in the mass market."

"In drugstores and discounters? That's not even in our distribution network. Derrick, all we need is a working capital loan."

"This is a great opportunity. It's called Rainbow Nails—"

"Hold it. I know Rainbow Nails. It's a color line for teenagers. It's not even in our league. We must maintain our image," she said, shaking her head. "We can't lose focus on our luxury positioning in the market."

Derrick passed a hand across his face. "You need to do this, Verena."

"No." She folded her arms. "We agreed on a loan, that's it."

Derrick raised a brow and tapped his wine glass, the tinkling of fine crystal shattering the silence. "Herringbone didn't agree on anything," he said in a measured voice. "This is the offer. I've seen your financials, and I suggest you listen to it."

Verena stared at him. A sinking feeling began to gather within her. She might need the money, but she had to proceed with caution. She slid her wine glass away from her. "I'm listening."

"Herringbone will advance funds for a minor equity stake in Valent. You'll take over Rainbow and reinvigorate that company. We'll take a seat on the board, contribute some management expertise, and grow the companies together."

Verena paused, taking it all in. "And then what?"

"We'll find a suitor, you sell and retire."

"Why would we want to sell?" She bit her lip, but the sinking feeling intensified. "I'm far too young to retire. My sisters will probably join the business someday, and our children, too. This is our family business."

Derrick met her gaze. "It's also your opportunity to provide for your entire family. Then they can do whatever they want with their lives." He reached across the table for her hand. "And so can you."

Growing more uncomfortable, Verena glanced down at his hand and shook her head. The idea for Rainbow was just too much. "I don't know, Derrick. This is so far outside of our business plan. I can't see how it makes sense for us."

"Herringbone can take your company to an entirely new level. We're talking millions of dollars, Verena. You must think of your family. Mia likes to travel, and she should do it in style. Who knows how many years she has left? And Anika and Bella, what if they don't want to work in the business? Don't you want them to be able to do anything they'd like?"

Verena considered his words. Was he really trying to help her, or just line his own pockets? Or both?

"When Asia is in full stride, can you really handle the business?" Derrick stroked her hand as he spoke, his voice softening. "Someday when you have children, would you really want to spend weeks in Asia away from them?"

"I suppose someone else could take those trips." She closed her eyes for a moment. Derrick sounded so sincere. He had some good points. "I don't know..."

"Remember the life we'd planned together?" Derrick's

voice dropped a notch, nearly mesmerizing her. "I've changed, I promise. We could still make than happen."

"Don't get any ideas." Appalled, Verena snapped her hand back.

"Verena, don't be like this."

Rubbing her forehead, she thought about the past couple of glorious days with Lance, but she had to face the grim situation before her. *This is my reality.* She had to make this work, no matter how hard it might be.

Sizing up Derrick's expression, she wondered how often she'd have to see him, though she'd hardly seen him when they engaged. Yet the thought of tackling another company, especially one so different from their own, was overwhelming.

The culture of Valent Swiss Skincare would change with new managers on board. She'd always run the business based on providing the best service to their guests. But this was big business.

"Derrick, I'll be honest, I don't know anything about running a business in the mass market. You say Herringbone will support this new venture?"

"Absolutely, I promise. As much as required."

She turned over the decision in her mind. *Something didn't feel right.* Yet, she was not in a position to decline. "I'll have my attorney look at it," she said, her words laced with caution. "If I decide it's not right for us, can I still count on the loan we need for working capital?"

Derrick shook his head. "This is the only deal on the table, Verena."

"But surely—"

"Roper made it very clear that unless you agree to these

terms, there is no deal."

"That doesn't make any sense. If VSS is a good investment, then why wouldn't Herringbone go ahead with it? Seems the addition of Rainbow Nails could destabilize our company. If anything, it would be the riskier proposition." Though she didn't have his experience, this didn't seem prudent. She stood to check on the roast. "What am I missing here?"

Wearily, Derrick drew a hand over his face. "You ask a lot of questions, Verena, and I have to admit, they're good ones. Here's the deal, as a defunct company, Rainbow is dragging down one of our portfolio funds, and we're trying to improve its returns, or its prospect of returns, because we need the investors in that fund to invest in our new fund. You know I have a big stake in this new fund, Verena."

He got up and stood behind her, his hand on her shoulder. "This could be our future. We could have an even larger stake in it together."

"Derrick, don't."

Not listening to her, he moved closer. "You'd be doing Herringbone—and your family—a big favor. And me."

She shrugged him aside to get a serving platter. "I don't know, Derrick."

Turning brusquely from her, he poured more wine for himself. "Look, I wouldn't have agreed to bring this deal to you if I didn't think you could do it."

He did have some good points about her family's needs, but his attitude was grating on her nerves. Tamping down her tension, she drew a breath. "I'm thinking of Mia, and of Anika and Bella, too. It could sell for millions, you say?"

"How often do you have the opportunity to secure their future? You could set up trust funds for each one of them. Think of the cost of their college education alone."

"I've already saved some for them. I really want them to have the opportunity that I never had to go to college. Twins are expensive."

"It's a lot of responsibility on your shoulders. I promise, you won't regret this. It's the right thing to do."

She threw him a look of caution. "I'll have to speak to my attorney and accountant. And Rainbow should be a separate company. If it doesn't perform, I wouldn't want it to hurt VSS."

"Of course, absolutely. I'll send the term sheet to you tomorrow. As long as you approve, we can move to the legal agreements immediately. And from then on," he added, "you'll be on the path to success."

Derrick made it sound so easy. He always talked about buying, building, and selling companies as if they were baseball trading cards.

She pulled on a pair of oven mitts. Glancing over her shoulder at Derrick, an involuntary shudder went through her. Herringbone's plan still didn't feel right to her.

Yet, she knew she might have to make the best of the situation for her family's sake. Her gut twisted as the thought of it. As a result, the business and life she had always known would change.

Perhaps it was time for change.

As she hefted the hot roasting pan, Derrick approached her from behind.

"How's that Beef Wellington? I'm starving," he said, clasping her bottom with his hands and squeezing for emphasis.

Or not. Fury seized her. How dare he touch her like that? After sliding the roast from the pan onto a platter, she picked it up and whirled around, anger blinding her reason. "Here you are."

The platter tilted in her hands. In a split second, the roast took flight, landing squarely on Derrick's polished Gucci dress shoes.

"What the hell?" Derrick leapt to his feet and yanked off his shoes. Bits of pastry crust crumbling from the roast swam in the juice puddling in his shoes.

"Oops." Verena leaned back against the counter, the platter dangling from her fingertips. "And don't you ever touch me again," she shot back.

Derrick scowled at her. "What's the matter with you? These are expensive shoes!"

"Obviously not anymore," Verena said.

Ripping off his socks, Derrick glared at her. "This is not funny. You could've hurt me."

She looked down at his gnarly feet. "Not with that set of toenails to defend you."

"And dinner. Look, it's ruined."

Verena couldn't suppress a wry laugh. "How about a salad? Or a pedicure?"

"You're nuts, you know that?" He grabbed a kitchen towel and began rubbing his shoes. "I'm out of here."

After Derrick stormed out in his bare feet, Verena grabbed her wine and sat down, surveying the damage and satisfied that she'd stood up to him.

On the counter, her phone vibrated with a text. She ignored it. Had to be Derrick, and she was finished with him.

As the wine warmed her throat, she couldn't help but wonder, had she just destroyed her only option? And her family business along with it?

18

Clad in his chef whites, Lance removed his hat and took a break from the Paris competition, striding outside to gather his thoughts. *Or get rid of them.* The memory of Verena and their last night together had been running like a tragic movie through his mind.

Outside, horns blared, jolting him back to the present. Watching the traffic jam on the street, Lance thought that if he ever needed a cigarette, it was right now.

But he'd promised Verena.

Instead, he strode into a café and ordered an espresso. Not that it would calm his nerves, but he'd had restless nights since Verena left and was in dire need of caffeine.

The day after Verena had gone, Lance had thrown himself into the competition he'd come to Paris for. Though he'd taken time to have to a hotel concierge arrange for a bouquet of white lilies and tuberose to be delivered to Verena's home.

He'd also seen Mia and the twins off when they departed to visit her sister in Switzerland. That sweet woman had clearly arranged this chance meeting in Paris with Verena, and he would be forever grateful to Mia for that.

Never had he had such a wonderful time, or felt such an incredible connection with a woman, as he had the last two days with Verena.

"Expresso, monsieur?"

"*Oui, merci.*" Lance sipped the espresso, turning his thoughts over in his mind.

Their last night had been nothing short of perfect.

Yet when he'd left her at the door to her room, she'd sounded so sad. What had she said? He'd been so enamored with her that he'd hardly registered her last words to him at the time. Mainly because what she said seemed so out of sync with the amazing evening they'd had dancing at Le Speakeasy and strolling the streets of the *arrondissement.*

Lance cupped his chin in his hand, thinking. *What were her words again?*

He'd said, *Paris won't be the same without you.*

Nor my life without you, she'd replied before she shut the door.

That's exactly what she'd said. He was sure of it.

Five little words.

Never had five words caused him so much grief.

Not until he'd returned to his room and emerged from his love stupor the next morning did her words really strike him.

He'd thought she meant that her life in Los Angeles wouldn't be the same without him until he returned.

He gulped the espresso. *Yeah, that's what my ego wanted to hear. But then she made it even clearer.*

So he tried to call her, but she was already on the plane.

He sent an email telling her how glad he was that they'd run into each other again in Paris. When she didn't reply, he grew concerned. By then the competition was in full swing and demanded his full attention.

The next time he tried to call, it was far too late and he didn't want to wake her. So he sent another email.

Still no reply.

Again he tried to call and text. She didn't respond, and his call went to voice mail.

She'd been worried that last day they were together. Was she in some kind of danger? Surely Mia would have called him if she had been.

Or did Derrick mean more to her than she'd led him to believe? He'd tried to warn her about that creep.

Cursing himself under his breath, he knocked back the rest of the espresso.

If only he'd been listening better that night. What had he done to turn her away? He recalled every detail of the evening but he couldn't think of anything he'd done, other than try to show her that she was the most important woman in his life.

And save her from drowning, even though he would've done that for anyone.

Walking back to the event, Lance grappled with what now looked like hard evidence. *Verena Valent dumped me.* But why?

He deserved an answer.

Yet he wasn't the kind of man to push a woman for one. He didn't go where he wasn't wanted.

She'd sure seemed to have genuine feelings for him. His certainly were. Or had it only been the magic of Paris?

He couldn't accept that, although he didn't want to come across as a stalker, and he feared he'd already reached out enough times to qualify for that status.

Smacking his forehead with his palm, he hurried back to the event. He needed to get his head back in the game.

The mysterious disappearance of Verena Valent from his life would have to wait until he returned to L.A.

19

Verena looked around the conference table in the VSS office. To her right, Lacey shifted uncomfortably. Lacey's yellow blouse was a burst of sunshine among the otherwise weary team on this dreary day. The company controller, Annette Margaux, along with the Vice President of Marketing, Pearl Cho, sat directly across from her. And at the end of the table was the VSS corporate counsel, Jack Epstein. They were all studying the last round of documents from Herringbone that Lacey had passed out.

Verena waited in the silence, listening to the rain pelt the windows and turning over options in her mind. After she'd dumped the Beef Wellington on Derrick's shoes, he had called her the next morning. *I deserved that*, he'd said, actually apologizing for being so forward with her. He assured her the deal was still on.

Even so, Verena had continued to try to find alternatives to the Herringbone deal. In the meantime, she had given her management team a few days to study the plan for Rainbow Nails that Herringbone had suggested. Everything about it was wrong, and she knew it, but if VSS wanted funds from Herringbone, they would have to find a way to make the deal work.

Unless she could find another option. How many calls had she made to bankers, friends, and private investors since she'd returned from Paris? She couldn't even count them. The economic news was worsening by the day, too.

As if she needed reminding.

"So, let me hear some of your thoughts on this deal." Verena asked her team. Even having to consider it went against her better judgement, but it was quickly becoming their only option.

Annette vehemently shook her head. "Rainbow is essentially a defunct company. There's no infrastructure, so we'd be responsible for rebuilding the company from the ground up. It will be costly. They have a huge inventory assortment—unless you trim the product line—so that will put a lot of pressure on the bookkeeping function." She peered over the rim of her stylish navy glasses. "We'll definitely have to add more people."

"And we can't really leverage our existing field support," Pearl said, brushing her jet black hair over one shoulder. "The team in the field is already stretched thin. I can call on a couple of major accounts, but after next month, my calendar is booked solid with our Asian expansion. Maybe we can outsource Rainbow's sales and marketing, or add another person to sell into those markets and oversee the field support."

"More expenses," Annette said, making notes. She ran a hand through her cropped blond hair.

"And then there's the added manufacturing and distribution management." Verena nodded, taking in her team's comments. "That's two more people." She jotted down figures on a tablet. *This is going to kill us.*

"Who will handle product development?" Pearl asked.

"Guess I'll have to come up to speed quickly on nail care." Verena felt utterly sick over the plan before her.

"And where will that fit in your current schedule?" Lacey asked. "Between three and five in the morning?

That's too much for you to handle alone."

Lacey always had her back. "Jimmy Don is taking over VSS product development, so that should free some of my time," Verena said.

Lacey snorted with disgust. "He's such a rude young man. What does he know about skincare?"

"Absolutely nothing. We'll have to train him." Grim laughter rippled around the conference table, although Verena held back her own vitriolic comment about Jimmy Don. "Jack, what's your opinion of the deal?"

Jack removed his glasses. "It's a tough deal to execute. Your resources are geared toward the luxury market. Even though Rainbow is a cosmetics company, it will require more support and a larger investment in inventory. Is Herringbone really serious about opening ten thousand doors this year for Rainbow's line?"

"That's right," Verena said. "They're trying to re-establish the ground they lost last year."

"Ten thousand doors—that's a lot of stores," Pearl said.

"And Herringbone's not giving us nearly enough money to support them," Annette added.

"Mass is different, many more stores per chain. They promise that we'll have access to whatever funds we need." Verena turned to Jack. "I know it's a lot of work, but do you think it's a fair deal?"

"It's stacked in their favor, for sure, but as long as they provide the support they've promised, you might have a shot at it." Jack put his glasses back on and scanned the term sheet. "Assuming there aren't any surprises in the final documents, I'd have to say it's not a bad deal, in light of the current economy. Though we would have been much better off with your original plan."

"I know, but I haven't been able get another loan commitment," Verena said.

Jack went on. "However, I don't see that you have much choice, and believe me, Herringbone is well aware of that fact. If you had access to other capital, you wouldn't even be considering this deal, in my opinion."

As if to punctuate his point, thunder cracked outside, shuddering the walls. Everyone fell quiet. Verena regarded her team. "Then should we consider it now?"

Annette cleared her throat. "We have less than thirty days of cash reserves, even with the personal credit card advances that Verena put into the business."

"So that's a yes," Verena said. "Unless I can find an alternative."

"Most of the other cosmetic companies are laying off people," Pearl added.

"At least you can find the talent you need for Rainbow," Jack said. "Plenty of people are looking for work now, ready to take what they can get."

"We've always run pretty lean," Pearl said.

"Herringbone doesn't think so," Verena said. "We'll have to make some staff reductions, or move some people to the Rainbow side."

Annette nodded. "Jimmy Don was questioning how much the estheticians make. He suggested we could terminate those with the most seniority, and bring in younger people who would work cheaper and require fewer benefits."

The room grew quiet again. Against a flash of lightning outside of the window and looming disaster within, Verena tried to stay calm, even though she was incensed by his suggestion. *Jimmy Don is an idiot.* Their reputation was built on excellent service and results. Their clientele went to VSS because their estheticians *were* the best.

"That's also age discrimination," Jack said. "Herringbone should know the law."

"Don't worry, we won't do that," Verena said. She wouldn't compromise their quality.

Annette spoke up again. "He was also asking if we could cut costs on ingredients, or change the product formulations, even on the medicated line. Or use generic products in the skincare services." She shook her head. "I didn't want to tell you."

"He *what?*" Anger built in Verena. "The only reformulations allowed at Valent are to *improve* the products. We will not lower our standards." *What a greedy imbecile.* What did Jimmy Don know about their business? She made a note to speak to Derrick.

The small group around the table fell silent.

Finally, Pearl cleared her throat. "We might have some natural attrition coming up, and maybe I can combine some territories in the field, reduce some staff there."

"Instead of a full-time bookkeeper, I can start with a part-time person," Annette offered.

Jack removed his glasses and began to clean them with a cloth. "In the spirit of the times, we can give you a rate reduction or stretch out payments on your legal bills," Jack said. "Valent has been a good client."

"I appreciate your efforts," Verena said. "I know you're really trying, and I will take each of you up on your suggestions. But that doesn't do much to change our financial situation. We expended a great deal of money to put Asia in play, and we did so on the promise of a working capital loan. Now that that's disappeared, and no other banks or investors are willing to step in, we're really in a bind."

Verena looked around the table and realized that the members of her trusted team feared for their jobs as well. Herringbone's plan was far from perfect, but as a leader, she needed to keep her team morale high. And that seemed nearly impossible.

"We have excellent prospects ahead in Asia," she said, raising her voice above the intensifying storm outside. "In fact, pre-orders have far exceeded what we thought we would do in the first month. That," she said, jabbing a finger in the air, "is our *reputation* making the sale, that and the enthusiasm of the sales teams on the floor. They trust us to deliver the best quality products, the quality we are known for. I assure you, we will continue to do that. And if we have to take on Rainbow Nails, that's what we will do."

With reluctance, her team nodded in agreement.

"We're with you, Verena, but frankly, I'm surprised they would burden VSS with Rainbow Nails right now," Jack said. "Those must be pretty important investors Herringbone is protecting. Who would Thomas Roper be afraid of?"

Who indeed? Verena shuddered to think. "I can only imagine." She hesitated. "Jack, did you confirm with Herringbone's attorney that the loan to VSS isn't available unless we take Rainbow? I mean, is there *any* circumstance under which they would revert to the original plan?" It seemed pointless to ask, but she was hoping for some small miracle.

192

Jack pushed back from the table with a deep sigh. "I tried. Completely off the table, Verena. I'm sorry."

"It was worth a try." She looked around the table, feeling everyone's concerns. "Well, team, it seems we're going into the nail polish business." But every fiber of her being warned her against it.

Verena sat outside of her favorite coffee shop on Robertson Boulevard sipping a latte and waiting for the caffeine to take effect. It wasn't far from Fianna's shop, which was already busy this Saturday morning. Fianna had opened her doors early for her semi-annual sample sale, and Verena watched as women lined up at the door. She was pleased for Fianna, and had told many of her clients about the sale. Any other time, she would have been there with them, but not today.

Feeling worn and frazzled from the events of the week, Verena had pulled on comfortable blue jeans with tall black boots and a crisp white shirt. Dark sunglasses obscured her puffy eyes.

Trying to find an alternative to the Herringbone deal, she hadn't slept much since she'd returned from Paris. With Mia and the twins just back from Switzerland, she had to get away from her energetic sisters this morning, even though she was glad they were back.

She glanced up in time to see Scarlett walking toward her.

"Good morning," Verena said. "Got your favorite mocha coffee." She slid a steaming cup toward her.

Scarlett eased into the chair next to Verena. "You're amazing, thanks. I worked pretty late last night." She pushed her sunglasses up onto her head, catching her dark coppery blond curls.

"You don't show it." Scarlett's face was clean and devoid of makeup, except for moisturizer. Her friend's complexion was flawless, a smooth testament to the benefits of good skincare, which Verena had helped her achieve.

Scarlett sipped her coffee, closing her eyes as an expression of gratitude crossed her face. "Ah, that's *bueno*." She sat back. "How's the financing problem going?"

Verena shook her head. "Complicated. Now Herringbone wants us to take on another company." Verena went on to tell her about the deal with Rainbow Nails. "It's an awkward alliance at best, but it's a requirement for financing." She paused. "Derrick is really encouraging it. Says it will benefit my family."

"You don't sound confident."

"It's not up to me anymore. If he's confident, I'm confident." Verena's mouth curved into a smile, although it didn't reach her eyes. She felt drained by the ordeal.

"You can still say no. Sounds like they're using Valent." Scarlett sounded indignant. "What are you getting out of it?"

Verena gulped her coffee, irritated that Scarlett thought she was giving up. "We get to stay in business, avoid terminating loyal, highly trained employees, and grow the company without worrying about how we're going to pay vendors and employees."

"Why can't you keep looking?"

"I have been," Verena said, exasperated. "Saying no to a deal like this is a privilege when you can afford it. If I backed out now, I'd be on the fast track to bankruptcy court. I've talked to every banker and private investor who'll take my calls. I'm flat out of options, Scarlett. I've run out of time."

"Okay, I understand, I'm sorry. Tough spot you're in." Scarlett waited for her to calm down. "If it makes you feel any better, you're not the only business struggling right now." She sighed. "What do you have to give up to Herringbone?"

Verena shrugged. "Minor equity. Some control, that is, we bring in some Herringbone talent, but my family still controls the board."

"For now."

"What?" Verena didn't like the sound of that.

Scarlett went on. "They'll find a way to take over, mark my words. Watch your back, Verena. You have a big red target on your shirt, whether you realize it or not. I've seen this happen before."

"What should I do?"

"Try not to let them push you into a corner. Fight to keep control."

"I'm trying." Verena frowned and stared into her coffee. "Herringbone's demands escalate daily, even though they agreed to the term sheet. With the economy eroding and layoffs leading the headlines, I fear power is slipping away, although I still have control of the board."

"You must retain that," Scarlett said, jabbing a finger in the air to make her point. "And they still want your business. Send me the documents, I'll look at them. You're not alone."

"That would be great. Every night I wake with a terrible feeling, and it takes hours to go back to sleep. If I can. Mia says it's my subconscious alerting me to danger."

"She's probably right."

"Still, I've got to make the best of it. Show Herringbone that Valent can rise to the challenge." Verena straightened her shoulders. "And we *will* succeed."

Scarlett's phone vibrated with a message. She read it with confusion, and then disappointment. Finally, anger crossed her face. Verena watched the storm of emotion that one short text had set off in her friend. "Scarlett, what's wrong?"

"It's not for me." She shook her head.

"Who sent it?"

"Johnny." Scarlett shoved a hand through her hair. "Mama was right." She spun her phone around for Verena to see the message sent to her in error.

Carla, mi amour, do we need orange juice for the mimosas?

"Who's Carla?" Verena asked.

"Carla Ramirez. We all went to school together. Looks like she and Johnny are dating. I've heard she's been warming a seat at the bar at the Polo Lounge while he works."

Verena studied her friend. "And why does that bother you? I thought you and Johnny were just friends."

"We've known each other so long. Too long, maybe. He wants to settle down, marry someone who wants to have babies and put on an apron."

"And what's wrong with that? I thought you wanted children someday. Did he tell you that?"

"He doesn't have to," Scarlett said, sniffing with disdain. "He's a man. It's in his DNA."

"Now who's being sexist? Come on, you don't really believe that." Verena slid a gaze toward Scarlett. "Why would it matter to you anyway?"

"It doesn't," she said, sputtering. "But as a friend, I don't want to see him make a mistake."

"So, tell him." Verena wondered what was really bothering her.

"I have to leave for New York in the morning." She gestured toward the phone. "And he's clearly busy today."

"You'll be back in a couple of weeks," Verena said. "You're taking the lead in that case here, right? And I can sure use your advice."

Scarlett nodded. "Johnny's love life is none of my business."

Verena stared at her. "Like *that* would stop you from saying what's on your mind?" She broke into a grin, and Scarlett started to chuckle at herself.

"Never has," Scarlett said.

"Didn't today."

Scarlett raised a shoulder. "I call it the way I see it."

"Remember the night at the Grammy party?" Verena burst out laughing, and soon the two friends were laughing so hard that tears came to their eyes.

People at nearby tables were looking at them, but neither of them cared. They both needed a good laugh to cut the tension in their lives.

"Oh, I can't stop," Verena said, wiping her eyes.

Thought they tried to recover their composure, the two of them sputtered with laughter every time they looked at each other.

"Let's get out of here before we run into clients," Verena said, gasping for breath. She pushed her hair from her eyes and pulled her sunglasses down.

Their arms around one another, they were still chuckling as they hurried across Robertson Boulevard.

"Verena!" Lance called out, but she didn't hear him. Peering from under the brim of his favorite baseball cap, Lance's heart clenched with anguish when he saw Verena and her friend hasten from the café.

She looked incredible in jeans and boots and dark sunglasses. Better than any of the Hollywood stars he'd met at the hotel.

He'd been in the corner nursing his morning coffee, recovering from his long trans-Atlantic flight and reading the newspaper. He left early in the morning to avoid traffic and liked to stop here before reporting for work at the hotel. As soon as he set foot inside the busy kitchen, it was nonstop action for the day. That's when he'd heard a familiar laugh carried on the breeze behind him. Laughter he'd wondered if he'd ever hear again.

He'd turned and spied Verena. She had been deep in an earnest conversation with the woman he recognized from the Polo Lounge—*Scarlett*, he recalled—but by the time he rose to say hello, they were off, laughing together over some private joke as they strode across the street, turning heads in their wake.

Waving, he called out, "Verena!"

He tried to race across the street after them, but the light changed and a car nearly hit him. Then they'd disappeared behind a long line of women that stretched down the sidewalk. He'd never find her now.

"Dammit!" Lance turned back. He stalked back inside the coffee shop.

All through the chef competition in Paris, she'd

intruded upon his thoughts. He was still at a loss to figure out what had happened between them.

Lance returned to his table and sat down, sorry that he'd missed her.

She'd made her choice, he supposed. As far as he was concerned, Derrick was a train wreck waiting to happen, but he hated to see Verena caught in a catastrophe, even if she had dropped him in Paris.

He drummed his fingers on the table.

If he could help it, he wouldn't let that happen. He punched in Verena's mobile number.

20

"You remembered," Verena said into the phone, her heart lurching. "Your flowers reminded me of the hotel."

She and Scarlett had just stepped into a specialty food shop on Robertson Boulevard when her mobile phone rang.

"You're back from Paris?" Verena knew she should hang up, but Lance's voice was like a salve to her wounded soul. Yet how was she going to handle him now?

Scarlett swung around with a puzzled expression.

"I'll never forget it either." Verena caught her lower lip between her teeth. *Never, as long as I live.*

Who's that? Scarlett mouthed silently.

When Verena shook her head, Scarlett's curiosity was piqued. Verena waved her off.

As Lance spoke, the sound of his rich voice eroded her resolve. She remembered how they had danced and how safe and loved she had felt in his steady arms. And that body of his...how he'd looked at the pool without a stitch on. An intense, warm feeling spread throughout her.

"How was the competition?" She couldn't help but smile as she listened to him. "Congratulations." He'd won an award with his entry of ginger-lemongrass crab stir fry.

Scarlett stared at her, a hand on her hip and her toe tapping, refusing to budge.

"At our house?" Verena paused, turning away from Scarlett. Mia and the twins had just returned from

Switzerland. "I know they would love that, but we already have an engagement that evening…no, I'm sorry, the whole weekend looks bad." *What was she doing?*

Verena swallowed, wishing she could accept his invitation to cook for them. "I loved seeing you in Paris, too. I'll never forget that you saved my life."

She hesitated, mesmerized by the sound of his gravelly voice rich with emotion and imagining the warmth in his eyes.

Scarlett ducked into her line of sight again. She was bursting with questions.

"Breakfast and a bike ride? Lance, I can't." She lowered her voice. "It's a complicated time for me." Once the words were out of her mouth, she could hear Lance's enthusiasm dim. Her heart ached right along with him.

"Maybe in a couple of weeks. I'll mention it to Mia and call you later." Verena clicked off, staring at the phone and wishing she could have spoken longer with him. And yet, their timing was all wrong. She couldn't let him distract her from what she needed to do with her business.

"Who was that?" Scarlett demanded. "Who's sending you flowers? And who saved your life? What happened?"

"The chef from the Beverly Hills Hotel, Lance Martel. We ran into him in Paris."

When Scarlett looked suspicious, Verena quickly added, "We were staying at the same hotel, and he pulled me from the pool when I hit my head swimming. It was all quite by chance." *Or was it?*

Scarlett let out a low whistle. "Some coincidence."

"That's all it was." Verena slipped her phone into her purse, her head swimming with conflicting desires.

201

"Are you sure?"

"Come on, I have to buy ingredients here for an old Swiss fondue recipe Mia is teaching us how to make tonight. Seems Anika and Bella fell in love with it in Switzerland." She pulled a list from her pocket. "I need a couple of cheeses. Gruyère, Vacherin Fribourgeois, and a bottle of white wine, kirsch—that's cherry brandy—and garlic."

"You're avoiding the question," Scarlett said. "You can't outmaneuver me, I'm trained to probe. And I don't believe one iota in coincidences."

If Verena was honest with herself, neither did she. "Who knows, maybe it was kismet," Verena said, eager to change the subject. "That's what Mia calls meant-to-be coincidences."

As soon as the words left her lips, a surge of discomfort flashed through her. *What if kismet were real? What if Lance and I were meant to meet again in Paris?*

When Verena swept through the back door with her groceries, she was surprised to see Mia bustling around the kitchen, happily singing a tune. She was dressed in an apricot linen blouse and white linen slacks, with a Chanel twill scarf at her neck pinned with a vintage diamond-studded brooch. Her hair and makeup were perfect. She'd clearly taken extra care for something special today.

"You look lovely, Mia." She placed her shopping bags on the counter. "Are you going out?"

"No, darling, I'm expecting company. An old friend, Pierre Chevalier, is stopping by for tea to welcome me home."

"That's thoughtful." Verena drew a glass of filtered

water from the faucet. *And unusual.*

"Camille said that he asked after me several times while we were gone. He asked me to tea at the Peninsula Hotel, but I suggested we have tea here. Much more intimate, don't you think?" She colored slightly. "I mean, why should we put ourselves on display and start tongues wagging?"

"Sounds like you might fancy him," Verena said, using one of Mia's favorite terms. She'd bet that was his handkerchief Mia had been carrying in Paris. She was guardedly happy for Mia, but who *was* this Pierre?

Verena tried to remember a time when she'd seen her grandmother with a man. Mia had dated a few times after Emile's death, but there wasn't anyone she really cared for. Then the cancer struck, and her son and his wife died in the accident. Her world had nearly imploded. Since then, Mia had dedicated herself to looking after her, Anika, and Bella. Verena glanced at her grandmother. Mia deserved a shot at happiness and companionship.

"Maybe there's someone you might fancy, too," Mia said lightly. "Remember Paris?"

Verena shot her a pointed look. "Let's not start this again. I'm far too busy."

"You've been seeing a lot of Derrick since we returned."

"It's not what you think. You know Derrick's company is financing our business."

Mia shrugged. "It's a woman's prerogative to change her mind."

"What century did you get that old saying from?" Verena said, chiding her with a smile and eager to change the subject. "What time will Pierre be here?" Verena

JAN MORAN

glanced at the new wooden clock on the wall that Anika and Bella had insisted they bring home as a souvenir from Switzerland. The clock was in the shape of a Swiss chalet, with carved figurines dancing along a ledge and acorns hanging from the pendulum chains. As she looked up, a little cuckoo bird jutted out to mark the hour with a whistle.

A knock sounded at the door at precisely the same time. "There he is now." Mia brushed her hands on her snowy white apron and hurried to the door.

Verena trailed behind her. She was curious.

Mia opened the door. "You're perfectly punctual. Come in, Pierre."

Removing his hat, Pierre Chevalier stepped inside. He whisked a bouquet of flowers from behind his back. "I searched for authentic Alpine flowers, but they're rarer than snow at the beach. The florist told me that daisies also grow in the Alps, so I thought these might do."

"What a cheerful mix of colors. And I'd like to introduce my granddaughter, Verena."

"Hello." Verena had to admit that he was impressive. Fine manners, impeccable sport jacket, well groomed. And he had eyes only for Mia.

Verena and Pierre exchanged pleasantries as Mia took Pierre's hat. They followed Mia to the kitchen, chatting as Mia arranged the blaze of purple, white, and yellow flowers in a vase and put them on the kitchen table. "Such a lovely sunny day, I thought we'd have tea outside on the patio."

Pierre said, "Verena, will you join us?"

"I'd like that." She was interested in learning more about him. And he took her mind off Lance and the business.

They seated themselves on cushioned chairs under the

awning, and Mia poured freshly brewed Earl Grey tea into cups. She sliced a fluffy angel food roll filled with strawberries and cream. "This is a traditional Swiss treat, and it was always Emile's favorite."

Verena saw a shadow cross Mia's face. *She probably didn't mean to say that.* Mia seemed nervous now.

Pierre fixed her in his sight with an intractable gaze, watching her every movement. "Emile was a lucky man."

Verena caught a whiff of Pierre's sandalwood cologne and noted his immaculate monogrammed shirt. It seemed he'd taken extra care today, too.

"And Ondine was a lucky woman," Mia said.

Pierre slid a wrinkled hand over hers. "They've both been gone a long time, Mia. Long enough, you know."

Mia reached into her pocket and withdrew the handkerchief she'd been carrying. "I forgot that I had this. I washed and pressed it for you."

A smile creased his face. "Keep it, my dear. It makes me happy thinking that you're carrying it close to you."

"Oh, I have been. Your handkerchief travelled to France and Switzerland with me."

Verena suppressed a smile. She was enjoying this. Why shouldn't Mia have someone in her life?

Pierre sipped his tea. "Next time, would you like me to accompany you? I could carry all the handkerchiefs you might need."

Feeling like she was a third wheel, Verena rose from her chair. "It's been a pleasure meeting you, Pierre, but I have some business to attend to."

"On a Saturday?" he asked, automatically rising from his chair as she did and helping to slide her chair out.

Mia said, "Verena is a hard worker, just like we were at her age."

"Yes, I am," she said to Pierre, noting his perfect manners. *Mia must like that.* "It's been a pleasure meeting you, and I hope our paths cross again soon." She added, "I'll be back for dinner later. Mia makes the most wonderful Swiss cheese fondue, and she's going to teach us how to make it this evening."

She left the table, bursting with happiness for Mia. It was so cute to watch the two of them courting. That was another one of Mia's terms. And he *was* handsome. Verena was dying to hear more, but she wanted to give them their privacy.

Verena grabbed her purse, got into her car, and started for the salon. Midway there, she stopped her car at a red traffic light and thought about taking a detour to the Beverly Hills Hotel. *Maybe I'll see Lance.* But then she thought about the business and the promises Derrick had made to fund the company. She sighed, feeling trapped.

When the light turned green, she turned toward the salon.

21

A few weeks later, Verena sat at her office desk, thinking. *Scarlett was right.* She had signed off on the term sheet with Scarlett's approval, and Jack had coordinated with Herringbone's attorneys to draft the documents. The deal should have been done.

However, Roper had delayed the rapid closing, though the effective date of the agreement hadn't changed. Only with Scarlett on her side had Verena been able to maintain her sanity.

Verena straightened the documents on her desk and put on her black jacket. When she had dressed that morning, she'd felt like she was going to a funeral, so she had dressed accordingly. "I'm going to lunch," she said to Lacey. "Please call me if the documents come back."

Lacey wagged her head. "I thought Herringbone wanted a fast closing."

"That's what Derrick said," Verena replied. "Could still be today, but I have to pick up a prescription the doctor called in for Mia."

Worry flashed across Lacey's face. "Everything all right with her?"

"The trip to Europe took a lot out of her, and she picked up a cold that has turned into bronchitis. She's had a hacking cough for weeks." This was exactly what Verena had been worried about. But Mia and the twins had such a wonderful time that it almost made up for it.

Verena couldn't remember the last time she'd seen Mia so happy. After burying a husband, a son, and a daughter-in-law, Mia deserved every bit of happiness that came her way. She'd been seeing Pierre until she'd become ill.

As soon as Verena walked into the house, she could hear Mia coughing. She made her way through the house to her grandmother's bedroom. After pushing the drapes open to light the room, Verena put her hand on her grandmother's warm forehead.

"We'll get this temperature under control soon," Verena said.

"So glad you've come, dear." Mia adjusted herself in her bed. "This cough is almost getting the better of me."

Verena shook her head. "Not for long."

Verena brought her a glass of water and Mia swallowed the tablets she gave her. Mia patted a spot on the bed. "Come sit by me."

Verena sank onto the fine cotton duvet. "Did you speak to Pierre this morning?"

"Of course. He calls every day," Mia said. "And have you heard from your Lance lately?"

Covering her feelings, Verena chuckled at her grandmother's choice of words. "He's hardly *my* Lance. He called and we spoke, but he understands how busy I am. So is he." She shrugged as if it didn't matter to her. Paris was quickly receding in her mind, blotted out by business. Had their connection even been real?

"I see," Mia said. "Well, tell me how your day is going. Any sign of the documents yet?"

"Not yet. With each draft Roper goes farther outside of the boundaries they established in the term sheet. Even when I agree, they come back with more requests."

"Sounds like this deal has gotten out of hand." Mia squinted at her. "Surely Derrick is helping you?"

"That's just it. Everything he says makes sense the way he explains it. But it's *not* what we agreed to in the beginning. And they know we need the funds more with every passing day."

Mia stared at her, her blue eyes still piercing in their intensity. "That's why they're stretching it out, my dear."

"It's not good business."

"No, it's not. You could tough it out. We have before, you know."

"At this point, that would mean not paying vendors or employees and that would put us out of business. It was easier with just the one salon."

Now they had a network of salons, with huge investments in product inventory in retailers across the United States and Europe, and more sitting at customs in several Asian countries. Verena wished she had seen this coming, but then, other companies far larger than VSS hadn't either.

Mia reached for Verena's hand. "I realize it's a lot more complicated now. For the record, I think you're doing a wonderful job. It's not easy—no one else really understands how difficult it is to run this business."

"Your support means so much to me."

"I wish I could help you more, Verena." A sad look washed across Mia's face. "I wish Emile and your father were still here with us." A hacking cough seized her, interrupting her thought.

Verena lifted the water glass to Mia's lips. When Mia recovered, she motioned to her slender frame. "This old body is wearing out on me," she said, her voice hoarse. "It's so frustrating, because I'm as sharp as I've ever been." She patted Verena's hand. "That's why you must always take good care of yourself."

"And I do, Mia."

"Not lately. You've been coming home later and later, and I know you're not sleeping well."

"I've been home every night by ten o'clock," Verena said. *Well, almost.* There had been one or two nights she'd stayed at the office until after midnight reviewing the documents that Herringbone and its attorneys kept changing.

"And working until two or three in the morning. You can't keep this pace up for long."

"When the deal is in place, I can ease up a little. I promise, Mia." Even as she was reassuring Mia, she feared that this oppressive workload was just the beginning. Derrick and Jimmy Don were barking orders faster than she or anyone on her team could respond to.

"I'd think Derrick would be more understanding."

"It's not his company, Mia. It's my responsibility."

"So what's the latest wrinkle in the deal?"

"They want to create a subsidiary for Rainbow Nails. I've been fighting it. It's important that Rainbow remain separate from Valent. And it's what we originally agreed upon."

"But they're pushing back."

"Seems their word isn't worth the paper it's written on. We agree to a point, and then Roper changes his mind. He knows we're at his mercy."

Mia coughed into her hand. "Are you making payroll?"

"Barely. We managed to pay the employees, and Mary

and Sasha each took a week of unpaid leave."

"You aren't taking a check, are you?"

Verena shook her head. "It's been eight weeks since I've drawn my salary." There wasn't any open credit left on her personal credit cards, either, but she hated to share that with Mia, who had always insisted they pay off all personal charges every month.

"That explains why you've been taking your lunch or coming home to eat at noon. Why didn't you share this with me earlier?"

"I wanted you and the girls to have a good time in Europe. It had been planned for so long."

"Well, we did use our travel mileage points for the airfare. And we stayed with my sister."

Verena smiled. "That was an enormous help, thanks."

"And if you need money, remember, I have a little tucked away."

"We're not going to touch the girls' college fund or your retirement. You earned it, and no matter what happens, you are *not* to touch those funds. It's all you and the girls have. What if something were to happen to me?" After her parents' accident, the possibility of unforeseen occurrences was very real to her, and something she always considered.

Mia sniffed with disdain. "What Roper is doing is an old ploy, you know, designed to starve the company into agreement."

"I realize that. Jack said he's never seen a legitimate venture capital company negotiate like this, and he's done hundreds of these kinds of transactions. They're not all bad, I'm sure, but Roper isn't a good representative of the industry."

"Can you speak to another fund?"

"The term sheet bars me from doing that, too. When I mentioned it, Derrick went ballistic. He said Roper would sue me and probably end up with ownership of the company."

Mia clasped her hand. "Keep fighting, my dear."

"I will. I'm not giving in. I just can't believe they've gone back on their word so much."

"Is Scarlett reviewing the documents for you, too?"

"She is, and she's helping me fight to retain our personal interests and stock shares, but it's tough."

Mia cleared her throat, taking it all in. "Did the company numbers fall short of their expectation?"

"Quite the contrary, our presales in Asia have far exceeded our projections. And even though some mid-price skincare lines are hurting for business, our sales at the high end have increased. The economy might be slowing, but luxury goods are still on fire, especially for our duty free clients."

"Hmm," Mia said, making a face. "Then that old buzzard Thomas Roper is just a greedy bastard."

Later that day at the office, Verena picked up a call that Lacey had routed to her.

"Jack, what's the word?"

"Still no deal," he said. "And Roper said he won't reimburse you for the personal credit card draws you took."

"What? Those were for the business, for payroll." She was astonished that Roper would deny that reimbursement. After all, he had agreed to it. A chill slashed through her. *I can't believe a word that man says.* She'd have to call Scarlett again.

"I know, I know. Verena, look, I spoke to Herringbone's counsel, and it appears this deal is in danger of not going through. Are you prepared for that?"

Verena sat back. The negotiation had gone on so long that the only option now was bankruptcy protection. "No."

"All right then, will you agree to this last point? You'll carry the personal debt you incurred, and try to make it up on the sale at the end. How much is it?"

Verena gave him a six-figure number.

There was a moment of silence. "You must have great credit."

"Had, Jack. Had." She felt sick to her stomach. Her entire world was imploding.

"Times are tough here, Verena."

"Our forecast is still excellent." Orders in Asia were increasing.

"True, but Herringbone is greedy."

Verena fell silent, remembering what Mia had said about Roper—*a greedy bastard*. Her grandmother rarely used such language. "That's the second time today someone said that."

Jack gave a sour laugh. "Well, it's true. Are you sure you don't have any other options?"

"I wouldn't be considering this deal if I did."

"So, you'll agree?"

"I'll call you back." She clicked off, then dialed Scarlett. After explaining the situation to her, Scarlett's advice mirrored Jack's.

Her head throbbing, Verena called Jack again. Feeling powerless, she choked out one word. "Agreed."

Two hours later the documents finally came through on the fax. Verena sat at her desk and began to review the redlined copies once more. A few minutes into it, she bolted up, and then punched Jack's number. "What's this in section 8.2?"

"Hold on, I just got the documents, too." She could hear him clicking through the copy on his computer. He cursed under his breath. "They want you to reduce your salary by thirty percent."

"I'm already making less than any other CEO they have in their portfolio company, and now I'm carrying enormous personal debt that must be serviced, thanks to Roper." She'd be making less than anyone on her executive team—and that included Jimmy Don. She recognized this as a psychological strategy to undermine her authority and strip her power.

"Verena, wait, you still have control of the board. Just agree to it, deliver the numbers you say you're going to, and then vote yourself a raise at the next board meeting."

Verena was quiet for a moment. "I can do that?"

"As long as you control the board." He paused. "The email says this is their final offer. If not received back by five o'clock, the deal is off the table."

"It's twelve minutes to five."

"They will probably hold to that. Or penalize you more for missing it."

Verena had a few choice words for Herringbone, but she held her tongue. "I'll have Scarlett call you."

Verena dialed her friend, explaining this last volley. She could hear Scarlett explode on the other end, but she promised to call Jack and Herringbone's counsel.

At two minutes to five, her phone rang. "Scarlett, what

should I do?" Her shoulders slumped as Scarlett spoke, and she could hardly breathe. "I understand. I'll sign the damned documents." She slammed the phone down, and then angrily scratched out her signature on several pages.

Lacey hovered at the door. "What can I do?"

Verena tapped the documents on her desk. "Fax these back to Herringbone right away. I'm leaving. If Derrick calls, have him call my mobile phone." She slammed her desk drawer shut and grabbed her purse. She noted the concerned look on Lacey's face. "Don't worry, it's not you, Lacey."

"Oh, I know, Verena," she said with a sad drawl. "I swear I've never seen such goings on."

"First, I want you to know that wasn't my idea, Verena," Derrick said, holding up a flat palm as he nudged the door closed behind him.

Verena glanced up from the report on her desk, barely able to contain her rage over the lengthy negotiations that had culminated yesterday. Arching a brow, she said, "You could have stuck up for me."

"Roper likes to score concessions in the last couple of rounds." Derrick crossed the room, the sound of his new shoes as sharp as nutcrackers on the hardwood floor. He came up behind Verena and placed his hands on her shoulders, gently kneading her neck.

"Stop it." Verena shrugged away from him.

"You must understand, it wasn't personal."

Verena expressed a puff of air between her lips and continued to read. He was so damned logical, and she was sick of it. The agreement had been amended so many times it was bleeding red ink.

"Come on, Verena, don't shut me out." Derrick circled her chair and then perched on the edge of her desk. Leaning toward her, he placed his hand over the report she was reading.

Brushing his hand away, she pursed her lips. "*Thirty percent?* That's extraordinarily personal, Derrick."

"Look at it as a temporary salary reduction. I can make it up to you."

"That's not the point. It was an underhanded tactic."

Derrick shrugged. "It's just the way he is. If he smells weakness, he goes in for the kill. It's sport to him. You should see all the trophy heads on his office wall."

Verena cringed at the thought of the deer and antelope heads Roper probably had. Supposedly he'd shot a lion in Africa last year, and it made her sick just to think of it. She tilted her chin. "I *refuse* to be another head on his wall."

Derrick reached into his pocket and fished out a small red velvet box. He slid it across her desk. "Here's a little something that should ease your pain."

She rolled her eyes, fury flowing through her veins like molten lava. "You have *got* to be kidding."

Derrick pushed his lower lip out in a contrite expression. "I was only the messenger on this deal, sweetheart. I told you he was a tough old buzzard."

"I have a different word in mind." She folded her arms in defiance. "Take your trinket. I don't want a consolation prize."

Derrick looked incredulous. "Don't you even want to see what I bought for you?"

"No. I'm not a little girl who's going to clap her hands and let you make everything all right," she said, spitting out the words with a vengeance. "This is my *family's* business, Derrick, this is our livelihood. We have *bled* for this business, you know that. Now, is this Roper's last sleazy move, or is he going to continue to pillage me and the company every chance he gets?"

"You wanted to play with the big boys, Verena." He leaned across the desk again, his lips curving into a mocking smile. "Learn the game."

Verena shoved her chair back and stood up. Picking up her report, she said, "Valent Swiss Skincare is not a game to be played."

"You came to us. What were you expecting?"

"Some semblance of fair dealing." She whirled around in a burst of anger. "You've become just like Roper." She spat out the last word, its taste vile on her tongue.

Derrick sauntered past her. "Toughen up, Verena." He tossed the small box into the air and then stuffed it into his pocket. "And you shouldn't turn down gifts from me." He paused at the door and glanced pointedly around her spacious office. "By the way, Jimmy Don will be in after lunch. You should decide where you're going to put him."

"I told you that moron is *not* welcome here." Verena balled her fist so tight her nails dug into the palm of her hand.

Derrick shrugged. "Roper's order. But I'll see what I can do for you."

22

"You could have kept them," Fianna said, taking the cape and scarf she'd given Verena for her Paris trip and hanging them on a rack behind the counter of her boutique. "But you can always borrow them again."

"I'd love to keep the black lace dress," Verena said. "I'm telling everyone who designed it."

Fianna grinned. "It's so perfect on you. Did you want to look around at my latest collection?" She went back to steaming a new dress she had just finished.

Verena's eyes roamed over the shimmery summer shades of Fianna's new designs, which were artfully arranged around the shop. "Wish I could, but I'm on a tight budget for a while."

Fianna frowned as she wielded the long arm of the clothing steamer. "Still dealing with Derrick?"

"It's complicated, but the deal is done." Verena was having suspicions now about how much Derrick actually had to do with the deal. Was it really all Roper?

"I can't believe how much you went through," Fianna said, shaking her mane of curly red hair. "It boils my blood to think of what that man did to you."

The front door opened with a jingle, and Fianna smiled at an artsy brunette woman. Turning to Verena, she said, "This is Elena, the jeweler next door I was telling you about."

"Delighted to meet you," Verena said. With her hair

FLAWLESS

coiled in a casual twist to reveal exquisite chandelier earrings, Elena looked like an artist. She was clad in black and had a tiny flower tattoo on her neck just behind her ear.

"Fianna always talks about your business," Elena said. "I should come by for a facial sometime."

"As my guest, I insist." Verena inclined her head, trying to place Elena's accent. "Australian?"

"I grew up there, although I was born in San Diego."

Suddenly Verena remembered something. "Can you repair a pearl clasp?"

Elena smiled. "Probably. Bring the pearls by sometime."

"Actually, I have them with me," Verena said. I'd put it in my purse meaning to have it repaired. Then I changed purses when I went to Paris and forgot about it. I just grabbed it again this morning."

"What luck," Fianna said.

Verena fished out a pouch and opened it. Elena ran her fingers reverently over the iridescent pearls. "Incredible quality, simply beautiful, and perfectly matched."

"These mean a lot to me. They belonged to my mother." The clasp had snagged on her hair and snapped.

Fianna gave her a sympathetic smile. "Take special care of those."

"I understand, of course." Elena inspected the clasp. "I can fix this, no problem."

Peering over Verena's shoulder, Fianna said, "Are you still carrying that ring around with you, too?"

"Wha—oh, I forgot." *Derrick's ring.* Verena had felt like throwing it at him. Now more than ever.

"Show it to her," Fianna said. "Maybe Elena can

recommend a good pawn shop for it."

"She's kidding," Verena said.

"Am I?" Fianna shot back. "He owes you."

"What kind of ring is it?" Elena asked.

Verena dug out the blue box and opened it.

"Engagement ring." Elena slid the large solitaire from its velvet nest.

"Guess it was meant for that, but no, I'm definitely not engaged anymore."

"Looks new."

"I never wore it. He bought it at Tiffany's in Japan not long ago."

"You could return it to the store in Beverly Hills." Elena peered at it.

"No, I'm giving it back to him." *The sooner the better.*

Holding the ring, Elena held a magnifying loop she wore around her neck to it. A shadow crossed her face and she looked puzzled as she lowered her loop.

"What's wrong?" Fianna asked.

Elena shifted uncomfortably. "I hate to see things like this happen." An uneasy expression creased her brow.

"Verena is one of my best friends," Fianna said. "You can be honest with her."

"Tell me what you saw," Verena said quietly, as more suspicions of Derrick gathered in her mind.

"That's not a Tiffany ring," Elena said. "Wherever he bought it—and I'm sure it wasn't at Tiffany's—well, they might have misled him. Although he probably knew what he was buying because it's marked."

"What are you talking about?" Fianna demanded.

Elena handed the ring back to Verena. "I look at a stone's characteristics, like how the facets are joined on top of the stone, inclusions, and the appearance of the girdle around the perimeter. But in this case, there's a marking inside of the ring to confirm it, as there should be. C.Z." She shook her head. "That's not a diamond, it's a cubic zirconia."

Verena's phone buzzed and she looked at the screen. "Speak of the devil. I'll take this outside."

"Derrick. What's up?" They spoke for a few minutes, and she answered a question he had. Then Verena said, "I can't believe you tried to get me back with a fake diamond."

The line was silent for a moment.

"I didn't want you to travel with an expensive ring," Derrick said. "Don't you think that's logical?"

Standing on the sun-drenched sidewalk outside of Fianna's shop, Verena gripped her phone to her ear. "Logical would have been to let me know exactly that," she said, hurling her words back at him. "Imagine my embarrassment in front of Fianna and Elena."

"They don't matter," Derrick said, huffing. "They're not your friends."

"Excuse me? Fianna is an old and trusted friend." He had often discounted her friendships, and it always annoyed her.

"She used to work for you," he said slowly, as if speaking to a child.

Verena couldn't believe what she was hearing. "And what difference might that make?"

"That's why she's your friend." His speech was even more deliberate.

Listening, Verena was incredulous at the turn of the conversation. Derrick did this often, swiftly switching the subject to another matter removed from the issue at hand.

"Back to the ring. It will be with Lacey. Get it from her." An interminable pause ensued and Verena stood watching the traffic flow on Robertson Boulevard, waiting for him to respond. Finally she said, "Derrick, I have to go," she said, measuring her words as he had done.

He huffed, but didn't respond, so she clicked off.

Staring at the blank screen on her mobile phone, she wondered what made some men do the dishonest, disgusting things they did, while other men had a completely different code of conduct.

Men like Pierre. And Lance.

As she thought about it, she realized she still had a decision to make.

Back in her office, Verena picked up the phone to place a call to one of her top buyers. As she was waiting on hold, Jimmy Don sauntered in.

"I'm on a call," she said evenly.

Oblivious to her comment, he plopped down in front of her desk.

Jimmy Don was driving her crazy. He was supposed to be her chief operating officer, but he was the one making assignments to her. Every time Verena threw a task back at him, he'd just stare at her with his pasty, pock-marked face and tell her it was Roper's orders.

He smirked at her while she was discussing the next season's order and promotions. With his surly demeanor fogging up her brain, she had difficulty concentrating.

"Excuse me, may I call you back? Something has just come up, and I'm afraid I have to tend to an emergency." Verena hung up the phone. "This had better be life-or-death urgent. That call was money in the door."

He tossed a piece of paper in front of her. "I'm reducing payroll. These layoffs are effective immediately. The bookkeeper is preparing their last checks, but Lynette won't give me the checks until you approve this. So, there it is. Sign it."

Verena glared at him. He had no respect for the women who worked in the company. "I assume you're talking about our controller, *Annette*. She was correct, but you don't tell me what to sign." She scanned the paper. He had scribbled a list of names. "Are you crazy? The first two women are pregnant."

"So? When I asked them the exact date they were leaving and returning, and a name and phone number to verify their child care, they didn't give satisfactory answers."

"Because they don't know exactly when they're going to *have* the baby. It's not a bus schedule, it's childbirth, and it's unpredictable. And you can't ask questions about child care."

"As an employer, it's my right."

"No it isn't." Verena's blood pressure soared. "We have laws in this state. You can't make inquiries like that, and you can't lay off pregnant women. The answer is no."

"Then how do we do it legally?" Jimmy Don stared at her.

Verena counted silently to three, and then picked up the phone and punched in Jack Epstein's number. "Jack, I'm putting you on speaker phone. Jimmy Don is arguing with me about terminating pregnant employees. Why don't you advise him on employment law so we don't get slapped with two lawsuits?"

As Jack lectured him, Jimmy Don's face began to redden. Half an hour later, Verena thanked Jack and hung up. "Satisfied?"

"I don't care. It's my decision and I'm going to fire them."

Verena stood up. "What's wrong with you? Didn't you hear a word Jack said?" His behavior was so disturbing. She'd often wondered if he was inexperienced, or ignorant. Now she realized he was just a stubborn, immature jerk.

"I heard."

"I hope so. That call just cost us a few hundred dollars of Jack's time. But the real issue is why you won't listen to me. I've been down this road before. I'll have a word with Roper myself. You can go now."

She stood waiting for an answer when, to her astonishment, Jimmy Don's face turned beet red and tears began to trickle from his eyes. *Why, the bully is crying.* This was just too much.

"Don't call Roper." He glared at her, wiping his eyes.

"No? Why shouldn't I? You barge around making everyone uncomfortable. You bring me plans that haven't been properly thought out. You insult our controller. You question my decisions. And about the generic brands you purchased for estheticians to use—every one of those products is going back. This is the Valent Swiss Skincare salon. We only use VSS products."

Jimmy Don sniffed with defiance. "Roper won't agree. He'd fire me and send in someone else. Don't waste your time."

Her skin prickled. This was a disaster in the making. She punched a button and Lacey came on. "Lacey, would you get Thomas Roper on the phone for me, please?"

Verena replaced the receiver and glared at Jimmy Don, checking her anger. "As CEO, it's my duty to inform our investor of any activity that puts the company at risk."

His face contorted, morphing to that of a conniving charlatan. "You do that and I'll tell him you're drinking at lunch, coming back drunk and abusing employees. Maybe even me." He pushed forward in his chair, clearly relishing her reaction.

Verena was horrified. *How dare he?* "You can't do that. That's blackmail."

"Not if I'm truly reporting what I've observed. Roper told me to report back on anything that might damage the company. In fact, he had a list of ideas." His lips twisted into a satisfied sneer. "They're waiting for you to make a mistake."

"I'm not going to make a mistake. I don't drink on the job and I don't fire pregnant women. You need to learn how honest business is conducted. What I don't understand is, you're smart. Why are you acting like this?"

As Jimmy Don blinked and wiped his nose, his haughty attitude cracked. "Look, I'm only warning you. You should be grateful. And if I don't say something, well, the next guy Roper sends in will. That's how Roper plays the game. You have to learn it. We all play by his rules."

Derrick's words shot through her mind. *Learn the game.* Instantly, Verena saw how it would play out. Roper made the rules and everyone played by them. *Even Derrick.* Her heart sank. Whatever trace of admiration she still had for Derrick's intelligence withered into a dry, dusty feeling that choked her. Roper had his greedy claws in everyone. But that was no excuse.

She strode to the door and flung it open. "Lacey, cancel that call. Jimmy Don is leaving now. And ask Annette to come to my office, please."

Verena whirled around to Jimmy Don and pointed to the doorway. "No one is fired without my approval. Now get out."

23

Thunder cracked overhead, waking Lance from a heavy slumber. With a groan, he peered outside. Heavy clouds had rolled in over the ocean, dousing the shore with steady rain. He had been looking forward to a long bike ride on the beach, but he'd have to make do with a workout at the gym.

A few hours later after he returned home, he slid open the wide screen doors on his covered balcony to let the scent and sound of the rain shower inside. There was a certain romance about this weather that spurred his creativeness, so after blending a protein smoothie with berries and greens, he pulled out his sketchpad and settled on the couch.

Creativity ran in his family and had led him to chef school, while his brother Aiden had developed a career in abstract art. Even though his skills didn't approach Aiden's, he still got pleasure from drawing and painting. With quick, flowing lines, he captured the crashing waves roaring in just beyond his condo.

After a while, he took a break. Glancing at his ocean painting on the wall, he was reminded of the day that he'd run into Verena. She'd taken interest in his hobby, and that had meant a lot to him.

Lance was growing increasingly concerned about Verena, yet he didn't want to appear needy or selfish. He was well aware of the commitments she had on her time, and he respected her for it. Yet he was also worried about her.

Seeing that it was around lunchtime, he reached for his phone and punched in her number. Maybe she'd have time to talk. It was Monday, the least busy day of the week at the hotel and his regular day off. Maybe at the salon, too. When Verena didn't pick up her mobile phone, he thought it might be tucked in her purse or maybe the ringer was off. He tried her office number.

Lacey answered. "Verena Valent's office. May I help you?"

He had to smile at her assistant's friendly southern drawl. This wasn't the first time he'd tried to reach her at the office. "Hi Lacey, it's me, Lance. Is Verena available?"

"Why, hey Lance. She's been mighty busy, but I'll check. I think I can get you through to her."

"Don't bother her if she's busy. It can wait." He could hear the woman's smile in her voice.

"Sometimes she needs a break. You hang on now, you hear?"

A few moments later, Verena came onto the line. "Hello Lance."

Her melodic voice weakened any resolve he might've still had. "You've been on my mind. Couldn't resist checking in with you."

"I'm really glad you did." She paused, silence filling the line.

She sounded weary, and Lance wished he could reach out over the phone to wrap her in his arms. "I'd love to see you again. How's later this week?" When she didn't reply, he added, "If you've had a rough week, I can come over and cook for you and the girls and Mia."

Another hesitation. "I'm afraid that's impossible."

"Want to talk about it?"

"Sorry, I really can't. Maybe you should—"

"Take care of you a little more?" He winced at himself. Wrong thing to say to a woman who ran her own company. Hadn't his mother taught him anything? But he didn't want to hear her tell him to find someone else, although if that's what she wanted, he could respect that. Yet her voice held a different note, one he knew well. Sheer exhaustion.

She laughed a little, but she still sounded distracted.

In an effort to lighten the conversation and get her to open up, Lance chuckled. "If I didn't know better, I'd think you were playing hard to get."

"I'm not playing, Lance. I *am* hard to get. I have a lot responsibilities. Maybe we should take a break."

Ouch. That hurt him for a moment, and then he realized how much she reminded him of his mother. "I understand. But I'm a patient man, Verena. If you need my help with anything, feel free to call on me."

She was quiet for a moment, and then she said, "You have no idea how much that means to me."

Actually, he had a pretty good idea. He'd watched his mother juggle an active family and still find time to pursue her dreams.

After saying goodbye, he swung around on his stool and gazed out over the Pacific Ocean, his heart full of compassion for Verena. Breathing in, he filled his lungs with the fresh sea air, never tiring of its power and beauty, or the omnipresent rhythm of its waves. Growing up near the ocean, this wonder of nature was part of his soul and where he often turned to rejuvenate his spirit when he was worn out from work. The sea held good memories for him.

When he was young, his mother had often taken him and his brothers to the beach to run off energy and explore nature.

Raising three boys, Lisette Martel had a lot of responsibilities and wasn't always immediately available to his dad. His parents were a team though, and his dad loved his mother all the more for tending to the responsibilities that benefited their family. Sometimes those were school functions for him and his brothers, or sometimes she had responsibilities during a film production.

He grinned. A lot of men might not have understood how the wrong dress could possibly be more important than having dinner on the table for her active family, but his father had always understood the big picture. The wrong dress could indeed derail a multimillion-dollar production.

Once, he recalled, an actress had become pregnant before filming, and the wardrobe had to be adjusted as it became apparent. If his mother neglected her professional responsibilities, her actions could endanger the production and those who had invested it or worked on it. It could diminish her ability to gain work in the future. Being creative and getting paid well for it not only provided his mom with a sense of accomplishment and self-esteem, but it also brought in an income that had helped underwrite her sons. Her mother was proud of that.

Some of the guys he knew didn't share his sentiments about strong women, but he admired them, just as his father still adored his mother. That's exactly the kind of woman he wanted in his life.

24

Verena had just finished another laborious report for Herringbone when the phone on her desk rang. Verena tapped the speaker button. "Yes, Lacey?"

"Scarlett is holding on line one," Lacey said. "And have you seen Jimmy Don?" She hesitated and lowered her voice. "There's a police investigator downstairs asking for him."

She tapped a nail on her desk. *That's interesting.* "Did the investigator say what it was in regard to?"

"Not a peep, he's got a mouth like a steel trap."

"I can't think of where Jimmy Don might be, unless he's off trying to fire someone else."

Verena switched lines to Scarlett. "Hey, girlfriend, what's going on?"

"I tried to reach you earlier, but Lacey said you were busy doing *facials?*" Scarlett's tone was incredulous.

"I know, it's been a while, but I had to lay off an esthetician. We're booked solid, and these are valued guests who have standing appointments. It's temporary. The last thing we need is gossip about how bad we treat our most loyal guests."

Scarlett turned serious. "Your corporate counsel just called me and we had a long talk. Are you alone?"

"Yes," Verena began, her curiosity piqued. "What did Jack Epstein want?"

"Close your door. You're not going to like this." Scarlett's voice was flat.

"It's closed." The tiny hairs of the back of Verena's neck bristled with apprehension.

"I received an email this morning from another attorney, one of Herringbone Capital's counsel. I just sent it to you. I'll wait while you open it."

Within seconds, the email appeared on the computer screen. Verena clicked it open and began to read. As she did, her first thought was one of disbelief, and then, shock.

"Are you still there, Verena?"

"I don't understand..."

"Herringbone is trying to take over your company. There's a new term sheet attached."

"They can't do that!"

Verena heard Scarlett sigh. "Yes, they can. I warned you about them."

"But Derrick said—"

"It doesn't matter what Derrick said, what matters is what is written in the agreement you signed. It says here that the Passari extension contract was to have been signed by now." Passari was one of their top retailers.

"Jimmy Don is working on it. He says it should be completed next month." Panic clouded her thoughts as she recalled her conversation with Jimmy Don. *We all play by his rules.*

"This means the company has violated a financial covenant."

"Because Passari is withholding payment until the new agreement is signed and new invoices are cut. Jimmy Don is working on this, Derrick knows that."

"I'm sure he does. Any issue with the Passari agreement getting signed?"

"No, but because Jimmy Don gave away a critical point

related to timing, Passari has no incentive to sign it until next month. I outlined the entire negotiation strategy for him, but he didn't follow it. He's an idiot." Verena had a sinking feeling. Hadn't Jimmy Don warned her about Roper?

"He's Herringbone's puppet. You realize he listened to your instructions and then turned them around on you. They set you up." Scarlett paused. "I'm really sorry, Verena."

As this knowledge set in, an intense chill of foreboding spiraled through her. Her teeth began to chatter.

Scarlett went on. "You have two options. One, they foreclose on the business and you get nothing. Two, the term sheet. Let's open that now. I'll go through it with you."

Nothing? How could that be? Numbly, Verena opened the attachment and began to read, her eyes glazing over.

"They'll release your personal guarantees from all loans to Herringbone Capital—that's five million bucks you'll be freed of, Verena."

Personal guarantees that Herringbone had insisted upon for loans to the Rainbow Nail subsidiary. Verena continued to scan the document on the screen. Her vision greyed, and light-headedness set in. *This can't be happening, this is insane.*

"Are you still with me?"

Verena blinked at the screen, trying to maintain her equilibrium. The words were shifting, but their meaning was clear. "I'm reading."

"All of your personally held formulas, trademarks, and patents, along with those of the company, will be transferred to them. Seems they were pledged for the loans."

"What? They can't do that." Anger gathered in her chest like storm clouds whipped by frenzied winds.

"They can. The company has no value without your intellectual property. Actually, I don't think the company has as much value without *you*, which is why I can't believe they're doing this. You're the creative genius, Verena."

"Then why is Roper doing this?"

"Because it's what he does." Scarlett said. "That's why people call it vulture capital. They can't help themselves. It never changes."

"But Derrick said—"

"Sorry to break it to you, but Derrick can't be trusted either. He's one of them. Their counsel mentioned that all decisions Herringbone Capital partners make have to be unanimous. Derrick's a partner."

He was. A minor partner, but a partner nonetheless. Verena closed her eyes, her mind reeling.

Derrick had to be in on this, no matter how many times he'd assured her that he was doing his best to help her. *He had been from the beginning.* Memories of promises and snippets of conversations roared through her mind. Now the pieces fit together like a puzzle. *Derrick is a lying bastard.* Blood rushed through her head, the veins in her neck throbbing.

Scarlett cleared her throat. "There's more, Verena. In exchange for the release of the personal guarantees, your stock will be reduced from eighty percent to thirty percent, and that will all be common stock. Phantom stock, really, since they have preferred stock, which is first in line on a sale. They have participation rights on the preferred stock, which was capped at a 6x multiple of their liquidation preference amount—far too much, if you ask me. Then there are their accumulated dividends. There's even more, but you get the picture."

Verena's head hurt like hell. She hadn't had much leverage in the negotiation process, and she had even less now. "Bottom line?"

"They're taking over the company and they get priority on all monies. Don't count on ever seeing anything. You might, but it's highly doubtful. When they sell the company, they won't be concerned about common stockholders."

When they sell the company.... Roper snapped his bony fingers and her family's livelihood was shattered. Gone in an instant. Lifetimes of work by her mother, her father, and her grandmother—all their labors had vanished. And for what? *Greed.* Thomas Roper and Herringbone Capital didn't have enough money?

"Finally, you're an at-will employee in the State of California, and they are terminating your employment." Scarlett paused. "But you wouldn't want to work for Jimmy Don anyway. Jack told me that he's being promoted to CEO."

That insipid little jerk couldn't wait to push me out of the way, Verena thought, fury coursing through her. *So this is it, this is how it's done. How owners lose their companies.* Now she understood.

"We can push back on some of these points and fight for severance, but I'll be honest with you, they've got the upper hand."

"Do everything you can, Scarlett."

"You know I will. Want to meet me for dinner tonight? We can review it more, and maybe I'll have a better answer for you by then."

"Okay, call me later." Her head was spinning.

"I will, as soon as I have something for you to review. Chin up. I love you, V. *Adios.*"

As if in a trance, Verena returned the phone to its cradle. She stared out the window, a mixture of shock, disbelief, and anger jostling in her mind. She thought about the jobs she had created and the loyal people who worked for her, and wondered what would happen to them. And what would happen to her. From job creator to unemployed—snap, and the world kicked you to the curb.

Hot tears of anger pooled in her eyes as she thought of Derrick and Herringbone, and of losing her company. She blinked hard.

She heard a soft tap on the door.

"What is it?"

Lacey's voice floated through the door. "It's me, Verena, can I come in?"

"Yes, of course." Verena swiveled in her chair, arranged a professional expression on her face to mask her turmoil, but she knew Lacey could see through it.

Lacey said, "Derrick called twice while you were on the phone. He's waiting for you at Spago. He's on line two, says it's urgent that you meet him there."

Verena stifled a sarcastic laugh. "Tell him I'm in a meeting," she said with a wave of her hand. "No. Wait. I'll take care of this right now." She picked up her purse and started out the door.

She drove the short distance to her friend Wolfgang Puck's restaurant and left her car with the valet attendants in front of Spago. "Keep it up front, please."

Verena stepped into the stylish restaurant, which was

buzzing with entertainment tycoons and stars, media personalities, and fashionable ladies-who-lunch. Verena nodded to the hostess, who recognized her. "Derrick is in the courtyard," the woman said.

When Derrick saw her, he half rose from his seat and pulled out a chair beside him for her. "How was your morning, sweetheart?"

Verena crossed her arms and remained standing, ignoring the proffered chair. "How do you *think* it was?" Her voice dripped venom.

"I suppose you saw the term sheet."

"So this is how it's done?" Her voice rose. "This is how you steal your former fiancée's company?"

People at surrounding tables began darting glances in their direction.

"Sit down, Verena," Derrick said in a hushed tone. "Let's talk about this."

"After what you've done to me, how can you think I'd sit down and have a meal with you? You're a deceitful, lying, conniving crook."

Derrick threw his napkin down and stood up, nearly pushing his chair over with the force of his action. He towered over her, glaring. "You didn't keep up your end of the bargain, Verena."

"Oh yes, I did. It was *your* man, Jimmy Don—and what kind of an idiotic name is that?—who stalled the deal with Passari. On *your* direction, I'm sure. Or Roper's. Those private strategy sessions you and Jimmy Don had—I wondered why I was excluded. Now I know. You were plotting against me."

With satisfaction, she saw his telltale tic, the throbbing

vein in his temple that began to bulge.

"Shut up, Verena, you lost your company, and you can't accept it."

"You *stole* it. There's a difference."

The restaurant had grown quiet. All eyes were on them.

Derrick's vein seemed ready to explode. When he didn't answer, Verena said, "The truth isn't good for business, is it, Derrick?"

"I told you to learn how to play the game." Derrick blew up, spitting his words. "Do you think anyone cares?" he yelled. "No one cares, Verena. *No one.*"

His words stung, but Verena continued with steady vengeance. "And to think at one time I wanted to marry you. You're a cold bastard." She jerked the blue box from her purse. "Here's your fake engagement ring." It tumbled across the tablecloth.

The manager approached Derrick. "Sir, please keep your voice down or leave the restaurant. You're disturbing other guests. We don't tolerate this behavior."

Derrick moved to leave, but he hesitated, eyeing the ring.

"Go ahead, take it, you can give it to whoever you call babe," Verena said. "I'm leaving."

The manager stood his ground. "It's time you left, too, buddy. No one treats a woman like that in my restaurant, especially not Verena Valent."

Derrick shot him a look, and then barged through the restaurant and out the front door, racing ahead of her to the valet attendant.

Verena strode through the restaurant, her head held high. She might have lost everything she had worked her entire life for, but she refused to lose her dignity.

As she passed a table, someone called to her and her heart sank. It was Greta Hicks, Derrick's ex-girlfriend and reporter for *Fashion News Daily*. Verena hadn't seen her since the event at the Beverly Hills Hotel.

Greta was with her publisher from New York. "Verena, care to comment?" she asked with a sneer in her voice.

"I just did." Verena continued through the restaurant, weaving among the tables, hearing people whispering as she passed. It seemed to take forever. Her face blazed with anger.

Outside, Derrick was yelling at the valet attendant about his car. Verena ignored him and pressed a bill into another attendant's hand. "Thanks for keeping my car in front." He held the door for her as she slid in, and then closed it behind her.

She pressed the gas pedal and whipped into traffic, leaving Derrick sputtering curses behind her on the curb.

And that's how I do it. She turned her car for home. She looked back and saw Derrick stumble and fall to the sidewalk. No one offered to help him up.

A few minutes later she pulled into her garage, got out of her car and walked straight into her bedroom, fury burning inside of her. She flung open the closet door and snatched several of Derrick's cherished Savile Row bespoke suits she had picked up from the dry cleaners for him when he'd been out of town. He'd never picked them up. A pair of scissors on her desk caught her eye. *Why not?* She heaved them onto the bed and went to work.

She shoved his clothes and everything he'd ever given

her into a black plastic garbage bag. She dumped it into the trunk of her car and wheeled out of the garage.

When Verena arrived at Herringbone's office building, she hoisted the garbage bag over her shoulder and strode in, ignoring the stares of passersby. When she reached their office door, she took aim with her high heel and kicked it open.

In the waiting room Verena recognized a pair of important female institutional investors from the state pension funds that she'd met a few months ago with Derrick. Everyone jumped, startled, and the receptionist hurried from behind her desk.

"Miss Valent, I'm so sorry about what happened," the young woman said. "I hate them all for what they did to you," she added, *sotto voce*. "I've decided to quit."

"Good for you, these men aren't your mentors."

Derrick and Roper raced into the room. Verena spun around, her anger spiraling.

"What are you doing here?" Derrick grabbed her arm, his fingers digging into her flesh, but she jerked away from him.

Never again would she allow him—or any other man—to hurt her.

"Returning your rags," she said, relishing her revenge, even though she knew it was a bit childish of her. Roper started to speak, but Verena cut him off. "Shame on you, Thomas Roper. You can both go to hell." Verena opened the garbage bag and shook out Derrick's shredded suits.

"What have you done?" Derrick screamed.

"Same thing you did to *my company*." As Verena flung jagged fabric in his face, morbid satisfaction surged through her.

The two investors edged toward the door. "Looks like now is not a good time," one of the women said.

"No, wait, I can explain." Derrick called to the women, pleading.

"We have nothing more to discuss with Herringbone Capital," the other woman said, frowning. "We don't like what we're seeing here."

With a satisfied nod to the two women, Verena brushed a thread from her sleeve and marched out of the building. As angry as she was, she had to admit one thing. *That felt good.*

Later that evening, she met with Scarlett at a café. Verena knew she'd been arguing all day with the other attorneys on her behalf. Scarlett hugged her when she saw her.

Verena had no appetite for food, so they ordered coffee. Scarlett told her the attorneys had been hammering away at the final points, but the net result was unchanged. Herringbone was taking over the company.

"I'm so sorry, but the battle is over," Scarlett said. "I just received some of the final documents from Herringbone's attorney. Do you want to look at them and sign them now?"

"I need a day, Scarlett. I'll sign tomorrow." She needed to review the legal documents with a clear mind.

"You'll have to pack up your office tomorrow," Scarlett said, taking her hand. "Or have Lacey do it for you."

Verena felt numb inside. "I'll take care of it."

25

The next morning, Verena dressed in somber black and went to her office for what she knew was the last time. She arrived early, unlocked the door, and climbed the stairs to her office. She passed the familiar photos of guests that Mia had proudly shared with her when she was a little girl. *It's the last time I'll see these.* She paused to fix them in her mind. This had been their legacy.

She strode into her office and opened her email. The first message contained the online edition of *Fashion News Daily.*

The headline read: *Valent Swiss Skincare and Herringbone Capital Battle for Control.*

Unable to read it, Verena turned her computer off. She knew what tomorrow's headline would read.

Lacey tapped on her door and pushed it open. "I'm so sorry, darlin'," she choked out, her shoulders shaking with grief. Verena wrapped her arms around her. She was going to miss Lacey, who'd been by her side at the office every day since her parents had died.

After a few moments Lacey pulled away, wiping her eyes. "Scarlett is on the phone for you. And that police investigator is back looking for Jimmy Don."

Verena gritted her teeth. "If I ever get my hands on Jimmy Don again, that officer will be investigating a homicide." *What I wouldn't give to snap that boy's neck.*

"He asked me if I knew Marvin Panetta." Lacey picked

at a thread on her lace dress. "Do you think Jimmy Don had anything to do with his death?"

Verena jerked her head up. "It was ruled suicide." However, Marvin's wife had been vehement in her disagreement of the assessment. *Could Jimmy Don have been responsible?* "But honestly, nothing would surprise me now."

Lacey glanced around the office. "Let me know when you need help...." Her voice gave out and another sob caught in her throat. She closed the door behind her.

Verena sat at her desk for the last time and picked up the phone. "Hello, Scarlett."

"Hi Verena." Scarlett's voice sounded strained. "They want you to sign some of the documents today. There will be more later, but these are important."

"Okay, I'll be through here shortly. I'll come by your office in a while." Verena swallowed a lump in her throat. Derrick and Roper hadn't wasted any time. With the news out, phone calls from business associates would start soon.

Scarlett agreed and hung up. Verena gazed around her office.

Three months ago, she had been planning the expansion into Asia, and their future looked bright. Today, she was broke, in debt, unemployed—and utterly devastated.

The only redeeming point was that she hadn't let Mia put her retirement savings into the business. Or the college fund.

Verena picked up the photo of her parents that had rested on her desk for a decade and brushed a speck of dust from the glass. She blinked, clearing her eyes. Somehow, she felt her parents were reaching out to her, offering her comfort. *I did the best I could,* she told them.

She blinked again and pressed a button on her phone. "Lacey, I'm ready. Would you come and help me pack my personal effects?"

After Verena signed the documents at Scarlett's office, she wound through the familiar streets of Beverly Hills on the short drive from the salon to her home. She was in an emotional fog. With her mind in turmoil, she missed a turn that she knew by heart.

How will I tell Mia? A wave of guilt crashed over her. Her grandmother had devoted her life to the business. Her mother and father had dedicated their all-too-brief time to Valent Swiss Skincare. And now, it was over.

Verena pressed a shaky hand to her mouth, her breath coming in short rasps. She'd managed to maintain her dignity at the salon. She'd called a meeting with all the employees—with the exception of Jimmy Don—during the short time in between skincare sessions, and thanked each person for their service and friendship over the years. *Together, we built something we can all be proud of,* she told them. Many of them were sobbing or fighting tears, and every one of the estheticians and team members hugged her before returning to their duties.

Missing another turn, Verena found herself lost in the neighborhood she knew so well. When she could no longer see through her tears, she pulled to the side of the road and stopped. She sank her face into her trembling hands, dreading the moment she'd have to tell her grandmother and break her heart.

Four filing boxes of personal effects from her office sat on her back seat. Four boxes of photos, mementos, press clippings, personal notes, and books. For all she had given to the business—all the hours and days and weeks and years. Her devotion, her ideas, her nurturing…her love. It was all condensed in four plain boxes.

A crumpled invoice sat on top. Jimmy Don had itemized every business lunch she'd paid for in the last five years—meetings with buyers, media interviews, and working lunches—all to advance the interests of the business. She had scanned the list and saw flowers she had sent to her top retail buyer when the woman's husband died, and the trip she had taken to New York to train the salespeople on a new account. He'd included birthday gifts for valued employees and dinners for employees who'd worked late into the evening for special events, such as the Academy Awards gala.

When Jimmy Don presented the bill, which was for thousands of dollars, it was the final insult. She knew Roper was behind it. What did Lacey always say? *You lie down with dogs, you get up with fleas.*

She had no intention of paying for those business expenses. She'd give it to Scarlett, who would contest the bill for her.

She couldn't remember how long she'd sat in her car, her emotions alternating between rage and sorrow, when a tap on the glass surprised her. It was a Beverly Hills police officer. She wiped her cheeks and rolled her window down.

"Everything alright, ma'am?"

Verena drew a deep breath. "Yes, thank you officer. I'll be fine, I just needed a moment to gather my thoughts."

He touched his hat and walked away, leaving Verena to compose herself before she had to face Mia. Finally, she turned the ignition and started for home.

"We've lost everything," Verena said, sitting on her bed and sobbing on Mia's shoulder. Since she'd arrived home, she'd been inundated with phone calls from people who had called the salon looking for her, only to be told that she no longer worked there. Her other salon managers and employees, vendors, and guests—they all offered their condolences, as if a death had occurred.

In a very real way, it had.

It was the demise of a dream, of a lifetime of work, of a way of life. Caring for treasured guests who had entrusted them with their skincare—and their heartaches and triumphs—for decades, even generations.

Running the salons, providing skincare, creating products—this was all Verena knew. *What will we do?*

"I'm turning in early tonight," Verena said, wiping her eyes. Anika and Bella had gone to a friend's house to spend the night and wouldn't return until morning. "I still can't believe what's happened. It's been a nightmare."

"And now it's over, Verena," Mia said, sounding numb. "You did the best you could under the circumstances. Don't look back."

"I can't stop thinking about it."

"And you won't, not for a long time. Losing a business is the death of an endeavor. We must accept death as part of life. Doesn't mean we like it, but it signals the end of one era and the beginning of another." Mia kissed her on the forehead and stood up. "A good night's sleep is exactly what we need. And don't worry, we'll think of something. We're smart women. No one can keep us down for long."

Mia closed the door. Verena flopped back on her bed,

her brain blazing. She had failed everyone—her grandmother, her sisters, their employees and guests. The salon had been a haven where women and men could count on being pampered, made to feel whole and healed. It had been a haven for her family, too.

Verena drew her knees up, tears burning her eyes. Scarlett had told her it was the worst time since the Great Depression for business lending, but she couldn't forgive herself, even though Herringbone's unscrupulous behavior was really to blame.

Anika and Bella would never take their place beside her in the business. The business with which she had been entrusted was gone.

Verena sobbed as she thought of Mia and the loss of her reputation. For decades Mia had enjoyed a certain status in town as the founder of Valent Swiss Skincare. She had been celebrated and lauded for helping women of all ages feel and look their best, and for helping awkward teenage girls blossom into confident young women.

Verena mourned the loss of their life's work. No longer could they aid those who suffered from acne, psoriasis, burns, scar tissue, birth defects, or skin cancer with Valent's medicated formulas, or simply make people feel more attractive and relaxed with other organic products and relaxing therapeutic services. Professionals whose careers hinged on their appearance depended on them.

But Jimmy Don didn't care. He planned to terminate their most experienced skincare specialists. "They're too expensive," he'd told her. Of course, those were Roper's words. And probably Derrick's, too. She remembered how he'd started grilling her about minor personal expenses.

Another sob wracked her body as guilt ripped through her. Others would soon lose their jobs, too.

The worst of it was that Scarlett had called her to say that Herringbone was demanding that she sign an agreement that would turn over all her intellectual property to Herringbone, including the products she'd been developing. She would be barred from working for competitors for five years, or selling to any retailer she'd ever been in contact with.

The final insult was that never again could she use her family name in skincare. Herringbone owned *Valent*. She choked as she wept.

Even her name belonged to Herringbone.

She allowed that some of the demands made sense to Herringbone, but it was terribly restrictive for a woman who had never done anything else, had studied and taught only this, and had committed her life to this cause.

As she thought of the restrictions against her future, another wave of anguish crushed her, sending her stomach into spasms. She rushed into the bathroom, retching from the disgust and disdain she'd had to swallow, her body expunging the injustices from her system.

Afterward, she lay on the cold tiled floor catching her breath, until once again, her body heaved against the cruelty that had been visited upon her. Her life, as she knew it, was over.

Again and again as the night drew on, her body purged itself of the evil she'd ingested, until finally Verena lay weakened and spent on the hard surface, feeling as if her soul had been shredded from her body.

Even then, the solace of sleep eluded her guilt ravaged mind.

She was still awake when the morning sun began streaming through the bathroom window. Finally drifting to sleep from sheer exhaustion, she woke again sometime later when footsteps pounded across the wooden floor and the door banged open. The twins had just arrived home from their sleepover.

"Verena, come quickly!" Anika's face was white. She pulled frantically on Verena's arm. "It's Mia, her chest hurts. You have to come right now."

Adrenaline snapped her from her groggy disorientation and she scrambled to her feet and raced through the house. Anika ran behind her. In Mia's bedroom, Bella sat holding a water glass and an aspirin bottle for her grandmother.

"It's my, my…heart," Mia managed to say, her eyes fluttering closed as she clutched her chest and crumpled over.

26

A sharp antiseptic smell assaulted Verena's nose and she shivered in the frigid air conditioning. She paced the length of the waiting room, her chest riddled with anxiety, her rubber-soled flip-flops squeaking on the polished linoleum floor. Anika and Bella were curled up asleep in bright orange chairs. They'd refused to stay at home.

Mia had been whisked from the ambulance and taken directly in for evaluation and stabilization. At one point, the doctor had come out to discuss bypass surgery, as long as Mia were strong enough to survive it. Verena learned that Mia had been assigned to one of the best cardiac doctors in the world, Dr. Omondi, who'd trained at Harvard Medical School.

Verena had called Mia's closest friend, Camille, and alerted Mia's sister in Switzerland, their great aunt Lara.

Now all she could do was wait and pray for Mia.

She hadn't slept at all last night, overcome with anguish at the horrible turn of events at the company. Mia had tried to console her, but in the end, her grandmother had suffered the ultimate price for Herringbone's treachery.

Every part of Verena's body ached with sorrow. She would never forgive herself, but the real perpetrator was Herringbone—Roper, Derrick, and Jimmy Don. Their sociopathic greed might have cost Mia her life. And for that, they would pay.

Verena didn't have it in her to exact the full measure of

revenge they deserved, but she prayed that somehow Mia's concept of karma would ensnare them. Verena had to believe that justice would be done, if not by courts of law, then by virtue of universal righteousness. Her father used to say, *what goes around, comes around.*

At times like this, she wished her parents were still alive. But the three siblings took care of each other. That morning, Verena had thrown on work-out gear and flip-flops before running out the door with them to follow the ambulance to the hospital. Anika, always the protective one, had asked a nurse for a toothbrush, toothpaste, and comb for Verena. Bella had visited the vending machine and brought back granola bars and fruit juice for all of them.

Verena placed her hands on her sisters' chests to check their breathing. This routine brought her a measure of comfort, but in an instant, panic seized her again. *What if Mia dies?* Verena choked back a sob.

She prayed Anika and Bella would not be robbed of their grandmother. *Not yet.*

Verena sank into a chair and covered her face with her hands. She was glad they'd gone to Europe. If this were the end for Mia, then at least her grandmother had accomplished her goal of introducing the twins to their heritage and cousins in Switzerland.

Not knowing anything was the worst of it. Other visitors had come and gone in the waiting room, but the three of them remained.

"Verena?"

She slid her hands from her face. "Camille." Tears welling in her eyes, she struggled to her feet and hugged her grandmother's dearest friend.

"It's alright, *ma chérie*, let it out. You'll feel better." Camille patted her back, murmuring words of support. "I'm trying to reach Dahlia, but I brought another friend, Pierre Chevalier." Camille turned as a smartly dressed man walked into the room.

"We've met," Verena said. "How are you?"

Pierre kissed her on each cheek in greeting. "Nice to see you again, Verena. I only wish the circumstances were better."

As they spoke, the twins began to stretch and yawn.

"Any word yet on her condition?" Camille asked, keeping her voice low.

"She's in surgery." Verena threw a look at the twins and whispered, "I hope Mia is strong enough to withstand the procedure."

Verena was relieved to see Camille, who had always been like an aunt to her. If Mia didn't survive, Camille could help her break it to the twins. It would be the most difficult thing she'd ever had to do. She couldn't even think about that. *Dear Lord, please don't take her yet.*

Camille put her arm around Verena. "We all have a limited number of days on earth, but Mia is a survivor. She's endured several bouts with cancer and emerged victorious. She has an indefatigable will to live."

Verena leaned into Camille, drawing strength from her force of will, taking comfort in the familiar perfume that Camille had blended, which permeated the stylish, nubby wool jacket she wore. Camille was a survivor of the Second World War and had met Mia after escaping to America. Verena wondered what Mia and Camille had been like then. Two young women who had become great friends. Verena thought about Dahlia, Scarlett, and Fianna. *They were probably a lot like us.*

Anika and Bella woke and rubbed their eyes. "Is Mia okay?" Anika asked.

"We'll know soon," Verena said, casting a pained look at Camille.

Pierre cleared his throat. "There's a decent cafeteria here. Would anyone like to join me?"

The twin scrambled to their feet. "May we?" they asked Verena.

"Of course. I'll stay here." Verena nodded her appreciation to Pierre. Something about him reminded her of Emile, the grandfather the twins had never known.

Pierre said, "We'll bring something back to you, dear. You've kept a long vigil."

Verena watched them leave, each girl holding one of Pierre's hands. She turned to Camille and they sat down. "I'm awfully worried about Mia. And there's something I have to tell you."

Camille took her hand, just as Mia had.

Verena cast her eyes away in shame, fidgeting as she spoke. "I lost the business, Camille. My grandmother's company. Mia tried to comfort me, but she's the one who suffered the most. I did this to her." A sob broke from her chest. "It's my fault."

Camille placed her hands on Verena's shoulders. "No, no, no, *ma chérie*. Mia called me last night, told me everything. It's that avaricious weasel, Thomas Roper, who did this. He's immoral, ill-mannered, and utterly rapacious. I have always despised that reprehensible little man." She expressed a puff of air between her perfectly drawn lips in disgust.

"You know him?"

Camille nodded. "But I didn't realize Derrick was in partnership with him. When you first started dating, Mia told me he was in some sort of banking." Her gaze slid away in remembrance. "Years ago, he ruined another woman I knew, a good friend. Stole her business and spun it off later to make millions."

"What happened to her?"

Camille pursed her lips and sighed. "She died, I'm afraid."

A chill crept over Verena. "I was much younger, but I think I remember this story. She committed suicide, didn't she?"

Camille bowed her head. "Yes," she said, and then raised her eyes. "But you and Mia are much stronger than she was."

Verena moistened her lips. *Are we?*

Several hours later when the cardiac surgeon emerged from surgery, her face was grim. Verena and Camille rose from their chairs. Verena clutched Camille's thin, veined hand, surprised at the strength of the older woman's grasp, though she was widely known for her iron will. As Verena braced herself, she realized there was no one she would rather have by her side. "How is Mia?"

"Your grandmother put up an amazing fight." Dr. Omondi pulled off her cotton cap and shook her head, her short, curly black and grey hair spiking at the crown. "She's resting in intensive care now, where we can continue to monitor her."

Verena gasped. The sudden dissipation of stress rendered her weak, and her legs buckled like jelly. She dropped onto a chair, still clutching Camille's hand. "When can we see her?"

"Soon, but limit the visit to a few minutes. She's weak and needs her recovery time."

"May I take the girls in?" Verena asked. They were still with Pierre.

The doctor nodded. "Mia talked about them quite a bit. I think it will be good for her to see them. You can all go in, but no excitement, and keep it brief."

Verena hardly heard the rest of what the doctor had to say before she left. She tilted her head back against the wall, expelling pent up emotions.

Camille crossed herself and murmured a soft prayer of thanks. Hugging Camille. Verena echoed her words under her breath, limp from the ordeals of the past twenty-four hours.

Pierre returned with Anika and Bella, and Verena shared the good news about Mia's survival. As he'd promised, Pierre returned with a club sandwich and an apple. Verena devoured the food with gusto.

When they were allowed to see Mia, they crept in on silent feet. Mia's face—nearly as pale as the white blanket that covered her—lit with joy when she saw them. An assortment of tubes and wires connected her to several monitoring devices that beeped in the background.

A nurse said, "We just removed her breathing tube. She'll be hoarse."

Verena sat beside her. "Grand-mère Mia," she said softly, reverting to the name she'd used as a girl for her grandmother, before she became simply Mia to her and the twins. She pressed her lips against Mia's cool brow, a sob of regret cracking her voice. "I'm so sorry—"

"Wasn't…your fault." Mia moved her head slightly.

Verena motioned to Anika and Bella to come forward. The girls took turns, wide-eyed and solemn, caressing Mia's hand and kissing her cheek.

After a few minutes, Anika and Bella left the room, while Camille traded places with them.

"Cold," Mia murmured.

Camille pulled a blanket from the foot of the bed to Mia's chest and tucked the sides around her. "If that's not enough, I'll have another one brought in."

Verena watched them and thought of how close she was to her own friends. Her grandmother and Camille had been friends for sixty years—they'd cared for one another through crises and celebrations, love and loss. They were survivors; soft and feminine on the outside, but with spines tough as steel when required. These women, they were her tutors in life. Verena lifted a corner of her mouth. *Who better to learn from?*

The cardiac surgeon walked in, clipboard in her hand. "How's my valiant patient?" Dr. Omondi checked Mia. "You're a real fighter, Mia Valent."

Mia lifted her head. "What's…that…your arm?"

Dr. Omondi pushed her sleeve up, revealing a fresh scar on her deep caramel-colored skin. "Burned myself in the kitchen, where I met up with a hot skillet," she said with a chuckle. "Was trying to make some of my native Kenyan dishes for my in-laws. Even docs have accidents, you see."

"Pretty skin…I have serum…minimal scarring." Mia's eyes flashed even as she struggled to speak.

Verena hastened to her side. "Mia, it's okay."

"Need serum. Bring…here." Mia was adamant.

"Your personal serum?" Verena leaned in close.

Mia nodded and pointed to the doctor's scar. "Return the...favor." A smile wreathed her smooth face and she closed her eyes.

"She needs her rest now." The doctor turned to Verena with interest. "What's this about a serum?"

"My grandmother started Valent Swiss Skincare. She's spent her life caring for people's skin." Verena smoothed Mia's hair. "She wants you to use her special serum, one she blended years ago. We never carried it in the salon, because it couldn't be mass produced. It's truly incredible."

"Your grandmother is quite a woman." Dr. Omondi lifted a corner of her mouth and made a note on her chart. "She's sedated, but make sure she rests. This is a critical period in her recovery."

Camille squeezed Mia's hand before she left. "I'll try to call Dahlia again," she said to Verena.

Verena stayed for a few more minutes, watching to make sure that Mia was breathing steadily, and praying that she would make it through the long night ahead.

The lunch rush was over and Lance surveyed the kitchen, directing his team and listening to comments about new seasonal dishes they'd recently added to the menu. He had a few minutes to prepare notes before his meeting with the head of catering about an important VIP wedding menu. *Quail, lobster, rack of lamb*...ideas whirred in his mind. This was the creative part of his job that he enjoyed the most.

His sous-chef called out to him, nodding toward the door to the adjoining dining room. "Chef, you have a visitor."

Lance looked up at the portly man. "Pretty busy here, can you take it?"

"I'd sure like to, that's one fine lady, but she said she had to see you. Something about Valent?"

Lance snapped his attention toward his sous-chef. "A blond-haired woman?"

"No, dark hair, but she's hot. And her perfume is fantastic. Oh là là." He smacked his fingers against his lips in the French fashion.

"You should be so lucky," Lance said, laughing. Wondering who it might be, he ran a hand through his thick chestnut hair in an attempt to tame it.

He'd invited Verena for another Saturday morning bike ride and breakfast after he'd returned from Paris, and even offered to make his award-winning crab for her entire family, but she'd declined. Worse, she hadn't returned a call from any messages he'd left. But he wasn't giving up. He pushed through the door.

A petite woman who did, indeed, smell wonderful—like gardenias, he noted—swung around. "I'm Dahlia Dubois, a friend of Verena and Mia Valent. We met at the Polo Lounge a while back. My grandmother, Camille Dubois, sent me here on a mission of mercy. Do you have a moment?"

27

"A heart attack is nothing compared to the cancer treatments I've been through," Mia said, shifting in her hospital bed so that she could complete her skincare regimen. After showing satisfactory progress during the night, she'd been moved from the intensive care unit to a room.

"Don't downplay this incident," Verena said, scolding her grandmother.

The life had returned to Mia's face. Verena had brought Mia's facial cleansers and moisturizers to the hospital, along with other personal items to make her feel more comfortable. Dahlia and Camille had visited earlier, and had brought an assortment of Dubois spa products.

Verena had also brought roses from Mia's garden, and the assortment of apricot, yellow, and pink blossoms filled the air with their delicate sweet scent, masking the antiseptic smell. She'd also plugged in soft music that they'd played at the salon to create a soothing oasis.

The door to Mia's hospital room swung open and her cardiologist walked in. "And how are you today, Mrs. Valent?" Dr. Omondi smiled as she checked Mia. "Your color is good." She scrutinized Mia's eyes and face. "You have the most amazing skin."

"Why, thank you." Mia smiled up at her doctor. "Now, about that burn you sustained. Verena, did you bring my serum with you?"

Verena withdrew an apothecary bottle from the bag she'd brought. "Here it is."

"Good, I'll take that. Dr. Omondi, do you mind? This is what I use on my face to keep my skin smooth and clear." When the doctor nodded her acceptance, Mia went to work.

Verena smothered a chuckle as she watched her grandmother administering her healing serum to the doctor's scar. *She's irrepressible.*

Mia smoothed the serum onto Dr. Omondi's arm, instructing the doctor on how to care for it. "I'll give you this bottle, but be sure to follow my instructions exactly. I think you'll be pleased with the results, and it won't take long."

Dr. Omondi thanked her and left to continue her rounds.

"You're incorrigible. You should be resting, and instead you're doctoring the doctors."

Verena had spent the night at the hospital, and when Camille and Dahlia arrived in the morning, she drove home to get supplies for Mia, snip her favorite flowers, and take a quick shower. She'd pulled on another pair of yoga pants and a tank top, brushed her hair into a ponytail, and returned to the hospital. At least she had plenty of time to spend with her now. She couldn't imagine going to work or answering to Jimmy Don today.

As devastated as she had been, a small part of her was glad the ordeal was over so she could be with Mia. But then, Mia wouldn't be here if it weren't for Thomas Roper and Derrick Logan. She clenched her jaw as a fresh wave of anger surged through her. *And they can go to hell.*

"Verena, you look disturbed." Mia shifted against her pillows. "You know, we have to put this behind us."

"I don't know if I can. That was your life's work, and our livelihood." Verena nervously chewed her lip, concerned about how they were going to survive. Verena didn't want to touch Mia's savings.

"I've found there's a gross misconception about life. We might get comfortable from time to time, but nothing in life is permanent." Mia blinked as the sun shifted brightly into the room, and Verena rose to adjust the blinds. "Life is ever-changing. Complacency is our worst enemy."

Verena folded her arms. "We *met* our worst enemy, and it was Thomas Roper."

"At least you never have to see Derrick again. I never did like that insolent, self-absorbed man." Mia sniffed with contempt.

"You were right." Verena stared out the window. "I tried to make the relationship work with him—even as friends, but there was always something missing… later I realized it was his heart. For a while, I actually thought he was looking out for us. By the time I realized he wasn't, it was too late."

"He's a sociopath. He and Thomas Roper are two of a kind, dear."

Verena lowered herself carefully onto the edge of Mia's bed. She cracked a knuckle, wishing she could punch them in the face. Nothing would be sweeter than revenge. She'd had a good start with Derrick's favorite suits.

"Don't do that, it's not ladylike," Mia said, sounding stronger.

Verena quirked a corner of her mouth at the admonishment. Her grandmother must be feeling better. "I can't believe they can get away with it," Verena said. "What they did was *criminal*. They stole our company right out from under us."

"To people like that, it's just business." Mia rubbed her skin where an adhesive bandage secured a monitoring device. "Frankly, you were working far too hard. Someday you'll want to start a family."

"If I ever meet Mr. Right, that is." Verena winced. "And that doesn't look promising, Mia. I have a unique situation. I'm not complaining, I'm just being honest with myself. I'm shelving those dreams until the twins are off on their own." She'd be thirty-three when they went to college, and nearly forty by the time they finished, if they wanted to go to graduate school.

Verena smiled wistfully. The chance of having children of her own was slim. Taking care of her grandmother and her sisters was far more important. Finding new employment was imperative.

What will I do? She'd never even interviewed for a job. She sat fidgeting with an edge of the sheet, wondering what her next step should be, heartsick over the turn of events.

Mia struggled to sit up, and Verena rose to assist her, plumping pillows behind her. She draped a soft shrug that Lacey had knitted around Mia's shoulders.

"What about that nice chef?" Mia asked offhandedly.

What about him? "He called a few times, but I was always up to my neck in business."

"He seemed awfully sweet. Good manners, good heart."

Verena thought about their time together in Paris. For a few days she'd actually enjoyed herself. She touched her lips, remembering the kiss they'd shared. She'd loved dancing with him, laughing and talking. He actually listened to her, unlike Derrick. *But no, it's impossible.* She had Mia and the girls to think about.

Oh, but it were possible... Just imagining Lance in her arms, a warm feeling spread throughout her.

Mia yawned and stretched. "I'd like to sleep this afternoon. No need for you to stay. Why don't you go home and have a rest, too?"

"You're such an independent woman, has anyone ever told you that?"

"My Emile used to say that to me."

Verena kissed her grandmother and closed the door softly behind her. She walked through the corridor and as she approached the nurses' desk, she saw a man leaning against the counter. A nurse motioned to her. "Miss Valent, excuse me, but this man would like a word with you."

"With me?"

"Yes, ma'am." The man flashed a badge. I'm Detective Cardiff with the Beverly Hills Police Department. Do you have a moment to answer a few questions about Jimmy Don Herald? I understand he used to work for you." When Verena arched a brow in curiosity, he added, "I visited the salon this morning. Lacey told me everything. Said I could find you here."

"Bad news travels fast. How can I help you?"

The detective led her off to the side and whipped out a notepad. "It's about Marvin Panetta. How did you know Mr. Panetta?"

"He was my banker, and a personal friend." Verena shook her head sadly, remembering the shocking events. "I never thought he was the kind of man who would take his own life."

The detective scribbled a note, nodding. "Did you ever hear Jimmy Don Herald say anything about Marvin Panetta?"

A chill snaked through her. "Do you think Jimmy Don was responsible for his death?" Marvin's wife had been adamant that her husband's death was *not* suicide, but murder.

The detective looked from one side to another, and dropped his voice. "We're following some leads, and would appreciate any information you might have or remember. In addition, do you know where Jimmy Don might be?"

"Come in," Scarlett said to Verena. "I have the rest of the documents in the conference room." Even though Verena had already signed some papers, Scarlett still needed Verena to sign the final set of agreements for Herringbone. "They're really rushing to have these executed and delivered. I told their counsel it was a bad time for you."

"It's okay. I'd rather get it over with." Feeling as if she were walking to the guillotine, Verena followed Scarlett through the Century City office of her law firm. Plush burgundy carpet softened her step, and polished ebony furniture gleamed against hunter green walls. Everything about the office was serious, from the law magazines in the waiting area to the expressions of people she passed.

They walked through the office. Verena said, "Scarlett, a detective from the Beverly Hills Police Department tracked me down at the hospital. He had some questions about Jimmy Don Herald and Marvin Panetta. Have you heard anything about this?"

"What a coincidence. I had to call Lacey this morning, and she mentioned that Jimmy Don didn't come into the office today. She asked if I knew anything, and said a detective had been trying to find him. Must have been the same guy."

"That's bizarre."

"That's Herringbone." Scarlett said, shaking her head. "Nothing surprises me now."

"What do you mean?"

Scarlett sighed. "You'll see." She held the door to the glass enclosed conference room.

Still clad in her casual yoga gear from the morning, Verena felt as if she were entering a fish bowl, soon to be devoured by sharks.

Scarlett shrugged out of her smartly tailored navy blue jacket and picked up two bottles of water. "Would you like coffee or tea?"

Verena eyed two tall stacks of documents on the table. "Have any vodka?"

"Actually, I do. One of the partners has a bar. Not that I hit the bottle, mind you. I'm two years sober next week."

"Congratulations," Verena said, pleased for Scarlett. "Just kidding. Let's get this over with." She unscrewed a bottle of water and took a long drink.

"I know this is the worst time to ask you to do this," Scarlett said, sounding apologetic. "Herringbone's counsel insisted and threatened other actions unless you sign off." She shook her head, sorrow in her eyes. "They're absolute bastards."

They sat down and Scarlett began to explain each document, and then showed her where to sign if she agreed.

After reading through several legal agreements, Verena's eyes began to glaze over. "Be straight with me,

Scarlett, is there any negotiating room on any of these documents?"

"Not really. You were out of financial compliance—quickly, I know, and through no fault of your own. Jimmy Don forced it, and I'm sure it was Roper's plan all along. Roper is the most loathsome, detestable man I've ever come across, and doesn't deserve the fine company you built up. Everything he did was legal, but certainly not moral. And as I've learned, it's not the first time he's pulled something like this on a company." She pointed to a document before them. "This intellectual property agreement is one we should examine in detail."

Verena nodded, listening to Scarlett's explanation and feeling sick to her stomach as she signed her family's assets away. "I wish I'd known this is the way venture capitalists operate."

"Not all of them do. Herringbone is in a class by itself." Scarlett leaned forward in her chair. "VC companies actually have their place, especially in bringing to market technological or medical advances that require vast outlays for research and development, but have enormous upside for everyone involved. Roper is definitely not one of the good guys in this industry. He's their equivalent of Bernie Madoff, and he gives them all a bad name. He took advantage of the economic situation to pounce on companies like yours."

"He's doing this to others?"

"Afraid so. That's what I discovered this morning."

Hearing that made Verena sick to her stomach. "What about the intellectual property?"

"The formulas, trademarks, patents, copyrights. It's all here. You could try to fight some of it, but honestly, you wouldn't win. The assets were pledged against the loan."

"It states, 'anything I've developed,'" Verena said, reading the agreement. A thought struck her and she looked up. "This covers me, but what about Mia?"

Scarlett raised a brow and scanned the document. "She's not mentioned at all. I think they assumed that anything she might have created was already in the company. She hasn't worked in the business for years, has she?"

"No," she said slowly, thinking.

"Then it only covers you."

"And this document? It limits where I can work and what I can do?"

"That's the one we discussed." Scarlett shook her head. "There's a lot in this one that reiterates what you had to sign earlier for the loan. Because of the non-compete agreement, you can't sell competing products to any of their existing retailers or those you ever called on. You can't work for any of the competitors listed there for five years, or offer employment to any employees. It's awfully restrictive, but in California, you can argue for the right to work. It's probably not enforceable. Of course, Roper can always come back and sue you."

Verena ran her finger down the list. It was exhaustive, and included every company she'd ever had contact with. Jimmy Don must have accessed their marketing and client databases. It was beyond restrictive; it was punitive. "What am I going to do? Skincare is all I know."

"You can start another company." Scarlett touched her arm in a sympathetic gesture. "Look at it this way. Roper is scared of your name and your talent, otherwise this agreement wouldn't be so restrictive."

"A lot of good that does me. I don't have the funds to build another business." *What in the world will I do?*

Scarlett pointed to a signature line. "This is the last signature needed."

This was her final official act for VSS. Lifting the pen, Verena hesitated over the thin black line, then quickly scrawled her name and put the pen down. "That's it?"

"It's all over now. I'm so, so sorry, Verena." Scarlett's eyes misted over as she hugged Verena, and the two women walked out.

28

That evening, Verena returned to the hospital. Outside Mia's hospital room, a commotion erupted in the hallway. "What on earth was that?" Mia looked alarmed. "Go see what's happening."

Verena hurried to the door. A patient had heaved a tray of food from a room into the hallway, and an attendant was cleaning it up while a nurse tried to reason with the patient. It was disgusting the way some people behaved. "Who would do that?"

At the same time, a nurse emerged from a room across the hall and called to another attendant. "It's Mr. Roper again in room two twelve. I need your help."

Verena stood rooted by the door, hardly believing what she'd heard. Glancing over her shoulder she said to Mia, "I'll be right back."

She sauntered down the hall, past the uproar, and caught a glimpse of the patient in room number two twelve. *Thomas Roper.* She clutched her throat and hurried back to Mia's room, fury shooting through her. She closed the door behind her and caught her breath.

"Whatever is wrong?" Mia frowned with concern.

Verena opened her mouth to tell her, but instantly thought better of it. Mia was here to recover. The last thing she needed was to worry about Thomas Roper—the man who stole the company she'd birthed—inhabiting a room a few doors away. "Someone didn't like the food, I suppose."

"Some people are so rude. What an unsavory, insufferable person that must be. I feel sorry for the staff for having to deal with people like that." Mia wrinkled her nose as if she'd encountered a rotten stench. "The food is certainly palatable, if a bit bland, but this is a hospital, after all, not a gourmet restaurant."

Verena always appreciated her grandmother's practicality.

They chatted for a while as the sun set. Camille came to visit again, and Verena stood and stretched. An idea had formed in her mind, though she had tried to ignore it. "I'm going to stretch my legs and make a call. I'll be back in a little while."

The hallway was quiet. Most guests had already left for the evening. She started down the long corridor, her rubber-soled shoes noiseless on the linoleum floor. She ducked her head against the glare of the fluorescent lights overhead.

The food tray incident from earlier in the day had lodged in her mind and now, anger coursed through her veins. *Room two twelve.* She ambled toward the room as if drawn by hypnotic suggestion.

She paused by the door, repulsed by the thought of Thomas Roper. *I should leave now.* She surveyed the empty hallway. Her mouth felt dry. Overcome by a sudden urge, she grasped the doorknob and turned it.

There on the bed lay Roper, his eyes closed. Was he dead? She crept farther inside, hardly daring to breathe, her heart thudding in her chest.

She stepped to the middle of the room between a vacant bed and Roper. With each breath he took, his chest rattled. Revulsion seared through her, rooting her to her spot. Digital monitors blinked and beeped, marking his bodily functions.

Another step closer and she could see the crepe-thin skin stretched across his flaccid arms and age-spotted face. *Here lies a man who values wealth above all else, even at the expense of others.* She shivered with abhorrence, her upper lip curling back. *This is who Derrick is modeling himself after.*

Disgust, hatred, and rage swirled through her and she shook uncontrollably. She imagined raking her nails against his arrogant face. Instead, she pressed her hand against her mouth and took another step, eyeing the wires and tubes that connected Roper to monitoring machines.

Standing next to him, she grimaced at the smell of his noxious breath, which filled the air with a poisonous stench on every exhale. Cold fury burned in her heart against his evil malevolence. *I hope he dies. The world will be better for it.*

As she stared at him, fierce wrath edged with madness blinded her reason. Calming her shaking limbs, she reached for a pillow and slid it from the vacant bed. The pillow's plump density was soft against her fingertips, its starched, crinkly cotton pillowcase cool in her palms. She pressed her mouth against it, and it robbed her breath.

As if in a trance, she lowered the pillow from her face, inching it toward Roper's putrid mouth. One quick motion, a firm hold—that's all it would take. Should she disable the monitors? She lowered the pillow until she could no longer see his malicious face, smell his foul breath.

One more finger's breadth would end her pain.

Or would it?

A loudspeaker crackled above her, jarring her from her dazed state. *No!* She jerked the pillow back, flung it onto the vacant bed, and raced from the room. Awakened, Roper called out, his voice raspy.

The door slammed behind her.

She leaned against the wall in the corridor and tipped her head back, gasping for air.

Thomas Roper had almost driven her to murder.

It's what he deserves.

But not at the expense of my life.

Blood roaring in her ears, she closed her eyes and tried to calm her thumping heart.

"Verena, are you alright?"

Am I hallucinating? Her eyes flew open. But no, that rich, gravelly voice was real, and she missed it so much. "Lance, what—"

He stared at her with alarm and pressed his warm hand against her forehead. "You're sweating, and your face is so red it looks like it's going to explode. Come with me right now."

Lance took her hand and led her across the hall to Mia's room. He stopped just outside of the door and put down the padded bag he carried. "Sit down on the floor and I'll get water for you. Mia doesn't need to see you like this." Lance raced through the corridor.

Verena slid to the floor and sat grasping her knees, her head buried against her legs. She couldn't believe how close she had come to murdering Thomas Roper.

Lance returned in a flash with a bottle of water. "Here, drink this." He knelt next to her and opened the bottle, and then smoothed strands of hair that had become plastered to her face. "You're under a lot of pressure. It's okay to crack sometimes. You're not made of stone."

She tipped the bottle of water up and let the water flow

down her throat. It was just what she needed to cool off. What a mess she was. Definitely not in the best shape to see the man who'd been haunting her dreams. "How did you know to come her?"

"Dahlia came to see me. She told me everything. About Mia...and the business."

"Oh, no," she mumbled, and swung her face away from him, acutely embarrassed. Tears pooled in her eyes, and she choked on a sob.

Lance wrapped his arms around her. "Let it out, Verena."

Tentatively, Verena rested against his chest, and found his steady heartbeat calmed her own racing heart. *How I've missed this man.* The familiar scent of his skin brought thoughts of Paris to mind.

Holding her, Lance rubbed her back, whispering to her. "You'll be okay."

Would she ever? Yet after a few minutes, she felt somewhat restored and raised her face to his. "You came to see Mia, so we should go in. She'll be glad to see you."

"I'd hoped you would be here, too." Lance slid his fingers along the line of her jaw.

A flicker of appreciation surfaced and she lifted a corner of her mouth. She was genuinely glad he was here. "Thanks for coming."

"I wish I'd come sooner." His deep voice reverberated in his chest.

"And I wish I'd returned your calls."

"Me, too. But you're forgiven." He grinned and helped her to her feet. He grabbed his bag, and pushed open the door to Mia's room.

"My dear Lance," Mia said, her eyes brimming with delight.

Lance crossed to her and kissed her hand, and then turned to Camille, who sat next to her, and did the same.

"Such a lovely aroma of food always clings to you," Camille said.

Lance opened his padded, zippered bag. "Maybe this is what you smell." He unloaded two large plastic containers and several smaller ones. Verena scooted a table close to the bed for him.

Mia clasped her hands. "Oh, you darling man. The food here is adequate, but certainly not gourmet. I admit I haven't had much of an appetite."

"I thought as much. Unfortunately, I only brought two of everything, but I can divide it three ways. And don't worry, it's all healthy."

"Smells divine," Camille said.

"I'm not really hungry, I had something earlier," Verena said. "Mia and Camille need to eat."

Lance raised an eyebrow toward her, but said nothing. He spread a tablecloth across the surface, added napkins, plates and silverware, and began to assemble the dinner. "This evening you're dining on sesame-crusted wild salmon in a white wine reduction sauce, with fresh pineapple mango salsa. Steamed broccoli on the side, along with quinoa lightly spiked with ginger, garlic, and scallions." After he plated the dinner and served it, Mia waved him to her side.

"You've made my day." Her eyes glistened as she gave him a peck on the cheek.

Verena could swear he blushed. "What, no dessert?" she asked, chiding him.

"How could I have forgotten?" He brought out two containers and opened one with a flourish. "Strawberry tarts with crushed almond crust, spa-style." He withdrew two half-sized bottles and wine glasses. "And, your choice of wine or sparkling water."

"Wine for me," Camille said, her eyes gleaming.

"Sparkling water for me," Mia added. "My medication might react with alcohol."

"Smart lady." Lance poured their requests, and then stepped back to admire his handiwork and watch the two women gush over his meal.

"You're amazing." Verena stood next to him, thankful that he'd come with such a thoughtful treat for Mia.

Mia took a forkful of the quinoa and her eyes fluttered with delight. "Verena, dear, I know you haven't had much to eat, why don't you and Lance go out and have a nice, quiet meal?"

"What a good idea," Lance said, taking Verena's hand. "Actually, I have to return to the hotel to check on a special event. Why don't you come with me?"

The feel of his hand sparked an avalanche of memories in her, but secretly, she was relieved. The vending machine food hadn't been satisfying, and she really needed to leave the hospital before she tried to murder Thomas Roper again.

"We'll be fine," Camille assured her. "I'll look after Mia tonight. And Pierre should be here soon."

"As long as you have two good friends to look after you." Verena bent to kiss Mia good-bye.

Her grandmother cleared her throat. "Verena, there's something you should know."

275

"What is it?" Verena saw Mia and Camille trade a pointed look. "Did you speak to the doctor again?"

"What? Oh no, nothing like that," Mia said. Her face lit with happiness, and she looked like she would burst. "I've been meaning to tell you that Pierre and I are becoming quite serious."

"Why, that's wonderful." Verena gave Mia another kiss on the cheek. Verena was surprised, but why should she be? Mia was a very attractive woman. "As long as you're happy."

Mia blushed. "He's a fine man. He was such a good husband to Ondine, and since both she and Emile are gone, we thought perhaps they wouldn't mind."

After they said their good-byes, Verena and Lance stepped out into the corridor.

"Wait, stop." Verena pressed a hand against Lance's chest. *Oh my God, it's Roper—and Derrick.* Verena pressed herself behind Lance. Her heart was pounding. "I don't want to see them," she whispered. A drama was unfolding before them.

A little way down the hall stood Thomas Roper, dressed in street clothes and cursing at the nurses. By his side was Derrick, wearing gym clothes and sweating as if he'd come straight from the gym.

"I don't care what you tell the doctor," Roper said to a nurse, jabbing the air with a bony finger. "I'm leaving. I'm for too busy for the nonsense. Bullshit, that's what this is, no more than a way for the medical community to line their pockets at my expense."

Derrick stumbled beside him, trying to keep up with the old man. "Sir, wait—"

"Let's go, Derrick. And don't you ever call an

ambulance for me again. Stroke, my ass. It was heartburn." Roper limped angrily through the hall. "Where the hell is Jimmy Don? I've been calling him all day."

"I, I don't know, sir." When Roper stopped at the door, Derrick took the old man's arm to offer support, but Roper jerked away.

"Don't insult me. I can walk by myself. Where's your car?"

"Parked right outside, sir."

"Give me your keys," Roper snapped. "I'll drive."

"Do you think that's a good idea?" Derrick raced ahead to open the door for him.

"Question my judgment again and you'll wish you hadn't."

The nurse that Roper had been berating shook her head. "He shouldn't be driving with those meds in him."

Another nurse snapped her head up. "He's under the influence. I'm calling the police."

Verena watched Derrick and Roper go, relieved that she was through with the despicable pair. She didn't know how she and her family would survive, but some things weren't worth the emotional aggravation. What did Mia always say to her?

Only one life to live, dear.

Verena threaded her hand through the crook in Lance's arm. "Let's go."

29

"Where are the twins?" Lance asked as he steered his convertible sports car out of the hospital parking lot. They'd waited until Derrick and Roper had left before they departed. Lance had the top down, and the summer evening air was mild.

"Anika and Bella are spending the night at a friend's house," Verena said. She ran her hands over her face, acutely aware of how haggard she looked. "They visited the hospital earlier. They've been worried about Mia, so it's good for them to be with friends right now."

"Poor kids, this is a lot for them, too. Let me know if I can help you with them. They're great girls. After I get off I can always make dinner and stay with them if you need to be at the hospital late."

How sweet of him. "It's more like refereeing sometimes."

Lance laughed, shaking his head. "My two brothers and I used to fight, too." He turned into a gas station and eased to a stop. "Hold that thought," he said, touching her hand. "I need to fill up."

A surge of electricity shot through her at his casual touch. She'd almost forgotten how much she enjoyed Lance's company. He lifted her spirits and made her laugh. Most of all, he made her feel appreciated and cared for.

She rested her head against the headrest. Everything had happened at once. The loss of the company, Mia's heart attack. And now she had to find or create work fast. She'd hardly slept in days and was becoming increasingly worried about their financial future. *What will I do?* She wished she could catch her breath, just for a while.

After he filled the gas tank, Lance swung back into the car, and then pulled out of the gas station. As they wound through the dark, quiet streets toward the hotel, flashing emergency lights winked ahead of them. Police cars had blocked off part of the street.

Lance peered ahead. "Looks like an accident just happened."

Verena snapped upright in her seat, instantly alarmed. "Oh, no, those poor people."

"I'm afraid we're going to have to go past it." Traffic had snaked to a crawl with one lane open.

"I hate to see accidents," Verena said, biting a knuckle. Thoughts of her parents' accident reeled back in her mind. Out of habit, she sent up a silent prayer.

"I understand." Lance touched her shoulder, empathizing with her. "Seems pretty bad. Looks like they smashed into the side of that building. Wonder how that happened?"

They rolled nearer and Verena turned away, but not before she saw two sheets covering bodies. *Dead bodies.* It upset her to witness such a horrifying event. She knew how it felt. Who were they? Did they have children waiting for them at home?

Lance squinted ahead. "There's a news crew."

Red lights flashed in Verena's eyes as a news reporter took her place in front of a mangled car and held up a microphone. Verena couldn't help herself; she peered closer. At once she recognized the reporter, who had been a frequent guest at the salon.

She stared past the flashing lights. *That car.* Verena gasped. "I think that's Derrick's Mercedes."

The reporter began speaking. With the convertible top down Lance and Verena could hear her clearly.

"Three, two, one… Hello, I'm Caroline Wilson reporting from Beverly Hills, and I'm on the scene of a one-car accident involving the world's wealthiest venture capitalist, billionaire Thomas Roper, who died just minutes ago. His partner, Derrick Logan, was a passenger in the car, and also died at the scene."

Derrick, dead? A cold wave of reality washed over her. Roper had insisted on driving. Despite her anger at Derrick, her eyes misted. What a dreadful way to die.

Another car screeched to a halt and she saw Greta Hicks of *Fashion Daily News* race to the crime scene in hysterics. "Let me through," she screamed. "Derrick Logan is my boyfriend. I was on the phone with him when it happened."

Verena stared transfixed, trying to look away but unable to break her gaze. *An hour ago, I nearly killed Roper.* Had she succeeded, Caroline Wilson would be reporting a far different story.

She watched Greta race to the scene. Evidently Derrick had never stopped dating Greta while they'd been engaged. He'd lied to her about that, too. Greta must have been the woman he called *babe.* Verena blinked. There was a time when that would have upset her, but now she was numb to an emotion as trivial as jealousy. She actually felt sorry for Greta. She blinked again, tearing her eyes from the grisly scene.

"What goes around, comes around." Lance shook his head as they passed the scene.

"My father used to say that. But never has it happened so quickly." Verena trembled, shaken at what she'd witnessed. *Karma.* That's what Mia called it. She wiped her eyes. Roper's evil deeds had turned on him, thus he had earned his demise.

Lance grew quiet as they drove on. Presently he said, "I know I offered to take you out for dinner, but if you're too tired, or upset, I can take you home and cook for you." He rested a hand on her shoulder. "I could pick you up in the morning and take you back to the hospital for your car."

His amber eyes harnessed the golden glow of the streetlight, reflecting their warmth. "Thanks," she said. "But if you don't mind, I'd rather not be alone tonight."

Lance took her hand gently in his. "That can be arranged."

When they reached the Beverly Hills Hotel, Lance drove around to the rear entry to park. They wound through the hotel to the kitchen, and he led her into his office, which was located off the kitchen. "I have to check on the event in the ballroom, but you can wait here."

Reaching behind his desk, he withdrew a bottle of cabernet sauvignon, uncorked it, and poured a glass for her. "Looks like you could use this. I'll be right back."

Verena sipped the wine, thankful for the calming effect it had on her. Her lips quivered and she realized she'd been shivering with shock, even though the night was warm.

A few minutes later, Lance returned with a small loaf of sliced rosemary bread, olive oil, nuts, and shaved parmesan cheese. "I don't want you to starve while I'm gone."

Unsettled by the accident, Verena ate slowly and sipped wine. Though the red flags had been waving during her relationship with Derrick, it hadn't been long since she'd discovered who he really was. Had he ever been genuine with her? Had he ever cared for her? Or had that just been a ploy to further his career and line his pockets?

After what Scarlett had told her, and seeing Greta tonight, the true picture came into focus for her. Derrick had never been honest with her. In the end, she thought, what a sad life he'd lived. She shook her head and took another sip.

By the time Lance returned, she'd managed to eat a few nuts and a couple of slices of bread with olive oil and cheese.

"Feeling better?" he asked, kneading her shoulders.

"I am, thanks." She smiled up at him. Just being around him soothed her spirits. She should have listened to her heart earlier. From now on, she would.

His eyes danced as if he had a secret. "Everything is running smoothly," he said. "The hotel isn't full, so would you like to stay here tonight? You could relax and have a swim—with me as your lifeguard, of course. No more repeat performances of that stunt you pulled at the pool in Paris."

"I don't know..." She hesitated, although she had to admit the idea sounded wonderful.

Yet Lance wasn't giving up. "We can have a good dinner and I'll arrange a massage for you afterward. You won't be alone tonight, but I'll be a gentleman, I swear."

Her heart warmed at the thought of spending the night

with him. Although her initial inclination had been to decline his offer, she remembered what Mia always said. *You only go around once.* "I'd like that," she said.

A grin lit his face. He reached into his pocket and pulled out a key. "A bungalow is ours for the night. I also called the hospital and told them that if they can't reach your mobile phone, to call you here at the hotel." He lifted a clean shirt and a pair of pants from the back of his door.

Verena suppressed a smile. He thought of everything. She looked down at her yoga pants and tank top, soiled from the day's wear. Almost everything.

Lance seemed to read her mind. "There are shops downstairs where you can pick up a change of clothing and anything else you might need."

She smoothed her hand along his muscular forearm. "Come with me?"

Lance covered her hand with his. "I'm all yours. And it's my treat. You've had a rough time."

She stared at him as if seeing him in a new light. He'd done so many thoughtful things for her and Mia today.

As they walked, Lance told her about the historic hotel. They strolled past the old fountain shop, and Verena couldn't help but smile as she admired the whimsical wallpaper with its pattern of green tropical leaves—a vintage throwback to the hotel's early days.

"A lot of celebrities sipped sodas at that counter," Lace said. "Elizabeth Taylor, Marilyn Monroe, and Princess Grace—even the Beatles. The hotel opened in 1912, so it's seen several waves of celebrities and local residents over the years."

Verena liked watching how Lance interacted with

people. His easy going style was light years from the way Derrick had dealt with others. Why had she ever wasted her time on Derrick?

Derrick. God rest his troubled soul.

She stopped by a stairway and kissed Lance lightly on the lips.

"What's that for?" he asked, surprise registering on his face.

She kissed him again. "For preparing dinner for Mia. For whisking me away when I desperately needed it. For tonight." She ran a finger down his chest, savoring their time together, however limited it might be. She'd have to return to reality tomorrow. The reality of Mia's recuperation, the reinvention of her career—whatever that might be—and too many bills to pay. But for tonight, at least she would not be alone.

Soon she found a boutique that appealed to her, and Lance helped her choose two outfits and a swimsuit, as well as matching sandals. While he browsed for swimwear, she slipped a sexy silk negligee she saw on sale into the bag. The saleswoman winked at her.

After they left the shop, Lance guided Verena through the hotel's manicured gardens, which overflowed with a riot of flowers, and past a rippling tiered fountain into the section where the pink stucco bungalows were located.

"Here we are," he said, opening a door. He scooped her up in his arms and stepped inside.

Verena was caught by surprise, but she loved his spontaneity. She felt light in his strong arms. The last few days had been a nightmare. All she wanted was to relax, have a good meal, and get a good night's sleep. *And feel these incredible arms around me.*

Drawing closer to him, their lips found each other's naturally. The moment he touched her mouth with his own was magic, and all the delights of Paris rushed back to her. This was the man she wanted.

"I really needed this break." She kissed him again. *And I need to laugh with a handsome chef*, she decided, adding to her list.

He put her down gently. "Hungry?"

"Starving, but I'd like to take a bath first." She needed to wash off the vile scents of Thomas Roper, Derrick Logan, and death.

Verena turned around and caught her breath, delighted at the spacious, sumptuous interior. A gleaming marble foyer stretched before them. A fireplace graced the sitting area, and a chandelier cast a soft, sparkling glow throughout the room. To one side was the kitchen and a dining area, and the bedroom was in the rear.

While she explored the bungalow, Lance opened a bottle of chilled champagne that had been delivered to the room.

Verena slipped off her shoes, curling her toes into the creamy thick carpet. The jade green marble bathroom had a deep soaking tub and a separate glass shower large enough for two. She leaned in to smell a bouquet of fresh lilies, trailed her fingers along the plush canopied bed, and pushed open a pair of French doors.

"We have our own private pool," Verena said, stepping into the enclosed patio. Tropical plants, twin topiaries, and an espaliered lemon tree were dotted around the space. An outdoor shower awaited them off to one side. She found herself thinking that people could fall in love here, and wondered how many people had.

"I feel an after dinner swim calling to me." Lance handed her a glass of champagne. "By the way, your bath is running, *mademoiselle*." He ran a hand down the length of her arm, and she felt a thrill at his touch. He'd put on jazz music, and she could hear the water running in the bathroom.

She shook her head in amazement. "Do you always think of everything?"

"I try to. I'm in the hospitality business, so I'm trained to anticipate what people might like to make them comfortable." Slipping a finger into her waistband, he tugged her toward him. "But for you, it's my pleasure."

Verena closed her eyes and sank into his embrace. His chest was firm against her touch, and she found herself remembering what he'd looked like at the Villa and Hôtel Majestic in Paris without a shirt. *Or pants.*

Lance ran his hands down her back, kneading the muscles between her shoulder blades. "You feel tense. I've booked a massage for you in the morning. But if you'd like one tonight, I'm happy to oblige."

"You're full service, aren't you?" Verena caught herself and blushed at her own remark. Should she rush into another relationship? Or was she being hasty? Maybe he didn't even want a girlfriend. And she came with a houseful of baggage, or so Derrick had told her. A dozen different scenarios rushed through her mind before she put a stop to them.

She thought of her parents and how their life had been cut short, and she couldn't help thinking of Derrick and

Roper and their accident tonight. Pushing her thoughts aside, she decided to live for today and for the loving man who stood before her now. *The essence of life is as fleeting as a heartbeat.* She sighed, enjoying the feel of Lance's arms around her.

Verena nuzzled against his neck and considered her grandmother's notion of kismet. A thought struck her. *What if Lance is the man I'm destined for?*

He kissed her on the cheek and let his lips linger against her neck. "Before we get seriously sidetracked, go bathe and relax. I'll hang up your new clothes."

"You're too much." She pulled away from him with a pang of regret.

After he left, Verena strolled into the bathroom. She checked her mobile phone, but there were no calls. Mia was probably resting.

Easing into the warm, verbena-scented water, Verena closed her eyes, reveling in the pure pleasure of the moment and hardly wondering what might happen next.

30

After hanging up the clothes they'd bought, Lance brought a bowl of strawberries to Verena. Bubbles were up to her chin and she was humming along with the music. He smiled at her, thinking she was the most genuine, beautiful woman he'd ever known.

She'd been knocked down hard and didn't deserve it. If he'd give him a chance, he'd gladly spend the rest of her life making it up to her.

Sitting on the edge of the tub, he picked out the juiciest, most succulent berry and held it out to her. He'd had a fruit plate delivered with the champagne. "Here's a little nosh to make sure you don't starve before dinner."

Verena caught it with her teeth and took a bite. "Mmm, delicious. Truly nature's dessert."

"You haven't seen anything yet." He kissed her and paused by the door, framing the image of her in the bubble bath in his mind, wanting to remember this moment forever. *Because this is just the beginning...*

Lance wandered outside to give her privacy to bathe and dress. He gazed up at the stars, thinking that he was the luckiest man alive. Tonight, he didn't want to hurry the evening, or put undue pressure on her. *I'd rather have the rest of our lives together*, he thought.

Was this even a possibility?

He wished he'd met her before she had to go through a relationship with a jerk like Derrick. Based on what he'd overheard between him and Roper that day in the hotel dining room, he was convinced Derrick had never meant to marry her, and had only used her to finagle her company for Herringbone.

Lance wished he had it in his power to wipe her slate clean. Instead, he would make it up to her by showing her what a wonderful woman she truly was. If he got the chance, he would treasure her for the rest of her life.

While Verena was bathing, Lance stepped outside to enjoy the night sky. With a clear sky overhead, the stars blazed with clear intensity, reflecting the way he felt on the inside. He spied the outdoor shower near the pool. The entire patio was enclosed with a high stucco wall for complete privacy. *Perfect.*

He hated to infringe on Verena's restorative solitude in the bathroom and the thought of an outdoor shower under the stars appealed to him. He stripped off his clothes and turned on the water.

Holding his head under the shower head, he let warm water glide off his back. Small bottles of shampoo and liquid soap sat on a ledge, so he lathered his hair, soaped up, and then ducked under the shower to rinse. He stood, letting the water pummel his back and enjoying how it felt. It wasn't until after he'd turned off the water that he thought about a towel.

"Damn," he muttered. He heard Verena giggle behind him.

"Looking for this?"

Lance glanced over his shoulder without turning to face her. "Oh, yeah, I completely forgot."

Verena stood in the doorway wrapped in a hotel robe.

She dangled a terry cloth towel from her fingertips—and looked far too sexy. Her dark sapphire eyes danced over his body with glee. "So, come and get it." She moistened her lips and swung the towel, playfully taunting him.

He pushed his wet hair back from his forehead. "If that's what you want." He began to turn toward her.

She screamed and flung the towel at him before racing back inside, her delightful laughter filling the air.

He caught the towel in midair and dried his hair and skin. Her laughter—warm and radiant as sunshine—tinkled in his ears and brought a smile to his face.

He hadn't heard her laugh since Paris.

If that was all he accomplished, he'd count the night a success. From what he'd seen, she'd been under far too much pressure for far too long. Although he wouldn't have wished death on Derrick, it was exactly what the man deserved for the way he'd treated Verena.

This was a woman who should be cherished. And he meant to do exactly that.

He wrapped the towel around his hips and stepped inside. "Got an extra robe?"

Verena peeked from the bathroom and handed him a bathrobe. "And where do you plan on sleeping?" she asked, laughing again.

Two can play at this game. "I think you'll be comfortable on the couch," he said, chuckling.

"Oh, you!" She lobbed a strawberry at him, and he caught it in his hand. As he bit into the berry, he wondered how the night would unfold.

31

Still laughing over the towel incident, Verena shut the bathroom door and sat in front of the vanity mirror. Brushing her damp hair back, she savored the image in her mind of Lance showering in the moonlight.

While she'd stood in the doorway watching him, long-repressed desire had surged through her. She'd enjoyed every minute and waited until he'd finished, liking what she saw. He hadn't known she was there until after he'd turned off the water. She giggled to herself again. She loved his playful nature.

Yet a question nagged the practical side of her mind, and she couldn't help but wonder if this was the right time for them. Her tattered emotions were raw from the ordeals she'd been through, beginning with the loss of her friend and banker, Marvin Panetta, and the ensuing financial disaster. Derrick's duplicity, Herringbone's take-over, Mia's heart attack. Her life had spiraled out of control.

In fact, she'd nearly committed murder a few hours ago. Was she in the right frame of mind to think clearly tonight?

Or was this exactly what she needed to soothe her battered soul?

As she'd watched Lance shower under the stars, she'd felt an emotion that was more than desire, more than sexual attraction. Is this what Mia had felt for Emile? What her father had felt for her mother?

Was it love? She wasn't quite sure, but she was sure of one thing. Being with him made her happy—simply happy, as if she belonged with him, and vice versa. Was that love?

She stared at her reflection in the mirror, imagining the answer might somehow emerge from her heart, but nothing was forthcoming.

Lance was dressed by the time she came out of the bathroom. He wore brushed black denim jeans and a white shirt that showed off his tanned face and sun-streaked hair. His amber eyes gleamed with appreciation of her. Although she'd dried her hair, she still wore her bathrobe.

"Your clothes are in the closet," he said, a grin playing on his lips. "Can't wait to see you in them." He shut the bedroom door behind him.

Verena opened the closet door and selected one of the outfits he'd bought for her. It was an ivory linen sundress that skimmed her slim figure and swirled around her ankles. She swept her long, wavy hair over her shoulder and stepped into the new, strappy high-heeled sandals. Turning to look at herself in the mirror, she saw a woman who now had hope in her eyes.

Smiling with satisfaction, she opened the bedroom door.

Lance let out a low whistle. "Magnificent," he said. "You look like an angel."

She kissed him lightly. "You're the angel, thank you."

Slipping his arm around her, he asked, "Do you have your phone with you in case Mia needs you?"

"I do." She kissed him again. "Thanks for being concerned."

"If we have to return to the hospital, the hotel driver

can take us." Lance took her hand in his.

"After your gourmet meal, I think Mia will sleep well tonight. And the doctor seems confident about her status."

They left the bungalow and strolled hand in hand to the main pool area, which was deserted at this time of night and where they'd first met.

Lance hugged her to his side. "I remember the first time I saw you here."

She smiled up at him. "Must have been kismet."

He escorted her into a private cabana with a striped green and white canvas awning, where a candlelit table for two had been set up. As they sat down, he said to her, "I think my kitchen team is nervous about serving us tonight."

"Why?"

"Guess I'm a tough customer." He threaded his fingers with hers.

Verena inclined her head, studying the serious expression on his face. "I haven't seen that side of you."

"I'm exacting, and I ask for excellence, because that's what our guests expect. Though if I have to correct an employee, I try to be positive, yet direct. And I always tell people when they do perform well. It's an art, I must say."

"That I understand."

He laughed. "They shouldn't be nervous though, because I couldn't be more relaxed tonight. I'm with the most beautiful woman in the world."

"Are you happy?" She searched his face for confirmation that he felt the way she did.

His eyes reflected the flickering candle light. "Infinitely happy. And you? You're had a rough time lately."

"That's true, but at the moment, here with you, I feel

hope for the first time in I can't remember how long." She closed her eyes and met his lips. A warm feeling rippled throughout her body.

"I share that sentiment," Lance said. "And I promise we'll dine in a leisurely fashion this evening."

The dinner was served in several courses that he had specially designed and directed. None of the dishes were on the menu; they were his own creations.

The first course was tomato bisque with fresh basil made from the ripest produce of the season, followed by a stacked tower of avocado, sushi, chopped lettuce, and melon garnished with caviar and surrounded with a slightly spicy mango sauce.

"Delicious," Verena said, taking a bite.

"It's a warm evening, so I thought you might like this," Lance said, when a half dome of crushed ice studded with fresh seafood was delivered. He poured more wine—a French Chassagne-Montrachet made from chardonnay grapes that Verena immediately decided was her favorite.

The full moon cast a glow over the main pool, and Verena watched an occasional breeze coax smooth currents across the surface. The evening was the perfect book-end to a dreadful period of time she hoped was behind her.

Biting her lip, she realized tonight might be all they would ever have. She couldn't be the kind of girlfriend he might want. She had Anika, Bella, and Mia to provide for— too many responsibilities for any man she'd ever known.

As long as Mia's recovery was on track—and it looked like it was—she had to look to the future. She wasn't sure what tomorrow would bring, but for tonight, she would put aside her to-do list and simply enjoy Lance's company.

Reaching for his hand on the table, she twined her fingers with his, and he lifted her hand to his face, kissing her fingertips as he did.

When a server brought dessert, Verena exclaimed over the chocolate mousse drizzled with raspberry liqueur.

"What's a fine dinner without dessert?" Lance's eyes crinkled with pleasure as he watched her.

As they enjoyed the dessert, Lance asked her about the twins, chuckling as she told him about Anika and Bella's silly exploits. She told him about her parents, and then about Mia and Emile, and the great love they'd had.

Lance told her about his parents in La Jolla and his two brothers who lived in San Francisco and San Diego, respectively. He spoke about them with such affection and this impressed Verena.

Although the moon was high in the night sky by the time they finished dinner, Lance asked, "Feel like a swim in our private pool?"

"That's the perfect end to the evening." *Well, almost perfect.* Her eyes roved over his firm physique, and she imagined what it would be like to—she stopped herself. Live in the moment, she reminded herself.

After strolling back to the bungalow, Verena slipped into the brightly patterned Pucci bikini she'd bought at the boutique. She met Lance at the pool and saw that he'd already changed into his swimsuit. She glided into the water, stroking from one end to another. Lance joined in, and they swam together for a few minutes until Verena paused at one end.

"It feels so good to stretch out through the water." She breathed in, savoring the moonlit scene around her and the handsome man by her side.

Lance shook water from his thick hair and pushed it back. With a fluid motion, he lifted her and eased her against his chest, their faces nearly touching.

As if it were the most natural thing to do, Verena closed her eyes and found his lips, caressing them with her own. Lance responded, deepening their kiss, and Verena was transported into another dimension of pure pleasure.

Before long, their swimsuits vanished. A blissful moan escaped Verena's lips as the water sluiced across her skin. The freedom of nudity heightened their desire, and Lance swept her from the pool and onto a cushioned chaise lounge.

Moonlight dusted Lance's powerful torso and his bronzed skin glowed against her fair, porcelain skin.

"If you're uncomfortable, we don't have to go on," he murmured.

She couldn't imagine breaking the spell, and urged him on, reveling in such passion as she'd never known. Every touch of his skin charged her with emotion.

Lance lifted himself above her, whispering his love for her, nuzzling her neck, her décolletage, her stomach. She stroked his broad back, marveling at how his powerful muscles rippled beneath his skin. What a beautiful man.

After making love, they lay sated in the warm night air, taking full advantage of the cocooned privacy. They were languid, in no hurry to move.

Finally, Lance scooped her into his arms and carried her to bed. Verena snuggled beside him under a fluffy, down-filled duvet, her hand splayed across his chest, her body formed to his. Drifting off, she dreamed she was sleeping on a cloud, folded into the tender embrace of angel's wings.

Hours later, against a dawning coral sky, they made love again. As Verena stretched in bed, Lance made cappuccinos for them.

"Ready for a morning swim?" He handed her a steaming cup.

"Hmm, sounds perfect."

After they finished their cappuccino, they swam in the nude in their private pool. Later, they dried in the sun's rays and traded massages. Verena loved the feel of his skin under her hands.

"Strawberries are in season," Lance murmured as they lay tangled together in bed. It was a decadent way to start the day, and now Lance was tempting her yet again—this time with his macadamia-encrusted French toast topped with strawberries. "I'll have my kitchen staff send ingredients."

"I could live here, you know." Verena stretched her limbs, drinking in the long expanse of Lance's well-toned body.

"Many people have."

"Just not on my budget," she said, laughing. She couldn't remember having laughed as much as she had since she'd arrived here with Lance. Being with him simply felt good.

"It doesn't take much to be happy," he said, kissing her on the tip of her nose. Lance rolled off the bed and plopped a robe onto the bed beside her. "In case you get cold." He shrugged into a matching robe before padding off barefoot to the bungalow kitchen.

Verena called Mia to check on her and Pierre answered the phone, saying that he'd spent the night on a cot next to her hospital bed. They chatted a little, and then Pierre put Mia on the phone. Verena was pleased to hear her sounding stronger. *And happy.*

After she hung up the phone, she turned on the television while Lance made breakfast. She flicked over to the local news channel, which was featuring the reporter who had been a guest at the salon—the same reporter she and Lance had passed at the scene of Derrick and Roper's accident. Verena moved closer to the television.

An image of the salon flashed across the screen as Caroline Wilson spoke. "The former chief operating officer of Valent Swiss Skincare, the Beverly Hills-based salon that was the subject of a recent take-over by Herringbone Capital, Jimmy Don Herald has been arrested today for the murder of Marvin Panetta, who was the CEO of National Western Bank."

Verena gasped. She'd known in her heart that Marvin wasn't the type to commit suicide, and now her faith in him had been vindicated.

The reporter continued. "Citing evidence found on Panetta's computer, police say Herald killed Panetta when the banker decided to go to authorities to report Herringbone Capital's illegal practices and threats. The coroner originally ruled Panetta's death a suicide, but the evidence points to Herald as a prime murder suspect. If convicted, Herald will be subject to life in prison."

Verena folded her arms, at once both shocked and satisfied with Jimmy Don's arrest. He'd always made her uncomfortable, and he had a blatant disregard for human kindness, morality, and the law.

Karma had caught up with Jimmy Don, too.

"In a related story," the reporter went on, "the deaths of Herringbone Capital partners Thomas Roper and Derrick Logan have paved the way for a portfolio acquisition by White-Weber, another local venture capital firm. Last month an earlier offer was turned down, but a White-Weber representative says he believes Herringbone investors will likely vote for a sale now."

Verena turned off the television, not caring to hear the rest of the story—it was too painful. Besides, it made no difference. She was on her own.

They ate by the pool and after bathing, Verena put on her other new outfit, a gauzy peach, one-shouldered sundress, and wound her hair into a bun. She packed her few things, including the new negligee she hadn't needed after all. When she put on her sunglasses, Lance told her she looked like a celebrity. "Watch out for the paparazzi lurking around the perimeter of the hotel."

As she and Lance prepared to leave, Verena cast an appreciative glance around the bungalow. It had been a perfect *intermezzo*. And now, Lance was going with her to see Mia again. Verena hoped her grandmother would continue to improve.

Lance cupped her face in his hands, his thumbs stroking her face. "You're so special to me," he murmured, his voice thick with emotion. "You have been from the moment I first saw you. It was all I could do to contain myself in Paris. I want to spend every free moment with you then, and I still do today."

Verena felt exactly the same way. *This is real.* She traced the length of his back, feeling the warmth of his skin through the thin shirt fabric. *This feels so right; this is love.* Her lips parting, she closed her eyes and found his mouth, silencing their words.

As they strolled to Lance's car and she slid in, another thought surged in her mind. Their timing was still all wrong. Now more than ever, she needed to commit herself to creating another career. How else would she and the girls survive? Although Mia had offered her retirement money to Verena, taking any part of the funds Mia had set aside for her retirement violated Verena's deepest principles.

Verena was worried. She couldn't share with Mia or the twins just how desperate their circumstances were. And the four of them were just too much responsibility for any man.

Even though Scarlett had assured her that the loss of the business was not her fault, that Herringbone had wronged her, Verena still blamed herself.

The fact remained that it was Verena's responsibility to provide the household income, and right now, she had no idea how she was going to do that.

Until she did, she could not permit herself the luxury of dating this man, no matter how much she cared for him.

Her family needed her.

As Lance pulled into her driveway, he put the car in park and turned to her. "You've been awfully quiet on the drive back."

"I have a lot to do once I open that front door. My life is pretty full, Lance."

He squeezed her hand. "I know it is. That's part of why I admire you so much. You handle great responsibilities with grace."

Verena kissed him softly and pulled away. Her heart shattered as she took the first step to do what she knew she must. "Lance, we have to talk," she began.

"Of course. What's on your mind?"

"This has been a wonderful, magical interlude, and you have no idea how thankful I am for all you've done." Biting her lip, she went on. "I have so much to do, I don't how we can keep seeing each other."

"Haven't I heard this before?" Lance asked, rubbing his chin.

"It's not that I don't care deeply for you, I do. But I have to focus on providing for my family first. I love them all, but they're a handful. You don't know what boisterous twins are really like. And when Mia returns, she'll need a lot of help." She pressed a hand to her heart and looked away. "We can't keep this up, and you deserve more."

"I understand a lot more than you realize." Lance took her hand and stroked it. "But you should know that I'm also a man who keeps his promises."

Unable to contain her emotions, Verena tore herself from him. Fleeing from the car, she didn't look back, even when she reached her front door.

32

Verena suffered through the next week in a blur of action. Between taking the girls to school, preparing dinner and washing clothes, helping them with homework, visiting Mia, talking with physicians, managing finances, and looking for work, she was exhausted.

She was sure she'd made the right decision again about Lance, but that didn't lessen the pervasive pain in her heart.

That day, she'd hurried from the car to the house so that he wouldn't see her break down. It wasn't until after he'd left and she'd dried her tears that she wondered what he'd meant about keeping promises.

After Mia's physician approved her release from the hospital, Verena gathered her grandmother's personal items from the room. "Ready to go home?"

"Indeed I am," Mia said. "I just wish I didn't have to leave in a wheelchair. I'm fine now." She picked up her handbag, a new one that Pierre had given her as a surprise. "Pierre is bringing dinner to me this evening at the house. You should go out with your friends. Speaking of which, how is that handsome young man, Lance? I look forward to seeing more of him."

"Not anytime soon, I'm afraid." Verena cast her eyes down, busying herself with Mia's books. Lance hadn't even called her this time. She dragged her thoughts back.

Mia threw her a curious look, but before she could say anything, the door opened, and Dr. Omondi stepped inside.

"We're going to miss you around here, Mrs. Valent."
Dr. Omondi sat next to Mia and rolled up the sleeve of her
white jacket, exposing the faded scar that Mia had been
treating with her special serum. "My skin is markedly
improved. What did you say is in your serum?"

Verena stood to one side, listening. She was interested
in hearing a doctor's perspective.

"That's my secret, doctor," Mia said. "It's something
I've blended by hand for years. Only recently my chemist
told me that it's now technically possible to suspend the
ingredients in a formula stable enough to be made in larger
quantities."

The doctor ran her fingers across her skin. "In my
professional opinion, this is the most effective topical
product I've seen." She scrutinized Mia's face, touching her
cheeks and forehead. "Your skin texture and elasticity is
amazing, too. You say you've been using this for years?"

Mia smiled with pride. "I have."

"You've spoken to your chemist again?" Verena
fastened Mia's skincare bag and looped it over her shoulder.
"I don't recall that."

"That's because we didn't discuss it. You were so busy,
Verena."

They said good-bye to the doctor and promised to
keep in touch about the serum. Verena wheeled Mia from
the hospital. To Verena's relief, she didn't ask about Lance
again.

During the short drive home, Verena's mind began to
whir. Mia told her all about the recent tests and new
formulations, as well as the payment terms the
manufacturer would extend to them.

As she listened to Mia talk, Verena began to grow excited. This could be a real opportunity, as long as the serum wasn't considered an asset of VSS. That was almost too much to hope for.

After Verena helped Mia into her room and made her comfortable, she sat by Mia and phoned Scarlett to tell her about the serum.

"Scarlett, I have you on speakerphone with Mia. Is there anything in those documents I signed that would stop us from developing a new line around Mia's formula?"

Scarlett was quiet for a moment before she spoke. "You signed the intellectual property agreements, Verena, but they only pertained to you. No mention was made of Mia. Does anyone else know of this serum?"

"Only my chemist," Mia said. "This is my personal formula."

Verena took Mia's smooth hand in hers. "Think carefully. Did you develop it before or after you worked at the salon?"

"Many years afterward." Mia nodded her assurance.

"Did you use the same chemist?" Scarlett asked.

Mia raised her brows. "No, I found a charming woman who's a top notch chemist to work on it for me."

Scarlett said, "Would she have thought she was making it for Valent?"

"Certainly not," Mia said, her eyes brightening and nodding with more enthusiasm than Verena had seen in her in a long time. "I paid her myself. And I was very careful about retaining all of my rights."

Verena leaned closer to the speakerphone. "Scarlett, I'm going to find a way to manufacture this line.

Herringbone can't keep Mia's products off the market. Or any that I develop after I'm gone, right?"

"No, but they can sue you if you sell into any of your old accounts. Including all the ones you spoke to or pitched in any way. Even though Roper and Derrick are gone, the agreements remain in place for the new owners."

That covered all the best retailers, large and small. "I have something else in mind," Verena said.

"Wouldn't be surprised if the new owners of VSS ask you to come back on board after Roper's estate is probated," Scarlett said. "They're a good company."

Verena was so excited about this new prospect, she wasn't sure she'd want to return to VSS even if asked. The new owners were another large company, and she preferred her independence. Unless this idea couldn't be produced.

"Looks like you have the green light on the serum," Scarlett said. "So go get busy."

"You bet I will." Verena gave Mia a hug. She had plenty of reasons to yield to depression, but seeing Mia happy and at home again spurred her on. *I can do this,* she told herself.

After they finished talking to Scarlett, Mia wanted to nap. The neighbor had given the twins a ride home from school, and Anika and Bella were busy in their room with homework.

With the house quiet, Verena took a pad of paper, sat at the kitchen table, and began to sketch ideas and tally numbers for a new line. She had good relationships with suppliers, and thought she could obtain payment terms, maybe thirty to ninety days.

She made a phone call to one of her former suppliers

for containers and packaging. They had heard about what had happened at VSS and were shocked that she was no longer part of the company.

After she told them about the new products she wanted to develop, they promised to extend generous terms. They also agreed to help her create packaging mockups that she could use to demonstrate and sell.

It wasn't much, but it was a start. She wouldn't need to pay for packaging or the serum and accompanying products for three months. They could start small with a minimum order. She let out a little sigh of relief. That wasn't much time, and there was still a lot to do.

Feeling somewhat buoyed, she turned her thoughts to sales and distribution. Although she couldn't sell to the stores that carried VSS products, some of the buyers she knew had moved on to other companies.

However, inventory was expensive to produce, and then she'd need working capital for co-op advertising, sales commissions, and training—which she knew she couldn't obtain. Selling in department stores, or even boutiques, required far too much money, even if she had ninety-day terms from her supplier and manufacturer. No, there had to be another way.

She tapped her pencil on the pad, thinking and staring into space.

What if she could multiply her efforts without hiring people in the field for sales and support? She thought about online sales. With targeted advertising, that was a real possibility. Sales could ramp up over time. Then her eyes rested on the small television in the kitchen.

An idea began to form, and one word floated to the

forefront of her mind. *Infomercial.*

She'd met one of the top infomercial producers, Wilhelmina Jones, a few years ago at a cosmetic industry event and had been impressed with her professionalism. This woman's company could manage television production, as well as order fulfillment.

The last time she'd seen Wilhelmina was the night of the Cosmetic Executives Worldwide event for the Women in Pink Foundation, where she'd been honored. They'd spoken briefly.

That was the same night she'd met Lance.

Reeling her thoughts back, Verena ran her fingers across her forehead. While an infomercial might not seem as upscale as the VSS high-end retail accounts, she'd heard successful ones made quite a lot of money. She could also raise the bar for excellence. The more she thought of it, the more the personal connection with customers inherent in an infomercial and direct distribution model intrigued her. She'd also have more flexible time to spend with her family, an idea she found most appealing.

If Wilhelmina had interest in her idea and could provide capital. And *if* she wasn't on the non-compete list.

Sucking in a breath, Verena quickly pulled up the document on her laptop. Searching it, she was thrilled to see that Wilhelmina's name or company were not on it.

Dahlia's grandmother knew Wilhelmina, too. Surely Camille would have her direct phone number. Verena called Dahlia and told her about her idea. "What do you think?"

"That sounds like a real opportunity, and you'd be great on camera," Dahlia said. "Wilhelmina might be interested, and she has a good reputation in the business world. I have her direct number right here."

Verena jotted the number down. "We might even add perfume to the line, something subtle and Zen-like. Would you be interested in supplying it?"

"Count me in. We could create an organic spa collection for you."

Verena grinned. Her idea was taking shape. "We should have coffee soon and talk about this."

"How about lunch tomorrow? I'm meeting Scarlett and Fianna at the Polo Lounge. Johnny has a table for us."

As much as Verena enjoyed it there, that was the last place she wanted to go now. After she'd broken off her relationship with Lance, seeing him would be far too painful.

"I'd love to, Dahlia, but I'm on a budget now." That much was certainly true. "Come over this weekend. I'll brew a huge pot of coffee and make brunch. The twins have also been baking Swiss pastries."

"Sounds great," Dahlia. "And let me know how it goes with Wilhelmina."

Verena hung up and gathered her thoughts. She blew out a breath to calm her nerves before she made the call.

An assistant answered and transferred her to Wilhelmina. Verena quickly pitched her idea in a couple of succinct sentences. Wilhelmina seemed interested and asked for more details, so she pushed on.

"Everyone knows Valent Swiss Skincare, and our new serum is more advanced than anything we've ever done. We're planning an entire line around it."

"I'd like to hear more," Wilhelmina said. "Mia is well known, and I'd like to showcase you on the air. Frankly, we could use an upscale skincare line at a higher price point. We can spin a story about how you left the company to create something even more special with your grandmother, who is an industry legend. Do you have any celebrity endorsements?"

"I sure do." Verena thought of her friend, the model Penelope Plessen, and other actresses and models she knew. And Dr. Omondi, who she thought would be good on camera, if she were amenable to it.

"Excellent. Are you free to meet tomorrow morning?"

Verena agreed, and then hung up the phone and did a little victory dance around the kitchen. She'd call Dahlia and let her know she'd gotten an appointment.

Mia had always said that a good name was worth more than gold, and in this case, their reputation was definitely opening doors for them. She'd brainstorm with Mia about a new name for the company and the product line.

Before she could call Dahlia back, she heard Mia's phone ring in her room. Mia answered it, and her animated voice floated through the house to Verena. Overhearing the conversation, she gathered that it was Lance.

"I'll have to think about that," Mia said. "I always loved my friend Julia Child's beef bourguignon and coq au vin. She was a VSS client in the early days." Mia paused, listening. "Why, yes, I love surprises. I'll see you in a few days then."

Raking her teeth over her bottom lip, Verena wondered how she'd manage to avoid him, yet she told herself again that this was for the best. Lance had cooked for Mia in the hospital, so what was the harm in her grandmother talking to him? He'd clearly promised her that he would make or deliver dinner one night.

Promised. Maybe that was the promise he'd mentioned that he would keep. Mia had a right to her friends, so Verena decided she'd simply make herself scarce that evening.

Yet as Verena stared from the window, she couldn't help remembering their magical night in the beautiful pink bungalow. She still ached with longing for him, for the touch of his hand, the sound of his laughter, the feel of his skin under her fingertips. She wished she could share this good news with him, but Mia probably would. He would understand how much this opportunity meant to her, in a way that Derrick never could have.

She recalled their visit to Paris. Lance had been so at ease with Mia, and Anika and Bella adored him. That day it had almost seemed as if they were a family. Verena sighed.

Yet if she believed that, she was deluding herself. *Too much baggage.* That was her lot in life as far as men were concerned. She loved her family, and there wasn't anything she wouldn't do to protect them and their way of life.

Though she'd denied her feelings, she couldn't deny that Lance had lodged himself in her heart. Verena rested her chin in the palm of her hand, her decision weighing heavily on her mind.

The next day, Verena chose her clothes with care. She dressed as if she would be on camera—that was the look Wilhelmina would want to see. She put on a vibrant red, Diane von Fürstenberg wrap dress and stepped into her red-soled, black Louboutin heels. In the beauty industry, a woman had to know her business *and* look chic and glamorous.

As a finishing touch, she applied cherry red lipstick and looped her mother's pearls around her neck for good luck. Fianna's friend, Elena, had done a beautiful job repairing the antique clasp. Today marked a new beginning for her career and her life, and she wanted a memento of her mother with her.

Brushing her hair from her face, she gazed into the mirror. It was time she pursued her own career dream. She needed this break for financial reasons, but she also wanted to prove her talent. Not only that, she wanted to take some business classes to learn more. She'd hardly slept last night—ideas and visions had been racing through her mind. She couldn't remember the last time she'd felt so inspired. Excitement surged though her.

When she arrived at the Sunset Boulevard offices of Wilhelmina Jones and Company, an assistant ushered her into Wilhelmina's office. A large glass table served as a desk, surrounded by potted palms and antique Persian rugs. Awards and skincare products filled a bookshelf.

"Verena, it's nice to see you again." Wilhelmina still wore her jet-black hair short with vivid burgundy streaks. She was a stylish CEO, and was often photographed for business and fashion magazines alike.

Wilhelmina motioned to a sofa, where they made themselves comfortable. "Start from the beginning, please. I want to hear all about your new concept. Then I'll share my thoughts."

Verena plunged in and told her the story of Mia's serum, Dr. Omondi's comments, and the verbal commitments she had for manufacturing and packaging.

She also told her about Dahlia, and their idea for an accompanying line of spa-inspired fragrances. Most important, she shared her need for project financing. Wilhelmina listened and occasionally made notes on a small pad.

An hour, then two hours, flew past. Wilhelmina's assistant tapped on the door. "Excuse me, but you asked me to remind you about your lunch reservation."

"Thank you, Gwen, we lost track of time," Wilhelmina said. She turned back to Verena. "Let's continue this over lunch, shall we?"

Verena agreed and followed Wilhelmina to her car, a white Bentley convertible. The sun was warm on her shoulders, and they were so engrossed in conversation Verena didn't think to ask where they were going. After driving a short distance on Sunset Boulevard, Wilhelmina turned into the Beverly Hills Hotel.

At a loss for words, Verena clutched the edge of her seat.

"This is my regular Friday spot," Wilhelmina said as the valet attendant opened her door. She laughed. "Sometimes I think I do more business here than in the office."

Verena had trepidation over the possibility of seeing Lance. She glanced at Wilhelmina. Their meeting was going well, and she needed to focus for the remainder of their discussion. They were getting down to the deal points now.

On the other hand, Lance was a chef. Didn't chefs belong in the kitchen? Surely she wouldn't see him in the restaurant. If she did, she'd be pleasant and professional. She got out of the car on shaky legs.

When they arrived at the Polo Lounge, Wilhelmina waved at Johnny. "Love your bow tie, darling. More men should wear them."

"Hello, Johnny," Verena said, and saw his face brighten.

Johnny flashed a smile and adjusted his purple paisley tie. "Right this way, ladies, your table is ready."

If Johnny was surprised to see her, he didn't let it show. That was his job, after all. He'd once told her he followed the tabloids just so he'd know not to seat feuding parties near each other.

They sat at a prime booth on the patio surrounded by the scent of jasmine. Ruby red and pink bougainvillea flowers arched around the booths. The patio was full of beautifully dressed people, and laughter bubbled all around them.

"I'm glad you brought your new concept to me." Wilhelmina steepled her hands. "Now, let's talk about how we might work together." She began laying out her vision.

Verena was excited as they shared ideas. As the conversation shifted to other topics, she found her attention mildly diverted as she glanced about for a tall, good-looking chef. Mentally chastising herself, she returned her full attention to Wilhelmina. This conversation was far too important.

Lance never appeared. Perhaps Johnny had warned him.

Verena relaxed after their tortilla soup arrived. It was a classic dish on the menu and as delicious as always. Their main course came—they had both ordered the salmon—and Verena wondered if Lance might have prepared it. She lifted her fork, remembering how he loved to cook and the meals he'd prepared for her.

She missed so many things about him. Regret coursed through her, and she swallowed her meal with some difficulty, even though it was delicious.

By the end of lunch, Wilhelmina made an offer to Verena.

"I'd like to join with you and Mia in this venture as a minor partner," Wilhelmina said. "You'll be a natural in front of the camera. We can film with mocked-up product, and take just-in-time delivery for orders. When do you think you'll have live product ready for fulfillment?"

Verena shared her projected dates, and then she asked about financing. She held her breath waiting for a reply.

Wilhelmina smiled. "I can assure you that I am able to fully fund this venture. It won't take as much as you think, because we produce as we sell, so the inventory investment is small. You're bringing much more to the table, your reputation, good will, and product and skincare knowledge. My attorney will send a fair agreement for you to review, and I assure you, it's nothing like Herringbone's agreement. Thomas Roper was a greedy old bastard."

Verena let out a small sigh of relief. "That's what Mia said, too. And he was."

"The best advice I can give you is to trust your instincts," Wilhelmina said. "Those who use Roper's playbook like to make things complicated to fog their true intent. Even though they took advantage of you, you have a good head on your shoulders, Verena. Trust yourself. I'm very excited about this."

Verena appreciated her comments. "I will. I admit,

sometimes my better judgment has been taken over by self-doubt, and then I discovered I'd been right all along." About a lot of things, she realized.

Verena tapped a fingernail on a crystal goblet in thought. A year ago, she would have never imagined the hell she'd been through.

Now she was emerging from the depths of her nightmare and stepping onto a brand new path. She sipped her water, thinking about how much she admired Wilhelmina, who had a sterling reputation as well as brilliant business insights.

Verena understood that it was time for her to forge ahead again in business. *Perhaps in other ways as well.* Verena looked up from the coffee they'd just been served and smiled. "I'm looking forward to working together."

"So am I." Wilhelmina extended her hand and they shook on it. "Here's to our new partnership."

Just then, an older, distinguished gentleman stopped by their table to speak to Wilhelmina, and while the two of them were engrossed in conversation, Verena spied Lance across the patio. As she watched him, her chest tightened, and she experienced a flash of insight.

"Excuse me for a moment," she said to Wilhelmina, and then slid from the booth.

Wearing his chef whites, Lance was weaving his way around the tables, greeting guests. He hadn't seen her yet.

She strode across the patio with purpose, only this time, she wasn't running away from him. It was time she lived her life. Time she spoke up for what she wanted in every facet of her life.

When Lance saw her, his lips parted in astonishment.

"Hello, Lance," she said. With a slight tilt of her head, she slipped her hand in his, and headed for the entrance.

Lance trailed behind her past her wide-eyed friends, Dahlia and Scarlett and Fianna, who were now seated at a table near the door, and past Johnny, who beamed and winked.

When they emerged from the Polo Lounge, Verena stopped and swung around to gaze into the depths of his eyes. Feeling more confident now, she plunged in.

"I made a mistake, Lance. I presumed to know what you wanted, or didn't want, in an effort to protect myself from getting hurt. I didn't think you'd want to have anything to do with a woman who had as much baggage as I do."

"That couldn't have been farther from the truth. I wish you had let me get a word in, but you raced from the car so fast an Olympic coach would've been proud."

She felt her face flush. "Then you don't mind?"

"So your life is a little complicated. Mine is, too." A grin spread across his face, and he swept her into his arms. "I know we can work it out."

"I have no doubt we can," she said, trusting her instinct. She'd been guilty of over thinking and making assumptions about what others wanted. From now on she was listening to her instincts and following her desires—her true north, as Mia called following your internal compass.

Wrapping her arms around his neck, Verena pressed against the length of him, happiness surging through her. She couldn't remember when she'd had such a perfect day. The thought of many more days like this brought a smile to her face.

"Verena, I've missed you so much." Lance's deep voice cracked with emotion, and he pressed his mouth against hers.

His kiss warmed her to her core. How could she ever live without this man in her life?

After a moment, Lance said, "I know you have a lot of demands on your time. I understand, I grew up in a large rowdy family, too. I can help. I'll cook, I'll make crab for Anika and Bella every night of the week if they want."

"Don't let them know that." She smiled and kissed him again.

"You should know that Mia has already put in her order. I promised that I'd continue to cook for her."

"So that was your promise." Verena laughed. "Do you think she was trying to get us back together?"

"She's a wise woman. Like you." Lance nuzzled her neck. "But the vow I mentioned was to you. In Paris, I told you that wherever we are, I promised to keep the magic alive for the rest of our lives. I meant it."

As she recalled that magical moment in Paris, Verena felt her heart thudding.

"I love you, Verena, and have from the first moment I saw you. I'll welcome everyone who comes along with you. I'm signing up for the entire menu, not just the à la carte choices. I've missed being part of a big family. We'll figure it out."

She gazed into his golden amber eyes, and realized she'd never felt this way with anyone else. This was magical, yet very real. "I love you, too, Lance. You're the man I've been looking for."

A loud whistle sounded behind them, followed by

cheers and clapping.

Verena and Lance turned around to see Johnny, Scarlett, Fianna, and Dahlia rejoicing for them. A few passersby glanced at the handsome chef and the blond woman in the red dress, but this was L.A., and nothing fazed people here.

"Keep it down," Lance said, laughing. "This is a place of business."

"Aw, get a room," Johnny said, and slapped Lance on the back.

Lance turned back to Verena and waggled his eyebrows. "Maybe there's one available."

Verena laughed and hugged him. "My meeting with Wilhelmina Jones is almost over, and I have great news to share with you—with everyone." She turned to her friends and smiled.

Dahlia let out a little squeal. "I'm so glad."

"Then it's time to celebrate," Lance said. "One bungalow, coming right up."

The End

Read on for an excerpt from *Beauty Mark*,
the next novel in the *Love, California* series by Jan
Moran.

To hear about Jan's new books first and get special
offers, join Jan's VIP Readers Club at www.JanMoran.com.

Beauty Mark

London, England

"Where is she?" Scarlett Sandoval sat in the tea room at Brown's Hotel in Mayfair waiting for her client to arrive. She was annoyed, as usual, at Fleur's perpetual tardiness. She ordered a second pot of tea and checked her watch. Even though they were traveling on a private jet to Los Angeles, they did have a schedule, something that frequently escaped the fashion designer's notice.

"I'll take a car to the airport," David said, rising from his chair and slipping a button through a buttonhole on his crisply tailored bespoke suit. "I don't want to get stuck in traffic. You're the best one on the team at handling her anyway."

"We'll see you there. Soon, I hope." Scarlett made a face. David Baylor was on the partner track at the same high profile law firm, Marsh & Gold, in Los Angeles. Years ago, when she'd been in the firm's New York office, and he'd been in Los Angeles, they'd threatened a cross-country affair, but now that she'd relocated and they were in the same city, they were glad they hadn't crossed the line. David was a good work friend, and had recently become engaged.

Her mother was right. At this rate she might never get married. Polite conversation bubbled across the room. Scarlett nibbled on a scone, and then checked her watch again. She glanced around the stylish room, which had been renovated in recent years. Antique fireplaces flickered in the corner, while contemporary art splashed color across the walls. Silver gleamed against white tablecloths, and VIPs of London filled every tapestry covered chair.

A flurry of activity erupted at the entry way to the Georgian townhouse in which Brown's had been established since 1837. The venerable old hotel was the law firm partner's preferred hotel in London. As the story went, Alexander Graham Bell made the first telephone call from the lobby at Brown's. Couldn't Fleur have managed a call on the gold-plated mobile phone usually glued to her ear?

Speak of the devil, thought Scarlett, dropping her buttered scone in shock. Fleur strutted into the room, and Scarlett realized what the commotion at the front door was about. Her client struck a defiant pose at the door, while a murmur rose across the room and the tea room manager hurried to speak to her. Waist-length purple hair matched her six-inch platform shoes, but it was the attire in between—or rather, the lack of it—that had the manager in a dither. Her sliver of a dress was definitely against the dress code at Brown's Tea Room. Why then had Fleur insisted on meeting her here instead of at the airport?

"Put this on my corporate account, please," Scarlett

whispered to the tea sommelier. After hastily grabbing her briefcase, she slid from the booth. She covered the room in long strides and hooked her arm in Fleur's, whisking her from the room.

"Hey, wait a minute," Fleur said, struggling to keep up in her platform shoes. "We need to get some shots."

That's when Scarlett saw the billionaire shipping magnate with whom Fleur had been pictured in the tabloids. The impeccable Vladimir Ivanov was having tea in a booth near the entrance with another woman. She sighed and checked her anger against her client. "The plane is waiting."

Scarlett nodded to the doorman, who was attired in a formal top hat and three-quarter length coat. He signaled for a black town car that had been idling on the quiet block. Out of nowhere appeared several paparazzi; they began snapping photos like mad. Fleur placed her hands on her hips and angled a shoulder in a provocative pose for them.

"Let's go, Fleur." Scarlett gave her a minute, and then grabbed her hand. This was not the brilliant legal career Scarlett had imagined while she was pulling all-nighter study sessions in law school. She slid into the backseat and let out a sigh of relief as the driver steered his way through London.

"Did you call them?" Scarlett had traveled with Gina "Fleur" Georgopoulos long enough to know that she often called paparazzi to keep herself in the headlines. A Greek native from the Bronx, she'd moved to London, adopted an accent, and took the world by surprise when she had one of her boyfriends buy billboards over Sunset Boulevard in Los Angeles. Soon everyone was asking, who is *Fleur of London?*

On some level—a low one, Scarlett thought—it was brilliant.

"If I'd just had the chance to speak to Vladimir, they could've gotten some great shots. Cover page stuff." Fleur sniffed. "I'll be lucky if those make it into print at all."

Fleur was known for her outlandish costumes. "Chin up, Fleur," Scarlett said. "I'm sure that outfit is print-worthy. Besides, you should be celebrating. This new cosmetics trademark deal is nearly complete. You're about to be one very wealthy woman." One of the top makeup companies in the world, High Gloss Cosmetics, was licensing the Fleur of London trademark for a new line of brilliantly colored products, including lipstick, eyeshadow, eyeliner, and mascara.

"Pour me a couple of shots of vodka then." Fleur smiled coyly and shoved on oversized sunglasses, her signal that she was through talking.

"I have a call to make," Scarlett replied, matching Fleur's smile. A bartender she was not.

Scarlett punched in a number on her phone. "We're on our way," she said, and clicked off. She had already had a long day of negotiations regarding the intellectual property uses, and now they were en route to Los Angeles for Fleur to meet with the company in person. It was the final phase in the deal. Fleur was a master of self-promotion who had, surprisingly, few other talents. She hired other fashion designers to create her line, dressed outlandishly, wore makeup more suited for Kabuki theatre, and dated billionaires. This got her a multimillion dollar deal that others worked a lifetime for and never realized.

When they arrived at the airport, Fleur gravitated

toward the partner, which was fine with Scarlett. In her mauve silk blouse and chic grey wool suit, she could hardly compare to the peacock style of Fleur. Not that she wanted to, though. Scarlett preferred being an advisor to her famous clients.

Most fashion designers and actors she worked with were creative and accomplished, and they worked well together with mutual respect, but occasionally an eccentric client like Fleur came along, and usually landed in her lap at the firm. Scarlett was one of Marsh & Gold's top intellectual property attorneys, and made the firm a fortune every year.

"Welcome aboard." Lucan Blackstone was her fifty-something boss from Los Angeles. Originally from London, Lucan seemed to be going through a permanent mid-life crisis. Fast cars, fast women, fast money—that was his motto. He traded in Teslas, Lamborghinis, yachts, and long-legged European models. Both men and women were attracted to his charm, his intelligence, and his silver-haired, movie-star good looks. He was the consummate rainmaker. Marsh & Gold partners often overlooked his missteps to keep his deals flowing.

Scarlett stepped into the cabin of a newly outfitted Boeing jet, which had replaced the Gulfstream 550 Lucan had deemed too small. The crew closed the door behind her, ready for wheels up.

She cocooned herself in a large white leather recliner, surrounded by creamy white and beige leather, polished burl wood trim, and every amenity one could want at fifty thousand feet. With a touch to a digital screen, she lowered the shade and adjusted her light. Her sparkling water and crudité vegetable plate had already been set out for her.

She might be cruising in luxury, but Scarlett had plenty of work to do on the twelve-hour flight. She'd learned to tune out whatever went on in the bar, or the stateroom behind her. She placed her laptop on the workspace in front of her and opened her briefcase, ignoring the blaring television, Fleur's incessant chatter, and Lucan's barking guffaws.

"Working the entire flight?" David asked. He'd already stretched out his large frame in the reclining chair. His hands were cupped behind his head.

"Some of it. We need to get this deal done. Just received the red-lined agreement back."

"Don't those High Gloss corporate attorneys have anything better to do? You'd think they were billing by the hour."

She felt the rumble of the jet engines as they prepared for take-off.

She shrugged. "Keeps us in business."

Lucan walked by on his way to the galley. "David, don't let us keep you up. Late night of partying with our English clients?"

"Sure, you know me, sir." David winked and Lucan playfully punched him on the shoulder.

"That's my boy," Lucan said.

Scarlett grinned. She happened to know David had worked much of the night, too. He'd called her to discuss points several times.

Lucan skirted the curved divans that followed the lines of the plane. No telling how many models had lined those seats, Scarlett thought. She was the only female in the firm who'd ever flown on this corporate jet, which was reserved for partners and their handpicked team, but there were plenty of women's things in the stateroom. Scarlett didn't want to know any more than she did. She kept her head down and kept working. "You've sure got him fooled."

"Lucan just wants to relive his misspent youth," David said with a chuckle. "Hey, thanks for your help last night. Couldn't have done it without you. Now, I've got to get some shut-eye," He snapped open a prescription bottle and poured out a couple of tablets. "Need an Ambien to sleep?"

Scarlett shook her head. "Not for me." A lot of consultants, attorneys, corporate finance pros, models, and entertainers who crisscrossed the globe on a weekly basis wolfed down Ambiens like they were Altoids. Shifting time zones could cause people to do that, Scarlett knew. In the old days it was alcohol, and she knew all about that from her father. She squeezed lime in her bubbly mineral water and took a drink.

"G'night, Scarlett." David pulled a sleep mask over his eyes.

"Night, David. I'll wake you when we arrive." Scarlett flicked a few keys on her keyboard and hooked up to the wireless service onboard. One advantage to flying private was that there were no annoying announcements asking flyers to turn off their electronic equipment on departure and take-off. Coupled with long security lines and layovers, private jets were massive time-savers that allowed the firm to squeeze maximum time from valuable employees to serve high-paying clients. The deals they worked on were often staggering in value, especially in the Mergers and Acquisitions practice. The airplane began taxiing, gaining speed as it hurtled down the runway.

A minute later the wheels lifted from the ground and Scarlett felt the pressure of her body heavy in the seat as the plane climbed through clouds to blue skies above.

Once airborne, Scarlett gazed out the window and watched London recede from sight. When she was young she had dreamed of traveling like this, but it wasn't as glamorous as she'd imagined. As a first year attorney, she'd taken red-eye flights, arriving at client's offices after spending the night on an airplane. Or the corporate limousine would shuttle her home at five in the morning, just long enough to shower and return for another demanding day, while she napped in the back seat en route.

But she'd committed her life willingly. Scarlett loved the law and had a strong sense of justice. Even as a little girl, she'd wanted to protect the good kids and stick it to the bullies. The intellectual stimulation never bored her, and she met fascinating, creative people in her beauty trademark work. She smiled. Instead of *trademarks*, her friend Johnny often teased her, shortening it to *beauty marks*.

She stifled a yawn, and made a mental note to call her mother when she landed. She'd missed her mother's birthday in London, but she promised to make it up to her.

Her family had moved to Los Angeles from Spain when she was a young girl. A few years later, after her father died of liver failure, and her brother Franco died in an ambush in the war in Afghanistan, Scarlett became her mother's sole support. She worked throughout school, received scholarships, took student loans, and lived frugally.

Scarlett's eyes welled as she thought of Franco. She and her brother had been so close. She missed his quick smile and sharp wit. Everyone loved him, and hardly a day went by that she didn't think of him. He was the bravest soul she'd ever known, and the best tribute she could give him was to emulate him and his approach to life.

As soon as Scarlett graduated from law school, she'd moved her mother from the barrio to the west side of Los Angeles, where she lived in a lovely little condominium and spent her time making baby clothes for children Scarlett might never have time to have.

Still, Isabel Sandoval didn't give up easily. Every time Scarlett visited her, she seemed to have another *nice young man* to introduce her to.

Somehow time had slipped away from Scarlett. It seemed that one minute she was twenty-four and graduating from law school, and the next minute she was thirty-two with a ticking clock. She'd been a bridesmaid so many times she'd lost count. Even if she met someone today, she'd probably be thirty-five before she had children. She'd always thought she'd have a family by now. And so did her old-school mother. She adored her mother, but the world was different today.

One of the problems was that she wanted to get to know a man well before she married. As an attorney, she'd heard far too many horror stories to jump into a relationship. Maybe that's what held her back, she thought, suppressing another yawn.

Scarlett put on headphones to focus on the detailed task at hand. Dinner came and Scarlett ate while she worked, anxious to finish the agreement during the flight. They crossed the Atlantic and the eastern seaboard. Judging from the time they'd been in the air, they were somewhere over the midwest United States, Scarlett figured. Finally, she hit save, closed her laptop, and got up to stretch.

She took off her jacket, and then wandered to the flight deck to say hello to the pilot and crew. "Hi, Jeffrey."

"Hi, Scarlett," the pilot replied with a grin, touching a finger to his forehead. The aircraft was on autopilot.

She chatted with Jeffrey and the crew about upcoming flight plans, which included the next European rugby match, snow skiing in the southern hemisphere, a fly fishing junket in Scotland, and Formula One and Grand Prix races. Lucan spent a fortune on entertaining clients, but it certainly paid off.

Scarlett was booked for Fashion Week in Paris, and the Cannes Film Festival, where she often negotiated licensing deals for many of her clients. She went to all the glamorous parties, but she was not there to play. Marsh & Gold partners expected her to bring in new business, and she did.

In truth, her manic work pace and extensive travel didn't allow for much of a personal life. She envied her friends who managed to balance their lives.

As she walked to the galley for tea, she thought of her good friend and client, Verena Valent, who, after having lost her family's legendary skincare salon to an unscrupulous investor, created another skincare line. Verena managed to blend work, the care of her twin sisters and her grandmother, and a new relationship. How did she do it?

But Scarlett knew the answer. It was the flexibility Verena had as an entrepreneur. She was always busy, but on a time schedule of her own making. It was the same with their other friends, such as Dahlia, whose family ran a perfume business, and Fianna, who was a fashion designer and owned a boutique.

For eight years Scarlett had been focused on working her plan, investing her life into her career, and making partner. After graduation, she had sat for two of the toughest bar exams in the country—California and New York—and passed them both on the first try.

She'd had several competing offers, but she'd accepted a generous one from Marsh & Gold. Now, she was next in line on the partner track. The decision would be made next week. A satisfied smile curved her lips. Soon it would be worth the years of struggle.

Scarlett picked up the green tea she'd brewed and sat down on the divan. She kicked off her shoes, took a few sips, and leaned her head back. She closed her eyes. It felt so good to relax. They still had a couple of hours before landing at the Van Nuys airport in Los Angeles, where the corporate plane was kept. She felt herself drift off.

Her dreams were quite realistic sometimes. "Mmm," she murmured, as someone stroked her shoulders and arms, which felt so good. She couldn't remember who he was, this man in her dreams, she couldn't see his face. If she opened her eyes… but her eyelids were heavy.

"Just relax," he whispered. He ran a firm hand down her throat and chest, pausing on her breast.

She smiled in her sleep. Who was this virile dream man who seemed so real? One of her old boyfriends, or someone she was yet to meet? She had to know. Straining against her slumber, she fluttered her eyes, trying to capture him.

As she did, she gasped, and shot bolt upright on the divan. "*What* are you doing?"

"Relax," Lucan repeated. He hovered over her, and his white dress shirt was unbuttoned. "You work so hard, Scarlett. A beautiful woman like you needs a break."

"Lucan, stop it." Scarlett glared at him. "We're not doing this. Get away from me."

"Come on, Scarlett." He twirled a lock of her coppery blond hair around his finger. "Who's to know? David's zoned out on Ambien. Fleur passed out in the stateroom from too much vodka." A smile curved his perfectly tanned face. "And the crew won't talk. So let's have fun."

"Absolutely not." Scarlett stood up, weaving a little on her feet from a mixture of exhaustion and air turbulence.

"Scarlett, Scarlett. So naïve in so many ways." Lucan patted the spot next to him. "Sit down. I'll have a couple of nightcaps made for us." He pressed a button and spoke to the crew. "I won't bite."

She touched the cabin wall for support and glanced around. Where could she go? The stateroom door was closed. David was snoring in the front of the cabin. But a crew member would be here any minute. She perched on the bench, leaving space between them.

"So, is there someone else in your life?" His voice was warm and amicable. "You can tell me. After all, you're going to be a partner soon."

"Lucan, I don't want to talk about my personal life." *Of which I have none*, she thought. And then, *partner*? Did he really say that? She scooted to the edge of the seat. "And I'm awfully tired."

He stared at her, his brilliant blue eyes crinkling with laughter at the corners. He was a virile, handsome man, and he knew it. His irresistible charm had made a fortune for the firm. "I have a little pick-me-up if you need it." He brought out a tiny vial filled with white powder. "Come on, loosen up, Scarlett."

"Look, I'm not into that. Please leave me alone so I can take a nap before landing."

"Let me help you relax," Lucan said.

She started to rise, but he pounced, knocking her against the back of the sofa. In a flash, he was all over her. Scarlett flailed, but he was a muscular man, and he pinned her down. She glanced over his shoulder and saw a female crew member delivering the two snifters of cognac Lucan asked for.

"Help me," Scarlett cried.

The petite dark-haired woman looked shocked, then angry. Scarlett reached out to her, pleading with her as she struggled under Lucan's weight. Suddenly, the crew member dropped the drink tray on purpose, and the glasses shattered on the table. "Sir, I'm so sorry!" she exclaimed. "Watch out for the glass."

Startled, Lucan rolled off her and jumped to his feet. "You idiot! What's wrong with you? Clean this up and get out." Lucan buttoned his shirt and fussed with his hair.

Scarlett sprang up and threw a grateful look to the woman, who scurried away to get cleaning supplies.

"Don't you *ever* do that again," Scarlett snapped.

"What? You're overreacting." Lucan spread his hands out in an innocent gesture. "Your honor, I'm innocent."

The crew member rushed back, but she took her time cleaning. "Need to clean this mess up," she said calmly, brushing her dark hair over her shoulder. Her name tag read *Lavender*. She flicked on a small vacuum cleaner.

Scarlett turned on her heel and marched to the flight deck. She was so livid she couldn't stay in the same cabin with him.

"David, we're almost home." Scarlett spoke loudly to wake her colleague.

"Huh? Oh, Scarlett, what'd I miss?" David lifted his eye mask and rubbed his eyes.

"Not a thing." She shot a look at Lucan, and he suppressed a grin. "It was the best kind of flight. Unremarkable." She wished she could slap that grin off Lucan's face. What on earth was he thinking? She was still fuming.

Fleur came stumbling from the stateroom, her purple hair and makeup in disarray, her gold-plated phone already pressed to her ear.

"Have a good sleep?" Lucan asked when she hung up.

Fleur yawned. "Yeah."

Lucan's eyes roamed over her. "I assume you want to swing by the hotel and freshen up before we go out."

"Sure. Whatever."

Scarlett bit back a reply. The man was indefatigable. Then she remembered she'd gone straight from a meeting in Studio City to catch the outbound flight for London. Her car was still at the office in Century City, near her townhouse in Beverly Hills.

"I've got a car waiting for us here," Lucan said, as if reading her mind.

"Thanks, but I'm meeting a friend," she said cordially. Why had he ruined their professional relationship? *What a jerk.*

When they scudded down the runway in Van Nuys, Scarlett breathed a sigh of relief, glad to be home. As they taxied, he gazed out the window at palm trees swaying against a mountain backdrop.

Lucan and Fleur got off the plane first. Scarlett gathered her laptop and exited the plane with David.

"Wait right here," Lucan said to Fleur. "I forgot something."

Lucan pushed his way past Scarlett, and she nearly dropped her laptop. She clucked her tongue. The man was an oaf.

Once inside the airport, Scarlett ducked into the women's bathroom to avoid Lucan pressuring her into joining them in the car. She was washing her hands when the petite, dark-haired crew member who'd come to her aid opened the door. Scarlett raised her eyes and met her gaze in the mirror.

"Hi." The woman drew her brows together. "Are you okay?"

"I guess so." Scarlett lifted a shoulder and let it fall. "That was fast thinking. I really appreciate what you did." She smiled. "My name is Scarlett."

"And I'm Lavender. Hey, we're a colorful pair," the young woman said with a grin. "My mother was a hippie."

"I have no excuse. My real name is Escarlata."

Lavender laughed. "Look," she said, turning serious, "I've been in situations like that myself, but you're a big attorney, right?"

"Not immune to idiots, though." She turned off the faucet and dried her hands.

"And he's your boss?" Lavender looked sorry for her.

Scarlett nodded.

"I left my last job because of sexual harassment." Lavender shuddered. "I don't need that in my life."

"No woman does." Scarlett was still furious. She was smart, but she was street smart, too. She was angry with herself for missing the signs. But Lucan was the one to blame.

They spoke a little more before Scarlett left to retrieve her luggage.

As Scarlett walked out, she saw Lucan ahead of her, so she hung back to avoid him. He glanced around and then tossed a package into the trash. She stopped, hoping he hadn't seen her.

Lavender caught up with her. "It's okay, I've got your back," she said. "He's gone."

Scarlett grinned at her new friend. "Thanks." As she was wheeling her luggage toward the taxi line, her phone rang.

"Hi *chica*, are you back from London?" It was Johnny Silva, her childhood friend from the barrio, who'd been best friends with her brother Franco. He was the maître d' at the Polo Lounge now.

"Just landed, and waiting for a taxi." She was glad to hear from him.

"You, in a taxi line? It's almost eleven at night. Thought Marsh & Gold always called a limo for you. Are they having budget cuts?"

"No, it just worked out that way." Scarlett didn't want to tell Johnny about Lucan. Ever since they'd been children, he'd always sprang to her defense. She'd never hear the end of it.

"I'm nearby. I'll come get you. Wait there."

When Johnny wheeled into the airport fifteen minutes later, Scarlett greeted him with a hug. "So glad to see you, Johnny. Thanks for the ride."

"Anything for my *chica*. Things were awfully quiet without you." Johnny lifted her luggage into the trunk of his vintage red Mustang convertible. He'd bought it years ago, and had restored it one piece at a time.

It was a warm evening, and he had the top down. As he opened the door for her, his glossy black hair shimmered in the evening lights. "Are you hungry?"

"A little. Dinner was somewhere over the Atlantic." Scarlett slid into the car.

"Want to head over to the hotel? Lance is working on some new dishes tonight."

"I'd like that," Scarlett said, finally relaxing after the long flight. She never had to be anyone other than who she was with Johnny. *Why can't romantic relationships be like this?*

As Johnny drove, they talked about their friends, Verena and Lance, who had been dating for a while. Lance was the executive chef at the Beverly Hills Hotel, the legendary pink palace on Sunset Boulevard in Beverly Hills, a favorite hotel of Hollywood stars throughout the decades. Johnny was the maître d' at the Polo Lounge, where the beautiful people still gathered and felt at home.

To the people who'd lived in Beverly Hills for many years, like some of Scarlett's friends and their families, the five-square-mile community would always be a little village, where doctors still made house calls, shops had private house accounts, and restaurants and delicatessens let regular customers run a monthly tab.

Today, Van Cleef & Arpels and Cartier glittered on Rodeo Drive, and tour buses lumbered along pristine residential streets, but the city still maintained its charm among residents, who could walk almost anywhere in the city—a rarity in the car-dependent culture of Los Angeles.

Not that many of them did, of course.

Johnny parked and they threaded their way through the back entrance of the luxury hotel. Outside, under pink archways, the open air terrace dining area was ablaze with red bougainvillea, green garden chairs, and white tablecloths.

They reached the front of the Polo Lounge, where Johnny showed Scarlett to a booth in the bar area. Dark green walls created a clubby ambiance, mirrors reflected the dazzling array of guests, and polo pictures and a green-and-white striped ceiling harkened to the hotel's early days. Strains of jazz floated in the air.

"Scarlett, welcome home," said a slender blond woman who was already seated in the booth. She wore a creamy silk sheath dress and pearls.

"Verena, it's so good to see you." Scarlett hugged her friend and scooted in beside her. "I feel like I've been gone forever." She loosened the collar of her blouse and smoothed her hair back.

"Seems like it. A month, wasn't it?" Verena's fair porcelain skin seemed to glow in the low lights. Whether it was from happiness or her new skincare line, Scarlett couldn't tell, but she was glad Verena was doing better. After all she'd been through with her business and her family, she deserved it.

"That's right. Milan, Florence, Paris, London." It

sounded exciting, but she'd often worked sixteen hour days. Still, she had to admit she met amazing people and dined in all the best restaurants. Working at the firm was like having velvet shackles.

"Has Johnny told you the news?" Verena could hardly contain herself.

"No, what's going on?"

Verena looked like she was going to burst with happiness. "I'll let him tell you."

Johnny winked at her. "I'll get Lance." He disappeared into the kitchen.

"Did Lance propose?" Scarlett touched Verena's left hand, which was bare.

"No, not that. Too soon for us." Verena's blue eyes were as brilliant as sapphires, and they glowed with excitement.

"When you're ready, we should talk about prenuptial agreements."

"I lost everything, remember?" Verena laughed. "But we're happy."

"You're creating new intellectual property now, trademarks, copyrights, service marks." Scarlett started to launch into a legal discourse, and then she caught Verena's amused expression. It was late, and she was being overzealous again. She couldn't help it; it was in her blood.

"Relax, Scarlett. Everything in time, Mia says."

At the mention of Verena's grandmother, Scarlett pressed a hand to her heart. "How is she?"

"Much better now. She's been released from the hospital. She's a real fighter. In fact, she and Camille went shopping today. You can't keep a fashionista down when

Neiman Marcus has its Last Call sale."

Scarlett smiled, imagining the two doyennes of beauty together. Camille was their friend Dahlia's grandmother; Camille had founded a perfume empire decades ago. Originally from Switzerland, Mia had established a skincare salon in Beverly Hills in the 1940s. After Verena's parents died in a tragic accident, Mia raised Verena and her two younger twin sisters.

Johnny appeared at the table, and with him was Lance Martel, the executive chef. They all greeted one another and sat down.

"I told Scarlett that you've been experimenting with some new dishes."

A half smile tugged at Lance's mouth. "Salmon or pork?"

"Salmon," Scarlett said.

"Good choice. I'll whip one up for you. Did Johnny tell you?"

Scarlett shook her head. "No, and I wish someone would. You're all killing me. What's going on?"

Johnny and Lance traded a look. "We're starting our own restaurant," Johnny said. "We'll finally be in a place of our own."

"Why, that's wonderful." Scarlett was truly happy for Johnny. Both men were talented, and had devoted followings. The restaurant business was tough, but if anyone could do it, these two could. "Congratulations. When, where, and what's the name?"

"Scarlett, slow down," Johnny said. "We just decided. As usual, you're several steps ahead of us."

Scarlett felt her cheeks grow warm and she laughed.

"Occupational hazard."

Lance excused himself and went to prepare Scarlett's meal while the three friends caught up.

When Lance returned with the salmon dish, it was one of the best preparations she thought she'd ever had. It was perfectly moist, and seasoned with fresh herbs. A citrus reduction sauce was just the right accent, and a bed of spaghetti squash and spinach balanced the fish. Scarlett realized she was starving.

After she'd finished eating, Verena and Lance left. Scarlett watched them go. She was elated for them, but she also wondered where the magic was that had brought the two of them together. Where was her magic?

"Would you like to have hot chocolate by the pool before I take you home?" Johnny asked.

Johnny knew her well. She'd almost forgotten how they used to drink hot chocolate together. "I'd like that."

They strolled through the hotel, past the old soda fountain shop and out to the pool. A server delivered the hot chocolate he'd asked for. They were seated at a table when Scarlett said, "You know what I'd like to do?"

"No telling," Johnny said, watching her with dancing eyes, dark as mahogany.

Scarlett slipped her feet from her high heels and rolled up her trousers.

Johnny laughed and followed suit. Soon the two of them were sitting at the pool, dangling their legs in the cool water, and cupping hot chocolate in their hands.

Scarlett tilted her head back and gazed up at the full moon, which cast shimmering shadows on the rippling water.

Johnny touched her chin. "Hold it right there. You have cat's eyes in this light, a gorgeous golden green. Simply beautiful."

As was Johnny. Lots of women adored him. Scarlett noted a dimple in one of his cheeks when he grinned. "What a funny thing to say, Johnny."

He shrugged. "I'm noticing the little things more." He waved a hand around. "Look at us. Good friends, a good place in our lives. We've come so far, *chica.* Let's savor our success."

"Who has time?" The partner track had sapped her energy. The memory of Lucan assailed her thoughts.

"What a sad comment." Johnny slid his hand over hers and held it. "We *have* to make time. Think about it. Life doesn't get much better than this."

Scarlett gazed into his eyes. Johnny always spoke with such passion. That's what attracted her to him. *Where, oh where, is a man like this in my love life?*

Still, it was good to have friends like Johnny. If only Franco were here with them now, the three of them laughing and teasing each other like they used to, so long ago.

Maybe her brother was looking down on them.

She rested her head on Johnny's shoulder and sipped her hot chocolate.

To continue reading *Beauty Mark*, visit your favorite retailer.

About the Author

Jan Moran is a writer and entrepreneur living in southern California. She writes contemporary and historical fiction, and nonfiction. Keep up with her latest blog posts at JanMoran.com.

A few of Jan's favorite things include a good cup of coffee, dark chocolate, history, spas, traveling anywhere, and a warm sunny beach. Jan is originally from Austin, Texas, and a trace of a drawl still survives to this day, although she has lived in Southern California for years.

Jan has been featured in and written for many prestigious media outlets, including *CNN, Wall Street Journal, Women's Wear Daily, Allure, InStyle, O Magazine, Cosmopolitan, Elle*, and *Costco Connection*, and has spoken before numerous groups, such as San Diego State University, Fashion Group International, The Fragrance Foundation, and The American Society of Perfumers.

She is a graduate of Harvard Business School, University of Texas at Austin, and UCLA Writers Program.

To hear about Jan's new books first and get special offers, join Jan's VIP Readers Club at www.JanMoran.com and get a free download. If you enjoyed this book, please consider leaving a brief review online for your fellow readers.

Made in the USA
Middletown, DE
29 June 2020

10890118R00203